AMERICAN SCHOOL TEXTBOOK

U0033906

VOCABULARY KEY

SCHOOL

TEXTBOOK

VOCABULARY KEY

GRADE 6

Michael A. Putlack

FUN學 美國英語課本

各學科關鍵英單 二版＋ Workbook

MP3

寂天雲 APP

如何下載 MP3 音檔

❶ 寂天雲 APP 聆聽：掃描書上 QR Code 下載「寂天雲－英日語學習隨身聽」APP。加入會員後，用 APP 內建掃描器再次掃描書上 QR Code，即可使用 APP 聆聽音檔。

❷ 官網下載音檔：請上「寂天閱讀網」（www.icosmos.com.tw），註冊會員／登入後，搜尋本書，進入本書頁面，點選「MP3 下載」下載音檔，存於電腦等其他播放器聆聽使用。

FUN 學美國英語課本

各學科關鍵英單 GRADE 6

AMERICAN SCHOOL TEXTBOOK
VOCABULARY KEY

二版

作者簡介

Michael A. Putlack

專攻歷史與英文，擁有美國麻州 Tufts University 碩士學位。

作　　　者	Michael A. Putlack
	Zachary Fillingham / Shara Dupuis（Workbook B 大題）
翻　　　譯	謝雅婷
編　　　輯	王婷葦／歐寶妮
校　　　對	王婷葦
封 面 設 計	林書玉
內 頁 排 版	林書玉
製 程 管 理	洪巧玲
出 版 者	寂天文化事業股份有限公司
發 行 人	黃朝萍
電　　　話	+886-(0)2-2365-9739
傳　　　真	+886-(0)2-2365-9835
網　　　址	www.icosmos.com.tw
讀 者 服 務	onlineservice@icosmos.com.tw
出 版 日 期	2023 年 11 月　二版二刷　（寂天雲隨身聽 APP 版）

郵 撥 帳 號　1998620-0 寂天文化事業股份有限公司
‧ 訂書金額未滿 1000 元，請外加運費 100 元。
〔若有破損，請寄回更換，謝謝。〕

國家圖書館出版品預行編目資料

FUN 學美國英語課本：各學科關鍵英單 Grade 6.（寂天雲
隨聽 APP 版）/ Michael A. Putlack 著；謝雅婷譯 . -- 二版 .
-- [臺北市]：寂天文化 , 2023.11

　面；　公分

ISBN 978-626-300-214-2（菊 8K 平裝）

1. 英語 2. 詞彙

805.12　　　　　　　　　　　　　　　　112016205

FUN學美國英語課本：各學科關鍵英單

進入明星學校必備的英文單字

用美國教科書學英文是最道地的學習方式，有越來越多的學校選擇以美國教科書作為教材，用全英語授課（immersion）的方式教學，讓學生把英語當成母語學習。在一些語言學校裡，也掀起了一波「用美國教科書學英文」的風潮。另外，還有越來越多的父母優先考慮讓子女用美國教科書來學習英文，讓孩子將來能夠進入明星學校或國際學校就讀。

為什麼要使用美國教科書呢？TOEFL 等國際英語能力測驗都是以各學科知識為基礎，使用美國教科書不但能大幅提升英文能力，也可以增加數學、社會、科學等方面的知識，因此非常適合用來準備考試。即使不到國外留學，也可以像在美國上課一樣，而這也是使用美國教科書最吸引人的地方。

以多樣化的照片、插圖和例句來熟悉跨科學習中的英文單字

到底該使用何種美國教科書呢？還有如何才能讀懂美國教科書呢？美國各州、各學校的課程都不盡相同，而學生也有選擇教科書的權利，所以單單是教科書的種類就多達數十種。若不小心選擇到程度不適合的教科書，就很容易造成孩子對學英語的興趣大減。

因此，正確的作法應該要先累積字彙和相關知識背景。我國學生的學習能力很強，只需要培養對不熟悉的用語和統合教學（Cross-Curricular Study）的適應能力。

本系列網羅了在以全英語教授社會、科學、數學、語言、藝術、音樂等學科時，所有會出現的必備英文單字。只要搭配書中真實的照片、插圖和例句，就能夠把這些在美國小學課本中會出現的各學科核心單字記起來，同時還可以熟悉相關的背景知識。

四種使用頻率最高的美國教科書的字彙分析

本系列套書規畫了 6 個階段的字彙學習課程，本套書搜羅了 McGraw Hill、Harcourt、Pearson 和 Core Knowledge 等四大教科書中的主要字彙，並且整理出各科目、各主題的核心單字，然後依照學年分為 Grade 1 到 Grade 6。

本套書的適讀對象為「準備大學學測指考的學生」和「準備參加 TOEFL 等國際英語能力測驗的學生」。對於「準備赴美唸高中的學生」和「想要看懂美國教科書的學生」，本套書亦是最佳的先修教材。

《FUN學美國英語課本：各學科關鍵英單》系列的結構與特色

1. 本套書中所收錄的英文單字都是美國學生在上課時會學到的字彙和用法。

2. 將美國小學教科書中會出現的各學科核心單字，搭配多樣化照片、插圖和例句，讓讀者更容易熟記。

3. 藉由閱讀教科書式的題目，來強化讀、聽、寫的能力。透過各式各樣的練習與題目，不僅能夠全盤吸收與各主題有關的字彙，也能夠熟悉相關的知識背景。

4. 每一冊的教學大綱（syllabus）皆涵蓋了社會、歷史、地理、科學、數學、語言、美術和音樂等學科，以循序漸進的方式，學習從基礎到高級的各科核心字彙，不僅能夠擴增各科目的字彙量，同時還提升了運用句子的能力。（教學大綱請參考第 8 頁）

5. 可學到社會、科學等的相關背景知識和用語，也有助於準備 TOEFL 等國際英語能力測驗。

6. 對於「英語程度有限，但想看懂美國教科書的學生」來說，本套書是很好的先修教材。

7. 全系列 6 階段共分為 6 冊，可依照個人英語程度，選擇合適的分冊。

    Grade 1 美國小學 1 年級課程 　　**Grade 2** 美國小學 2 年級課程

    Grade 3 美國小學 3 年級課程 　　**Grade 4** 美國小學 4 年級課程

    Grade 5 美國小學 5 年級課程 　　**Grade 6** 美國小學 6 年級課程

8. 書末附有關鍵字彙的中英文索引，方便讀者搜尋與查照（請參考第 14 頁）。

強烈建議下列學生使用本套書：

1. 「準備大學學測指考」的學生

2. 「準備參加以全英語授課的課程，想熟悉美國學生上課時會用到的各科核心字彙」的學生

3. 「對美國小學各科必備英文字彙已相當熟悉，想朝高級單字邁進」美國學校的七年級生

4. 「準備赴美唸高中」的學生

MP3

收錄了本書的「Key Words」、「Power Verbs」、「Word Families」單元中的所有單字和例句，和「Checkup」中 E 大題的文章，以及 Workbook 中 A 大題聽寫練習文章。

How to Use This Book

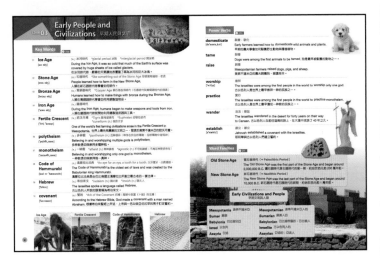

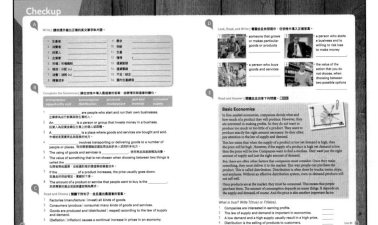

Checkup

Table of Contents

Introduction
How to Use This Book

AMERICAN SCHOOL TEXTBOOK

VOCABULARY KEY

Workbook

GRADE 6

Michael A. Putlack

FÜN學美國英語課本

各學科關鍵英單 二版

Unit 01

A Listen to the passage and fill in the blanks.

🎧 121 | **Basic Economics**

In 1._____ economies, companies decide what and how much of a product they will produce. However, they are interested in making 2._____. So they do not want to produce too much or too little of a product. They want to produce exactly the right amount necessary. So they often pay 3._____ to the law of supply and demand.

This law states that when the supply of a product is low yet demand is high, then the price will be high. However, if the supply of a product is high yet demand is low, then the price will be low. Companies want to find a 4._____. They want just the right amount of supply and just the right amount of demand.

But, there are often other factors that companies must consider. Once they make something, they must 5._____ it to the market. This way, people can purchase the product. This is called distribution. Distribution is often done by trucks, trains, ships, and airplanes. Without an 6._____ distribution system, even in-demand products will not sell well.

Once products are at the market, they must be consumed. This means that people purchase them. The amount of 7._____ depends on many things. It depends on the supply and demand, of course. And the price is also another important factor.

B Read the passage above and answer the following questions.

_____ 8. If companies want to make money, they must _____.
   a increase the price of their more affordable products
   b have as many products on the article at once
   c sell their company's products
   d have the right amount of supply and demand

_____ 9. "Companies want to find a median." In this sentence, the word "median" is closest in meaning to something _____.
   a in the middle   b expensive
   c at the high end   d cheap

_____ 10. According to the article, what is an important factor in consumption?
   a The way a product tastes.
   b The way a product is priced.
   c The way a product is distributed.
   d The way a product looks.

Unit 02

A Listen to the passage and fill in the blanks.

🎧 122 **The Earth's Climate Zones**

There are three main climate zones on the Earth. They are the tropical, temperate, and polar climate zones.

The tropical zones are found near the 1._____. Basically, they are found between the Tropic of Cancer and the Tropic of 2._____. In general, the tropical zone has hot weather most of the year. Many areas in the tropical zone have very wet weather, but this is not always the case.

The temperate zones are the largest of the three main climate zones. One temperate zone lies between the Tropic of Cancer and the 3._____. The other temperate zone lies between the Tropic of Capricorn and the 4._____. Most of the world's population lives in temperate zones. Temperate zones are neither too hot nor too cold. They experience 5._____ seasons all year long. For the most part, the weather is not too 6._____ in these places.

The polar zones are found north of the Arctic Circle and south of the Antarctic Circle. The weather in these places is 7._____ cold. Few people live in these places. Few animals live in them as well.

B Read the passage above and answer the following questions.

_____ 8. What is this article mainly about?
- a Where most people in the world live.
- b The different areas of climate on Earth.
- c The Tropics of Cancer and Capricorn.
- d Changing seasons and extreme weather.

_____ 9. According to the article, tropical zones _____.
- a always have wet weather
- b have little rain
- c usually have hot weather
- d are found above the Tropic of Cancer

_____ 10. "For the most part, the weather is not too extreme in these places." In this sentence, "extreme" means _____.
- a hot
- b cold
- c moderate
- d unusual

Unit 03

Listen to the passage and fill in the blanks.

🎧 123 **The Story of Israel**

In the past in the Middle East, there were many different 1._____. People often prayed to many gods. There were mountain gods. There were gods of rivers, lakes, and seas. There were all kinds of gods. However, one religion began that 2._____ only one god.

There was a man named Abram. He was said to be a 3._____ of both Noah and Adam. He lived in a land called Canaan. There, the god Yahweh made a 4._____ with Abram. Yahweh promised Abram many descendants and said that the land he was living on would forever be theirs. In return, Abram had to worship only Yahweh. Abram agreed. His name changed to Abraham, which means "father of many nations."

Abraham's descendants through his son Isaac became the 5._____. Isaac and his wife Rebecca later had twins: Jacob and Esau. Jacob's descendants founded the twelve tribes of the Israelites. They made the city 6._____ the center of their political power. For a time, they were powerful. Later, they were made 7._____ and taken to Egypt. It was in Egypt that Moses would later free the Israelites and return them to their land many years later.

B **Read the passage above and answer the following questions.**

_____ 8. "There, the god Yahweh made a covenant with Abram." In this sentence, "covenant" means _____.
  a conversation   b plan
  c discovery   d agreement

_____ 9. What did Yahweh make Abram promise?
  a To change his name.
  b To have many children.
  c To worship only him.
  d To keep a secret.

_____ 10. Who freed the Israelites from slavery?
  a Yahweh.   b Abraham.
  c Isaac.   d Moses.

4

Unit 04

A **Listen to the passage and fill in the blanks.**

🎧 124 | **Early Indus Civilization**

In the Indus Valley, which is in modern-day India and Pakistan, an early civilization formed long ago. It lasted from around 2500 B.C. to 1500 B.C. It is also 1._____ the Harappan civilization.

The people in the Indus Valley civilization mostly farmed the land. So they knew the secret of agriculture. This let them stop living as 2._____. But they were not just farmers. They also built many cities. Archaeologists have found several 3._____ where there were cities. They built palaces, temples, baths, and other buildings. They also planned their cities on a 4._____ pattern. So they were laid out in squares.

The people of the Indus Valley were advanced in other ways, too. They made pottery. They made objects from both copper and 5._____. And they even had their own writing system. It was based on 6._____. But it has not yet been translated.

The Indus Valley was one of the world's first civilized areas. Little is known about it. But 7._____ are learning more and more every year.

B **Read the passage above and answer the following questions.**

_____ 8. Which statement below best expresses the main idea?

a The Harappan civilization had its own writing system.
b Pottery was important for the Harappan civilization.
c An ancient civilization existed in the Indus Valley.
d The Harappans were known as good warriors.

_____ 9. Which of the following is NOT true of the Harappan civilization?

a They invented a writing system.
b They knew how to farm.
c They built palaces.
d They made iron objects.

_____ 10. "Archeologists have found several settlements where there were cities." An "archeologist" is someone who _____.

a solves math problems
b searches for lost people
c digs for old objects
d sells paintings

Unit 05

A **Listen to the passage and fill in the blanks.**

🎧 125 | **Rome: From Republic to Empire**

According to legend, the brothers Romulus and Remus founded Rome in 753 B.C. Rome grew larger until around 620 B.C., when a group of people called the Etruscans 1._____ it. The Etruscans ruled Rome for 111 years. In 509 B.C., the Roman people 2._____ King Tarquin the Proud. They were free again.

The Romans made a new kind of government. It was called a republic. Under the republic, they 3._____ a small number of people to be their leaders. These leaders were called 4._____. Up to 300 of them could be elected to the Senate. For the next 500 years, Rome remained a republic.

Rome began to grow more powerful. It soon controlled all of the Italian 5._____. From 264 B.C. to 146 B.C., it fought the Punic Wars against Carthage. The Romans won and became the masters of the 6._____. Soon, the republic was enormous. But it became 7._____. A general—Julius Caesar—challenged the rule of the Senate and became a 8._____. Yet he was murdered in 44 B.C., and the republic was ruled by three leaders. Eventually, those three men fought each other. Octavian won and became the first Roman 9._____. The republic was gone. Now it was the Roman Empire.

B **Read the passage above and answer the following questions.**

_____ 10. Who were the patricians?
- a Roman emperors.
- b Brothers Romulus and Remus.
- c People elected to the Roman Senate.
- d Supporters of Julius Caesar.

_____ 11. "Soon, the republic was enormous. But it became corrupt." A word that has a similar meaning to "corrupt" is _____.
- a dishonest
- b poor
- c challenged
- d changed

_____ 12. What is closest to the main point the author of the article wanted to make?
- a The Roman Empire was the most powerful government in history.
- b Julius Caesar was a powerful dictator.
- c It took many years for the Roman Empire to develop.
- d An empire is much more powerful than a republic.

Unit 06

Listen to the passage and fill in the blanks.

🎧 126 | **The Spread of Islam**

In 632, Muhammad died. He was the founder of Islam. At his death, there were few
1._____. And they had very little land. But after Muhammad's death, Islam
began to spread 2._____.

Soon after Muhammad's death, Muslim leaders selected 3._____ to govern
the Muslim community. During the reigns of the first four caliphs (from 632 to 661),
Islam spread throughout the Arabian Peninsula. By 661, Islam conquered land from
Persia in the Near East to Egypt in Africa. From 661 to 750, the Umayyad
4._____ ruled the Islamic world. They spread Islam throughout northern
Africa. In 711, an Islamic army crossed the Mediterranean Sea and entered Spain.
In a few years, they had 5._____ Spain. The Muslims went north and entered
France. But, in 732, Charles Martel defeated an Islamic army near Tours. The
Muslim advance to the north was stopped.

Meanwhile, the Muslims could not defeat the 6._____ in the east. They
advanced on Constantinople several times. But they always lost. Later, however,
the Ottoman Empire arose in the east. It challenged the Byzantines. By the fifteenth
century, the Byzantine Empire was weak. In 1453, the Ottomans conquered it.
They made Constantinople their 7._____. From there, they would rule a vast
Islamic empire until the twentieth century.

B Read the passage above and answer the following questions.

_____ 8. "During the reigns of the first four caliphs (from 632 to 661), Islam spread
throughout the Arabian Peninsula." A similar word to "reign" is _____.
- a control
- b victory
- c defeat
- d election

_____ 9. "Meanwhile, the Muslims could not defeat the Byzantine Empire in the east.
They advanced on Constantinople several times." Whom does "They" refer
to in the sentence?
- a The Byzantine Empire.
- b The Muslims.
- c The people from Constantinople.
- d The people who believe in Jesus.

_____ 10. What is the main idea of the article?
- a Mohammad started Islam.
- b Islam grew as a religion over a period of time.
- c The Ottomans were very powerful.
- d Muslims tried to bring their religion north.

Unit 07

Listen to the passage and fill in the blanks.

🎧 127 | **The Reformation**

For centuries, the Catholic Church dominated life in Europe. But many 1._____ in the Church were corrupt. They were more interested in money and living a good life than in religion. Some people were 2._____ about that. One of them was Martin Luther. In 1517, he posted his 95 theses on a church door in Wittenberg, Germany. They were a list of his 3._____ about the Church. This was the beginning of the Protestant Reformation.

Luther did not intend to form a new church. He only wanted to reform the Roman 4._____. But the Church called him a 5._____ and excommunicated him. This caused a split in Germany. Many of the German people disliked the Church. But they wanted to remain Christians. The Reformation soon turned 6._____. In Germany, Catholics and Protestants fought against each other. This happened until 1555. That year, the Peace of Augsburg allowed every German prince to choose to be Catholic or 7._____.

At the same time as the problems in Germany, the Reformation quickly moved across Europe. Men like Jean Calvin and Ulrich Zwingli led their own protests against the Church. Soon, new Protestant sects were founded. There was the Lutheran 8._____. There were Presbyterians and Baptists. There were also Calvinists. And, in England, the Anglican Church was founded when Henry VIII 9._____ from the Roman Catholic Church.

B **Read the passage above and answer the following questions.**

_____ 10. What is the main point of this article?
- a The Catholic Church used to dominate life in Europe.
- b The Reformation was led by many different people.
- c Henry VIII founded the Anglican Church in England.
- d Martin Luther posted his 95 theses on a church in 1517.

_____ 11. Who started the Protestant Reformation?
- a John Calvin.
- b Henry VIII.
- c Ulrich Zwingli.
- d Martin Luther.

_____ 12. "The Church called him a heretic and excommunicated him." Someone who is "excommunicated" is _____.
- a removed from the Church
- b made a leader of the Church
- c praised by the Church
- d paid by the Church

Unit 08

A Listen to the passage and fill in the blanks.

🎧 128 ┃ **The French Revolution**

In France in the eighteenth century, life was difficult for most people. The ruler of France was the king. He ruled by 1._____. This was the idea that God had chosen the king to be the ruler. This meant that the king could do anything he wanted. There were also nobles with great power in France. The 2._____ mostly lived good lives, too. But the rest of the people had difficult lives. They were poor, had little or no land, and had no freedom.

In the 1780s, the world was changing. The Americans had won their 3._____ with England and become free. The French people wanted the same thing. King Louis XVI and his wife, Marie Antoinette, were 4._____ rulers. They taxed the people. But the people became tired of their poor lives. So, on July 14, 1789, they rebelled. They stormed the 5._____ on that day. It was a prison in Paris. They freed the prisoners and took the weapons that were there. The French Revolution had begun.

The French Revolution was very violent. Louis XVI was 6._____ during the revolution. More nobles and clergy were killed, too. Thousands of people died during the revolution. In the end, the 7._____ was destroyed. But France did not become a 8._____ like the people had hoped. Instead, Napoleon Bonaparte, a general, became the emperor of France. He would then lead France to war with many European nations until he was finally defeated in 1815.

B Read the passage above and answer the following questions.

_____ 9. What is the main idea of this article?
- a Poor people started the French Revolution.
- b Napoleon was the first emperor of France.
- c Louis XVI believed he spoke for God.
- d Americans caused the French Revolution.

_____ 10. What was the first thing that happened in the French Revolution?
- a The king was killed by angry people.　b The Bastille in Paris was stormed.
- c Napoleon became emperor.　　　　　d Government switched to democracy.

_____ 11. "So, on July 14, 1789, they rebelled." Another word for "rebel" is _____.
- a run　　　　b talk
- c fight　　　 d produce

9

Unit 09

A Listen to the passage and fill in the blanks.

🎧 129 **The Great War**

For centuries, European countries had fought each other. But, from 1914 to 1918, there was a different kind of war. It was a world war. At that time, people called it the Great War. Later, it was called World War I (WWI). At first, people thought it would just be another war. By the time it ended, millions were dead. And many people were horrified by the 1._____ of war.

Before WWI began, many European countries had 2._____ with each other. They promised to defend other countries if they were in trouble. On June 28, 1914, Archduke Francis Ferdinand of Austria-Hungary was 3._____ in Sarajevo. The Austrians quickly declared war on Serbia. However, because of the different alliances, what should have been a small war became an 4._____ one. The Central Powers led by Germany, Austria-Hungary, and the Ottoman Empire were on one side. The Allied Powers led by England, France, and Russia were on the other side.

The Germans 5._____ attacked France. However, the German advance was stopped. Neither side could move against the other. Thus 6._____ warfare began. For four years, each side succeeded in killing many of the other's soldiers. 7._____ and airplanes were used in war for the first time. So were 8._____. Finally, the war ended. But it didn't end war. Around two decades later, World War II began. It was an even worse war than WWI had been.

B Read the passage above and answer the following questions.

_____ 9. Which statement below best expresses the main idea?
- a The Great War was started by Austria.
- b The Great War came to an end in 1918.
- c The Great War was a different kind of war.
- d World War II started two decades after the Great War.

_____ 10. Which of the following is true?
- a Airplanes were not used in the Great War.
- b The Great War started in Russia.
- c France was an Allied Power in the Great War.
- d The Great War lasted for over six years.

_____ 11. "The Austrians quickly declared war on Serbia." The word with the same meaning as "declare" is _____.
- a poison
- b pray
- c say
- d attend

Unit 10

A Listen to the passage and fill in the blanks.

🎧 130 **Globalization**

In the years after World War II, the world greatly changed. Much of this was due to new 1._____. For instance, the jet was developed. This increased the speed that people could travel. There were also advances in 2._____. Computers and the Internet were invented. It became much easier for people to communicate with others all around the world.

This has led to the spread of globalization. Basically, the world is becoming a smaller place. In the past, what happened in one country 3._____ affected other countries. Or it took a long time for any 4._____ to occur. But the world is different today. Because of globalization, what happens in one part of the world can affect places all around it.

Thanks to globalization, people can now do 5._____ more easily with those in other countries. When you go to the 6._____, you can see various foods from all of the different countries.

This happens because of globalization. Also, people are learning more about other countries these days. This leads to more 7._____ about other countries. In the age of globalization, there has not been a single 8._____. And the world is becoming richer. Globalization has surely been good for the world.

B Read the passage above and answer the following questions.

_____ 9. According to the article, what has led to globalization?
  a Easier ways of communication.   b Business.
  c Different foods at supermarkets.   d No world wars.

_____ 10. What is the main idea of this article?
  a Globalization is good for the world.
  b People should start learning more about other countries.
  c It's harder to do business in a globalized world.
  d People don't like going to the supermarket these days.

_____ 11. "In the past, what happened in one country rarely affected other countries." In this sentence, the word "rarely" has the opposite meaning of the word _____.
  a once   b never
  c usually   d only

11

Unit 11

🎧 131

A Listen to the passage and fill in the blanks.

The Five Kingdoms of Life

There is an amazing 1.＿＿＿＿＿＿ of life on the Earth. Scientists have classified all forms of life into five different kingdoms. Each kingdom has its own characteristics.

The first is the 2.＿＿＿＿＿＿ kingdom. There are about 10,000 species in it. The members of this kingdom are prokaryotes that are unicellular. Its members include various kinds of 3.＿＿＿＿＿＿ and some algae.

The second is the 4.＿＿＿＿＿＿ kingdom. There are around 250,000 species in it. The members of this kingdom include protozoans and some kinds of algae.

The third is the 5.＿＿＿＿＿＿ kingdom. There are around 100,000 species in it. Members of this kingdom are similar to plants. But they do not use 6.＿＿＿＿＿＿ to create nutrients. Mushrooms are members of this kingdom.

The fourth is the Plantae kingdom. There are around 250,000 species in it. Plants, trees, flowers, and 7.＿＿＿＿＿＿ all belong to this kingdom.

The fifth is the Animalia kingdom. It is the biggest with over 1,000,000 species in it. It is formed by 8.＿＿＿＿＿＿ animals.

B Read the passage above and answer the following questions.

＿＿＿＿ 9. The biggest difference between the Fungi Kingdom and the Plantae Kingdom is members of the ＿＿＿＿.
- a Fungi Kingdom include flowers
- b Plantae Kingdom include mushrooms
- c Fungi Kingdom use pollination
- d Plantae Kingdom use photosynthesis

＿＿＿＿ 10. "Scientists have classified all forms of life into five different kingdoms." A word with a similar meaning to "classified" is ＿＿＿＿.
- a sorted
- b planned
- c designed
- d prepared

＿＿＿＿ 11. The article is mainly about ＿＿＿＿.
- a the number of species in each kingdom
- b the characteristics of each kingdom
- c the color of the living things in each kingdom
- d the largest and smallest kingdoms

Unit 12

Listen to the passage and fill in the blanks.

🎧 132 **Gregor Mendel**

These days, scientists can do amazing things with 1._____. They can modify the genetic structure of plants. This can let them produce more fruit or grain. Some are even 2._____ to diseases. But the field of genetics is very young. It is barely over 100 years old. And it was all started by a 3._____ called Gregor Mendel.

Gregor Mendel enjoyed gardening. He especially liked to grow 4._____ in his garden. While doing that, he noticed that some pea plants had different 5._____. He saw that some were tall while others were short. The colors of their flowers were different. And there were other differences, too. He wanted to know why. So he started experimenting with them.

Mendel started 6._____ plants with one another. He learned about dominant and recessive genes this way. He created 7._____, which are plants that carry the genes of different plants. He grew many generations of peas and learned a lot about them. What Mendel learned became the basis for modern genetics.

Mendel did most of his work with peas in the 1850s and 1860s. But, at first, people 8._____ his work. It was not until the early twentieth century that people began to study his research. Then they realized how much he had really 9._____.

B **Read the passage above and answer the following questions.**

_____ 10. "But the field of genetics is very young." In this sentence, what is the meaning of "the field of genetics is very young"?
   a Research into genetics isn't considered fact.
   b Most genetic research isn't taken seriously.
   c Genetic research hasn't been around for very long.
   d People are still deciding if genetics is worth studying.

_____ 11. Another good title for this article is _____.
   a Dominant and Recessive Genes   b The Crossbreeding of Plants
   c The Best Way to Grow Peas   d The Basis for Modern Genetics

_____ 12. "Some are even resistant to diseases." A word with the same meaning of "resistant" is _____.
   a familiar   b unattractive
   c supportive   d opposing

Unit 13

Listen to the passage and fill in the blanks.

🎧 133 **Pollination and Germination**

All plants reproduce somehow. This allows them to produce 1._____ that will grow into mature plants. There are two important steps in plant reproduction. The first is pollination. The second is germination.

Most plants have both male and female 2._____ organs. However, they must come into contact with each other in order for the plant to reproduce. This happens through pollination. 3._____ from the male part of a plant must reach the female part of the plant. This can happen in many ways. The wind may sometimes blow the pollen from one part to the other. But this is very 4._____. Many times, animals such as bees, butterflies, and other insects pollinate plants. As they go from plant to plant, pollen gets 5._____ to their bodies. When they land on a new plant, some of it 6._____. Many times, this pollinates the plant. Once the pollen goes from the anther (the male part) to the stigma (the female part), the plant has been pollinated and can start to reproduce.

The other important step is germination. Germination happens after a plant's seeds have been formed. At first, the plant's seeds are 7._____. However, when they germinate, they come to life and begin to grow. If the conditions are good, then the seed will become a seedling. Eventually, it will 8._____ and become a plant.

B **Read the passage above and answer the following questions.**

_____ 9. According to the article, what is the first step in the reproduction process of a plant?
- a Germination.
- b Pollination.
- c Reproduction.
- d Maturation.

_____ 10. "As they go from plant to plant, pollen gets stuck to their bodies." A word with a similar meaning to "stuck" is _____.
- a attached
- b infected
- c formed
- d created

_____ 11. Another good title for this article is _____.
- a The Maturation of Plants
- b Pollination by Bees
- c The Steps of Plant Reproduction
- d How to Grow Plants from Seedlings

Unit 14

A Listen to the passage and fill in the blanks.

 134

The Carbon and Nitrogen Cycles

Carbon is one of the most important 1._____. All living things are made from carbon. But it is constantly changing forms. This is called the carbon cycle. In the atmosphere, carbon is often present in the form of 2._____. This is a compound that has one carbon atom and two oxygen atoms. Plants breathe in the carbon dioxide and use it to produce 3._____. The carbon then becomes part of the plants. These plants die and then often get buried. Over time, these plants may turn into fossil fuels like coal or 4._____. People later burn these fossil fuels, which releases carbon dioxide into the atmosphere.

Another important element is nitrogen. There is also a 5._____. Nitrogen is actually the most common element in the atmosphere. Around 80% of the air we breathe is nitrogen. We don't need nitrogen like we need oxygen. But nitrogen is still important.

There is often nitrogen in the soil. Plants 6._____ the nitrogen from the soil. When people and animals eat the plants, they release the nitrogen into their bodies. 7._____ in people's and animals' bodies can fix the nitrogen so that the bodies can use it. Later, when the people and animals die and 8._____, the nitrogen returns to the soil or the atmosphere. Then it can be reused again.

B Read the passage above and answer the following questions.

_____ 9. Which of the following statements is TRUE?
- a Nitrogen from dead plants turns into fossil fuels.
- b Everything that is living has carbon in it.
- c We don't need oxygen like we need nitrogen.
- d Around 80% of the air we breathe is carbon.

_____ 10. Dead, buried plants eventually turn into _____.
- a oxygen
- b carbon dioxide
- c elements
- d fossil fuels

_____ 11. "Bacteria in people's and animals' bodies can fix the nitrogen so that the bodies can use it." In this sentence, the word "fix" is closest in meaning to _____.
- a repair
- b change
- c fasten
- d hold

Unit 15

A Listen to the passage and fill in the blanks.

 135   **The Immune System**

Every day, the body is 1._____ by bacteria, viruses, and other invaders. It is the body's immune system that fights these invaders. It helps keep the person healthy. The immune system is made up of various cells, tissues, and organs.

2._____ are very important. They are also called leukocytes. They move through the body in 3._____. There are two types of leukocytes. The first try to destroy invading organisms. These are phagocytes. The second are lymphocytes. They help the body remember various invaders. This way, it can destroy them in the future.

Antigens often invade the body. The body then produces 4._____. They fight the antigens. If the antibodies succeed, they will always remain in the body. This lets the body fight the disease again in the future. This is very effective against viruses.

People are often born immune to certain diseases. This is called 5._____ immunity. But there is adaptive immunity, too. This happens when the body 6._____ threats to it. It then learns how to defeat them. Also, thanks to 7._____, people can become immune to many diseases. Vaccinations help improve the strength of the immune system.

B Read the passage above and answer the following questions.

_____ 8. White blood cells are also called _____.
- a leukocytes
- b antigens
- c viruses
- d antibodies

_____ 9. "Every day, the body is attacked by bacteria, viruses, and other invaders." A word with a similar meaning to "invaders" is _____.
- a attackers
- b visitors
- c burglars
- d frauds

_____ 10. Which of the following sentences is closest to the main idea of this article?
- a Our body has ways to defend itself.
- b Some people get sick easier than others.
- c Vaccines help to save people's lives.
- d Bacteria, viruses, and diseases are everywhere.

A Listen to the passage and fill in the blanks.

🎧 136

Volcanic Eruptions

Sometimes, volcanoes suddenly erupt. They spew tons of ash, gas, and
1._____. They might even kill large numbers of people. What is it that
makes a volcano erupt?

Deep in the Earth, there is usually a lot of 2._____. Also, the temperature deep
underground can be very high. In fact, it is often high enough to melt rocks. Melted
rock that is beneath the ground is called magma. The magma is constantly trying to
move up toward the 3._____. Under the earth, there are large pools of magma
that have gathered together. These are called magma 4._____. These magma
chambers often exist beneath volcanoes. Eventually, the pressure beneath the earth
becomes too great. The magma forces its way to the surface. This causes a volcano
to erupt. When a volcano erupts, it often 5._____ ash and gas. It can also
expel magma. Magma that is on the surface is called lava. The lava often creeps down
the sides of the volcano until it eventually cools and 6._____.

The size of the eruption depends on the amount of pressure that is released. Some
volcanoes release a steady amount of lava. These have a low amount of pressure.
Other volcanoes erupt 7._____. They can shoot ash miles into the air. They
can expel lava and gas very far in the area. These are the most dangerous
8._____. Mt. Vesuvius, Krakatoa, and Mt. St. Helens all had explosive
eruptions that killed many people.

B Read the passage above and answer the following questions.

_____ 9. Which of the following can be another good title for this article?
a How Large Are Volcanoes?
b Where Are Most Volcanoes Located?
c What Causes A Volcano to Erupt?
d Who first discovered why volcanoes explode?

_____ 10. "They spew tons of ash, gas, and lava." A word with a similar meaning to
"spew" is _____.
a bury   b hold
c expel   d carry

_____ 11. According to the article, the size of an eruption depends on _____.
a the size of the volcano   b the temperature of the magma
c the age of the volcano   d the amount of pressure released

Unit 17

Listen to the passage and fill in the blanks.

🎧 137 | **Mass Extinctions**

Every once in a while, a mass extinction occurs on Earth. When this happens, large numbers of 1._____ all go extinct at once. Scientists have identified at least five mass extinctions during Earth's history. During these mass extinctions, up to 95% of all life on the planet was killed. The last mass extinction happened about 65 million years ago. Scientists refer to it as the K-T Extinction.

65 million years ago, the Earth looked very different. There were no humans. Instead, 2._____ ruled the land and the seas. This was a time called the Cretaceous Period. Then, suddenly, there was a mass extinction. Scientists are not exactly sure what happened. But most of them believe that an 3._____ or comet struck the Earth. This caused a 4._____ change in the planet. Large amounts of dust were thrown into the atmosphere. This 5._____ the sun. No sunlight could reach the Earth, so many plants died. The animals that ate the plants then died. And the animals that ate those animals died, too.

The K-T Extinction killed all of the dinosaurs. And about half of the other species on the planet died, too. Of course, all life did not die. In fact, some life flourished. After the K-T Extinction, 6._____ began to increase in number. Eventually, humans 7._____. So, without the K-T Extinction, humans might not ever have existed.

B **Read the passage above and answer the following questions.**

_____ 8. Which of the following statements is not TRUE?
  a Scientists know that an asteroid caused the mass extinction.
  b Dinosaurs experienced mass extinction millions of years ago.
  c Mammals increased in number after dinosaurs became extinct.
  d The Cretaceous Period was 65 million years ago.

_____ 9. "Of course, all life did not die. In fact, some life flourished." The word "flourished" is similar in meaning to _____.
  a improved   b suffered
  c decomposed   d ruled

_____ 10. What is the main idea of this article?
  a Dinosaurs used to rule the earth, but now humans do.
  b A mass extinction changed the earth millions of years ago.
  c Not all scientists agree on the cause of the K-T Extinction.
  d When the sun is blocked, plants and animals die.

Unit 18

A Listen to the passage and fill in the blanks.

🎧 138 **Ocean Resources and Conservation**

Oceans cover around 71% of the Earth's surface. And they are full of many different resources that can benefit 1._____.

For one, the oceans are a great source of fish and seafood. Fisherman from numerous countries sail the oceans to catch fish for people to eat. However, humans are catching too many fish. Fish 2._____ are starting to become smaller. So humans need to be careful. They should not 3._____ areas. Instead, they should catch smaller numbers of fish. Then, more fish can grow and 4._____ the oceans.

The oceans also have many valuable resources beneath their floors. For instance, oil and natural gas are 5._____ from beneath the seafloor in many places. But, again, humans need to be careful. Sometimes, oil 6._____ release large amounts of oil into the water. This can kill many fish, birds, and other sea creatures.

There are even large amounts of certain ores beneath the ocean. Gold, silver, and other 7._____ metals could be mined in the future. And people can even use the oceans for energy. 8._____ energy could provide cheap and abundant energy in the future. But we need to take good care of our oceans. They have many resources, but we need to 9._____ them, too.

B Read the passage above and answer the following questions.

_____ 10. According to the article, what are two negative things happening to oceans?
  a Tidal energy and mining.
  b Fishing and energy production.
  c Valuable resources and ore.
  d Oil spills and overfishing.

_____ 11. "Tidal energy could provide cheap and abundant energy in the future." A word with the opposite meaning of "abundant" is _____.
  a clean   b limited
  c expensive   d difficult

_____ 12. What is the main idea of the article?
  a Oceans provide us with useful food resources.
  b Fishing in oceans must be stopped.
  c People need to protect ocean resources.
  d Cheap energy can be produced by oceans.

19

Unit 19

A Listen to the passage and fill in the blanks.

🎧 139 **Atoms and Their Atomic Numbers**

All atoms have different numbers of protons, neutrons, and electrons. The protons are 1._____ charged and are in the nucleus. Neutrons are also in the nucleus. But they have no charge. And electrons 2._____ the nucleus. They have negative charges. The number of protons and neutrons in an atom is often—but not always—the same.

Every element has a different number of 3._____. This helps make it different from another element. An element's 4._____ is the same as its number of protons. For example, hydrogen has only 1 proton. So this means that it has an atomic number of 1. It is the first element on the 5._____ of elements. Helium is the second element. It has an atomic number of 2. This means that it has 2 protons in its nucleus.

There are more than 100 different elements. Scientists often recognize them according to their atomic numbers. 6._____ is the basis for all life on Earth. Its atomic number is 6. 7._____ is an important element. Its atomic number is 8. Iron is another important element. 26 is its atomic number. Gold has an atomic number of 79. And 8._____ atomic number is 92.

B Read the passage above and answer the following questions.

_____ 9. According to the article, what helps to make elements different from each other?
   a The strength of the nucleus.
   b The amount of time they have existed.
   c The number of protons each has.
   d Whether or not they are charged.

_____ 10. This article is mostly about _____.
   a the importance of protons and neutrons
   b what makes atoms different from each other
   c the number of atoms in the universe
   d positive and negative charges within atoms

_____ 11. _____ is the basis for all life on Earth.
   a Oxygen   b Hydrogen
   c Helium   d Carbon

Unit 20

Listen to the passage and fill in the blanks.

🎧 140 **Energy and Environmental Risks**

In the modern age, human society runs on energy. Most machines need electricity to operate. Humans have many different ways to create electricity. But some ways are 1._____ to the environment.

For example, 2._____ are the most common kind of energy. They include coal, oil, and natural gas. First, people have to 3._____ them from the ground. This can sometimes harm the environment. However, scientists are creating cleaner and more efficient ways to do that these days. So the environment is not damaged as much. But when people burn these fossil fuels, they can 4._____ gases that might harm the environment.

Tidal energy is another way to make electricity. This uses the ocean 5._____ to make electricity. But some kinds of tidal energy can kill many fish and other sea creatures. Also, dams can create lots of clean 6._____ energy. But dams create lakes and change the courses of rivers. So they can change the environment very much.

Nuclear energy is a very powerful form of energy. It is cheap. It is also very clean. But many people are afraid of it because it uses 7._____ materials. Also, there have been some accidents at nuclear power plants in the past. But the technology is much better these days. So many countries are starting to build more nuclear power 8._____ now.

B **Read the passage above and answer the following questions.**

_____ 9. What is the main idea of the article?
- a Human society runs on energy.
- b Most machines need electricity to operate.
- c There are different ways to use energy.
- d Energy production can harm the environment.

_____ 10. What is the most commonly used type of energy?
- a Nuclear energy.   b Tidal energy.
- c Hydroelectric power.   d Fossil fuels.

_____ 11. According to the article, why are many people afraid of nuclear energy?
- a It can destroy sea creatures.
- b It's cheap and not good for the economy.
- c It uses radioactive materials.
- d It creates lakes and changes the course of rivers.

A Listen to the passage and fill in the blanks.

🎧 141   **Square Roots**

You have probably 1._____ a number by itself before. For example, two times two is four. (2×2=4) Four times four is sixteen. (4×4=16) Five times five is twenty-five. (5×5=25) And ten times ten is one hundred. (10×10=100) When you multiply a number by itself, you are 2._____ it.

However, what happens when you do an inverse operation? An inverse operation of squaring is finding the 3._____ of a number. When the divisor of a number and the result are the same, then that is the square root of the number.

For instance, the square root of 4 is two. ($\sqrt{4}$=2) Why is that? The reason is that four divided by two is two. (4÷2=2) The 4._____ and the result are the same. Also, the square root of 49 is seven. Forty-nine divided by seven is seven. And the square root of 100 is ten. One hundred divided by ten is ten.

However, not all square roots are whole numbers. In fact, they are usually 5._____ numbers. For example, what is the square root of three? It is not a whole number. Instead, it is 1.73205. It actually goes on to 6._____ because it can never be solved. And how about the square root of six? It is 2.44948. It too goes on to infinity and cannot be solved. Actually, the 7._____ of numbers have square roots that are irrational numbers.

B Read the passage above and answer the following questions.

_____ 8. "However, what happens when you do an inverse operation?" In this sentence, "inverse" has a similar meaning to _____.

- a opposite
- b complex
- c simple
- d mathematical

_____ 9. Which of the following statements is TRUE?

- a An inverse operation of squaring is finding the square root.
- b Most numbers have square roots that end after three numbers.
- c All numbers have square roots that can be calculated.
- d Forty-nine divided by seven is five.

_____ 10. Another good title for this article is _____.

- a Square Roots of Irrational Numbers
- b Finding the Square of Numbers
- c Calculating Whole and Irrational Numbers
- d How to Calculate Square Roots of Numbers

Unit 22

A Listen to the passage and fill in the blanks.

🎧 142

Probability and Statistics

The probability of something is the chance that it will happen. This is often expressed as a 1._____. For example, if you flip a coin, the probability of it being heads is fifty percent. If you roll a die, the probability of it being the number one is 16.67%, or $\frac{1}{6}$. You can 2._____ the probability by taking the number of ways something can happen and dividing it by the total number of 3._____.

Statistics, on the other hand, is the field of math that collects, organizes, and interprets data. Once data has been collected, one of the easiest ways to analyze it is with 4._____. For data that involves probability, circle graphs—or 5._____ —are the best to use. These can be divided into 100 percentage points. Perhaps there is a fifty percent chance of something happening, a twenty-five percent chance of something else happening, and a twenty-five percent chance of something different happening. This can easily be shown on a circle graph.

On the other hand, other statistics are best recorded on a 6._____. These are simple charts with an x-axis and a y-axis. For example, perhaps the person is recording some students' best subjects. The classes are English, math, science, and history. These classes go on the x-axis, which is 7._____. The number of students that do well in each class goes on the y-axis, which is 8._____. This makes the data easy to see and to interpret.

B Read the passage above and answer the following questions.

_____ 9. Probability can be expressed as _____.
    a circle graphs or percentages   b ratios or pie charts
    c percentages or fractions   d bar graphs or fractions

_____ 10. Another good title for this article is _____.
    a Why Probability Is Better than Statistics
    b How to Best Organize Probability and Statistics Data
    c Collecting, Organizing, and Interpreting Statistics Data
    d Building an Accurate Bar Graph

_____ 11. "This makes the data easy to see and to interpret." A word with a similar meaning to "interpret" is _____.
    a classify   b organize
    c collect   d understand

Unit 23

A Listen to the passage and fill in the blanks.

🎧 143 **The Metric System**

The metric system is a system of 1._____ that uses the base-10 system. It measures length, volume, weight, pressure, energy, and temperature. There are several units in the metric system. But, since it uses the base-10 system, 2._____ them is quite easy.

The meter is the unit used to measure 3._____ in the metric system. But there are also millimeters, centimeters, decimeters, decameters, hectometers, and kilometers. So, in 1 meter, there are 10 decimeters, 100 centimeters, and 1,000 millimeters. Also, in 1 kilometer, there are 10 hectometers, 100 decameters, and 1,000 meters. The most 4._____ units of length are the millimeter, centimeter, meter, and kilometer.

The liter is the unit used to measure 5._____ in the metric system. However, there are also milliliters, centiliters, deciliters, decaliters, hectoliters, and kiloliters. The method to convert them is the same as for meters.

The gram is the unit used to measure 6._____ in the metric system. The most common units of weight are the gram and the kilogram. There are other units, but they are not commonly used.

Finally, the metric system uses 7._____ to measure temperature. 0 degrees Celsius is the temperature at which water freezes. 100 degrees Celsius is the temperature at which water boils.

B Read the passage above and answer the following questions.

_____ 8. Which of the following statements is TRUE about the metric system?
- a There are 100 centimeters in a kilometer.
- b The most common units of lengths include milliliters and kiloliters.
- c The metric system uses Celsius to measure volume.
- d Grams are used to measure weight in the metric system.

_____ 9. "But since it uses the base-10 system, converting them is quite easy." A word with a similar meaning to "converting" is _____.
- a multiplying
- b adding
- c changing
- d recording

_____ 10. Another good title for this article is _____.
- a Calculating the Metric System
- b An Unused System of Measurement
- c Liters, Grams, and Kilometers
- d Measures and Units of the Metric System

24

Listen to the passage and fill in the blanks.

🎧 144 | **Dimensions**

The physical world we live in has three dimensions. These three dimensions can all be measured and 1._____ on a graph. They are length, width, and depth.

Length is the first dimension. It is represented by a simple line. On a three-dimensional graph, it is represented by the x-axis, which runs 2._____.

The second dimension is width. When an object exists in two dimensions, it can take the shape of a 3._____ , such as a square, rectangle, triangle, or circle. In other words, it can be represented in both length and width. On a three-dimensional graph, width is represented by the y-axis, which also runs horizontally.

The third dimension is depth. It is also called height. When an object exists in three dimensions, it can take the shape of a 4._____ , such as a cube, pyramid, sphere, or prism. On a three-dimensional graph, depth is represented by the z-axis, which runs 5._____.

The fourth dimension is 6._____ . Scientists have a name for a cube that exists in four dimensions. They call it a tesseract.

So how many dimensions are there? Scientists are not sure. Some believe that there may be eleven dimensions. Others claim that there are even more. Right now, scientists are searching for 7._____ dimensions. They have not found any yet, but they believe they exist.

B **Read the passage above and answer the following questions.**

_____ 8. Which sentence from the passage is closest to the main idea?
   a Some believe that there may be eleven dimensions.
   b Length is the first dimension.
   c Scientists have a name for a cube that exits in four dimensions.
   d The physical world we live in has three dimensions.

_____ 9. "Some believe that there may be eleven dimensions." When you "believe" something, you don't _____.
   a doubt it   b like it
   c trust it   d depend on it

_____ 10. "On a three-dimensional graph, depth is represented by the z-axis, which runs vertically." Which of the following is the opposite of "vertically"?
   a Fashionably.   b Mostly.
   c Horizontally.   d Casually.

Unit 25

Listen to the passage and fill in the blanks.

🎧 145 | **Types of Poems**

Poets have many different types of poems to choose from when they write. They can write very long or very short poems. They can write about many different subjects. And they can write with different 1._____ and in different meters.

One of the oldest types of poems is the 2._____. This is a very long poem. It can often be thousands of lines long. An epic poem is typically about a hero and his 3._____. There have been many famous epic poems in history. The *Iliad*, *Odyssey*, *Aeneid*, *Beowulf*, and *Gilgamesh* are just a few of the many epic poems.

On the other hand, many poems are very short. 4._____ are one type of short poem. They are poems with fourteen lines. Usually, the last two lines in a sonnet rhyme. Sonnets can be about many different topics. William 5._____ wrote many famous sonnets.

6._____ can be long or short poems. Each stanza in a couplet has two lines. The last word in each line rhymes.

7._____ are very short poems. They only have four lines. And cinquains have five lines. Limericks are also poems with five lines. And haikus are poems with only three lines. The first and third lines have five syllables. And the second line has seven syllables. They are some of the shortest of poems.

B **Read the passage above and answer the following questions.**

_____ 8. "And they can write with different rhyme schemes and in different meters." In this sentence, "schemes" has a similar meaning to _____.
  a formats
  b themes
  c lengths
  d words

_____ 9. Which of the following statements is TRUE?
  a There aren't many famous epic poems.
  b Most poems are very short.
  c Epic poems can be thousands of lines long.
  d Shakespeare was famous for his haikus.

_____ 10. What is the main idea of the article?
  a There are many different types of poems.
  b The epic poem is the best type of poem.
  c Shakespeare was the world's greatest poet.
  d Ancient poetry is more popular than modern poetry.

Unit 26

A Listen to the passage and fill in the blanks.

 146 | **Greek and Latin Roots**

English has more words than any other language. Why is this? One reason is that English 1._____ words from many other languages. Then it turns these words into new English words. Many of these words come from Greek and Latin. These are called roots. By studying roots, a person can learn the 2._____ of many different words in English.

For instance, the root hydro comes from Greek. It means "water." From that root, we get the words hydrate, dehydrate, hydrant, 3._____, and many others. The root aster comes from Greek. It means "star." From aster, we get the words 4._____, asterisk, astronomy, astronaut, and many others. Geo also comes from Greek. It means "earth." The words 5._____, geometry, and geography all come from it.

Of course, there are many roots from Latin, too. For instance, the root vid means to "see." From that root, we get video, visual, visualize, and many others. The root script means to "write." From it, we get transcript, 6._____, and others. And port means to "carry." From that root, we get transport, 7._____, export, and import, among others.

Without borrowing from other languages, English would have very few words. But, thanks to Latin and Greek—and other languages, too—English has many, many words.

B Read the passage above and answer the following questions.

_____ 8. This article is mainly about _____.
- [a] how Greek and Latin have many English roots
- [b] the number of roots in the English language
- [c] why English is the most popular language
- [d] how English uses roots from Greek and Latin

_____ 9. According to the article, which of the following statements is TRUE?
- [a] Roots from English are used in Greek and Latin.
- [b] English has more words than any other language.
- [c] The root "vid" means "video" in Latin.
- [d] English has many words because it is the oldest language.

_____ 10. "One reason is that English borrows words from many other languages." In this sentence, "borrows" could best be replaced with the word _____.
- [a] steals
- [b] lends
- [c] uses
- [d] writes

A Listen to the passage and fill in the blanks.

🎧 147 | **Common Proverbs**

Proverbs are short 1._____ that people sometimes use. They typically pass on some type of wisdom. The English language has a very large number of proverbs.

One proverb is "2._____ makes the heart grow fonder." It means that people usually have good memories of events or people from the past. Of course, at the time, they might not have thought much of them. However, over time, the "absence" changed their memories, so they remember the events or people 3._____.

"All that glitters is not gold" is another important proverb. Gold is very valuable, and it glitters brightly. But many other things glitter, too. However, they may not be valuable. In fact, they may even be harmful. So this proverb is a 4._____. People should be careful because not every shiny, good-looking thing is like gold.

"He who hesitates is lost" is a popular expression. This proverb tells people not to hesitate. They should make a 5._____ and go with it. If they hesitate or wait too long, they might lose an important 6._____.

Finally, "It's no use crying over spilt milk" is another common proverb. Sometimes bad things might happen to a person. But that person should not cry about it. Instead, the person should accept what has happened and 7._____. That is the meaning of that proverb.

B Read the passage above and answer the following questions.

_____ 8. "If they hesitate or wait too long, they might lose an important opportunity." In this sentence, "hesitate" has a similar meaning to _____.
- a worry
- b pause
- c decide
- d focus

_____ 9. The proverb "Absence makes the heart grow fonder" means _____.
- a people remember good things about those who are no longer around
- b not everything that is shiny and good-looking is valuable
- c people will miss opportunities if they wait too long
- d people should accept bad things that have happened and move on

_____ 10. This article is mainly about _____.
- a how proverbs were invented
- b why English has so many proverbs
- c the most important English proverbs
- d popular proverbs people use

A Listen to the passage and fill in the blanks.

🎧 148 **Classical Art**

The ancient Greeks loved art. They made all kinds of works of art. This included pottery, paintings, sculptures, and murals. The Greeks even considered their buildings to be works of art. So they made beautifully 1._____ buildings as well.

Many examples of pottery have survived from ancient Greece. Pottery in ancient Greece had two functions. People used it to eat or drink from. And they used it for decorations. Many Greek 2._____ have beautiful pictures painted on them. These pictures often show stories from Greek 3._____.

Sculpture was highly prized in ancient Greece. The Greeks made sculptures from either stone or bronze. Many stone sculptures have 4._____ to today. But few bronze sculptures have. The Greeks 5._____ the people in sculptures exactly as they looked in real life.

As for 6._____, many Greek buildings still exist today. One important feature of these buildings is their columns. The Greeks made three types of columns: Doric, Ionic, and Corinthian. Doric columns were the simplest. They had very plain designs. Ionic columns had flutes, or lines, carved into them from the top to the bottom. They were also more decorative than Doric columns. Corinthian columns were the most decorative ones of all. Their tops—called 7._____—often had flowers or other designs on them. And they also had flutes.

B Read the passage above and answer the following questions.

_____ 8. "Sculpture was highly prized in ancient Greece." In this sentence, "prized" is most similar in meaning to _____.
- a priced
- b valued
- c guarded
- d carved

_____ 9. This article is mainly about _____.
- a types of classical art
- b ancient Greek art
- c Greek mythology
- d kinds of columns

_____ 10. According to the article, pottery in Greece was used for eating, drinking, and _____.
- a ceremonies
- b decoration
- c mythology
- d building

Unit 29

A Listen to the passage and fill in the blanks.

 149 | **From Baroque to Realism**

From around the late sixteenth century to the early eighteenth century, there was a new type of art in Europe. It was called Baroque. There were Baroque artists in every European country. So they all had slightly different styles. But there were many 1._____ that Baroque artists shared.

For one, there were often 2._____ between light and dark in Baroque paintings. The artists also focused on movement. And they stressed 3._____ in the figures they painted. This was one way they tried to show emotions in their paintings. The works of Baroque artists also had symbolic or 4._____ meanings. Many Baroque artists painted religious topics, too.

One very important characteristic was that Baroque artists were 5._____. So they painted their subjects as realistically as possible. They knew about 6._____ . So they could show things such as size and distance. They were also able to use the 7._____ in their paintings very well. This ability made many Baroque artists quite famous. Today, people still admire the works of artists such as El Greco, Rembrandt, and Caravaggio.

B Read the passage above and answer the following questions.

_____ 8. According to the article, which of the following statements is TRUE?
  a Baroque artists tried to show emotion in their paintings.
  b Painting realistically was not a goal for Baroque artists.
  c Facial expressions weren't important for Baroque artists.
  d Baroque artists tried to avoid religious topics.

_____ 9. "Today, people still admire the works of artists such as El Greco, Rembrandt, and Caravaggio." In this sentence, "admire" has a similar meaning to _____.
  a purchase
  b discuss
  c respect
  d copy

_____ 10. Another good title for this article is _____.
  a Art from the Late 1500s to the Early 1700s
  b El Greco, Rembrandt, and Caravaggio
  c Use of Perspective in Baroque Art
  d The Light and Dark of Realistic Paintings

A Listen to the passage and fill in the blanks.

🎧 150   **The Classical Period of Music**

The years between 1750 and 1820 saw some of the greatest music ever created. This time is now called the Classical Period of music. Among the 1._____ who wrote during this period were Mozart, Beethoven, Haydn, and Schubert.

By 1750, people were getting tired of the 2._____ Period. So they worked on new forms of music. Thus arose the Classical Period. It has several important characteristics. For one, the 3._____ of the music often changed. In a single piece of music, there was not just one mood anymore. Instead, the mood could suddenly change anytime during a piece. The same was true of the 4._____ of the music. Music from this period followed several different rhythmic patterns. There were often sudden 5._____. Or the music would suddenly go from being very slow to very fast or from very soft to very loud.

Also, music from the Classical Period has beautiful 6._____. The works the composers created are typically easy to remember. Of course, they are still 7._____ works. But the ease with which people can remember them has helped increase their 8._____. Even today, the works of composers from this period are among the most popular of all classical music.

B Read the passage above and answer the following questions.

_____ 9. Why did the Classical Period of music begin?
- [a] Because people were tired of the Baroque Period.
- [b] Because Mozart's music suddenly became famous.
- [c] Because classical music was fashionable in Europe.
- [d] Because people wanted to hear very slow melodies.

_____ 10. "So they worked on new forms of music. Thus arose the Classical Period." What is the meaning of "thus" in this sentence?
- [a] Almost like this.
- [b] In addition to this.
- [c] Despite this.
- [d] Because of this.

_____ 11. Which statement best summarizes the passage?
- [a] Classical composers are well-known in every country around the world.
- [b] Music of the Classical Period is sophisticated and still popular today.
- [c] The Classical Period was between 1750 and 1820.
- [d] Classical music has only one rhythmic pattern and one mood.

Answer Key

Unit 01
1. free-market 2. profits 3. attention 4. median 5. deliver
6. effective 7. consumption 8. d 9. a 10. b

Unit 02
1. equator 2. Capricorn 3. Arctic Circle 4. Antarctic Circle
5. changing 6. extreme 7. constantly 8. b 9. c 10. d

Unit 03
1. religions 2. worshipped 3. descendant 4. covenant
5. Israelites 6. Jerusalem 7. slaves 8. d 9. c 10. d

Unit 04
1. known as 2. nomads 3. settlements 4. grid
5. bronze 6. pictographs 7. researchers 8. c 9. d 10. c

Unit 05
1. conquered 2. overthrew 3. elected 4. patricians
5. Peninsula 6. Mediterranean Sea 7. corrupt 8. dictator
9. emperor 10. c 11. a 12. c

Unit 06
1. Muslims 2. rapidly 3. caliphs 4. dynasty 5. captured
6. Byzantine Empire 7. capital 8. a 9. b 10. b

Unit 07
1. priests 2. upset 3. complaints 4. Catholic Church
5. heretic 6. violent 7. Protestant 8. sect 9. broke away
10. b 11. d 12. a

Unit 08
1. divine right 2. clergy 3. revolution 4. oppressive
5. Bastille 6. beheaded 7. monarchy 8. democracy
9. a 10. b 11. c

Unit 09
1. carnage 2. alliances 3. assassinated 4. enormous
5. swiftly 6. trench 7. Tanks 8. chemical weapons 9. c
10. c 11. c

Unit 10
1. technology 2. telecommunications 3. rarely 4. effects
5. business 6. supermarket 7. understanding 8. world war
9. a 10. a 11. c

Unit 11
1. variety 2. Monera 3. bacteria 4. Protista 5. Fungi
6. photosynthesis 7. bushes 8. multicellular 9. d 10. a
11. b

Unit 12
1. genetics 2. resistant 3. monk 4. peas 5. characteristics
6. crossbreeding 7. hybrids 8. ignored 9. accomplished
10. c 11. d 12. d

Unit 13
1. offspring 2. reproductive 3. Pollen 4. ineffective
5. stuck 6. rubs off 7. dormant 8. mature 9. b
10. a 11. c

Unit 14
1. elements 2. carbon dioxide 3. nutrients 4. petroleum
5. nitrogen cycle 6. absorb 7. Bacteria 8. decompose
9. b 10. d 11. a

Unit 15
1. attacked 2. White blood cells 3. lymphatic vessels
4. antibodies 5. innate 6. recognizes 7. vaccinations
8. a 9. a 10. a

Unit 16
1. lava 2. pressure 3. surface 4. chambers 5. expels
6. hardens 7. explosively 8. eruptions 9. c 10. c 11.d

Unit 17
1. species 2. dinosaurs 3. asteroid 4. tremendous
5. blocked 6. mammals 7. evolved 8. a 9. a 10. b

Unit 18
1. humanity 2. stocks 3. overfish 4. repopulate
5. pumped 6. spills 7. valuable 8. Tidal 9. conserve
10. d 11. b 12. c

Unit 19
1. positively 2. orbit 3. protons 4. atomic number
5. periodic table 6. Carbon 7. Oxygen 8. uranium's 9. c
10. b 11.d

Unit 20
1. harmful 2. fossil fuels 3. mine 4. release 5. tides
6. hydroelectric 7. radioactive 8. plants 9. d 10. d 11. c

Unit 21
1. multiplied 2. squaring 3. square root 4. divisor
5. irrational 6. infinity 7. majority 8. a 9. a 10. d

Unit 22
1. percentage 2. determine 3. outcomes 4. graphs
5. pie charts 6. bar graph 7. horizontal 8. vertical 9. c
10. b 11. d

Unit 23
1. measurement 2. converting 3. length 4. common
5. volume 6. weight 7. Celsius 8. d 9. c 10. d

Unit 24
1. charted 2. horizontally 3. geometrical figure
4. solid figure 5. vertically 6. time 7. extra 8. d 9.a 10. c

Unit 25
1. rhyme schemes 2. epic 3. adventures 4. Sonnets
5. Shakespeare 6. Couplets 7. Quatrains 8. a 9. c 10. a

Unit 26
1. borrows 2. meanings 3. hydrogen 4. asteroid
5. geology 6. inscription 7. portable 8. d 9. b 10. c

Unit 27
1. expressions 2. Absence 3. fondly 4. warning
5. decision 6. opportunity 7. move on 8. b 9. a 10. d

Unit 28
1. designed 2. ceramics 3. mythology 4. survived
5. depicted 6. architecture 7. capitals 8. b 9. b 10. b

Unit 29
1. similarities 2. contrasts 3. facial expressions
4. moralizing 5. realists 6. perspective 7. space 8. a 9. c 10. a

Unit 30
1. composers 2. Baroque 3. mood 4. rhythm
5. pauses 6. melodies 7. sophisticated 8. popularity
9. a 10. d 11. b

Workbook 聽力閱讀試題本

Syllabus Vol. 6

Subject	Topic & Area	Title
Social Studies ● History and Geography	Social Studies	Economics
	Geography and Culture	World Geography
	World History	Early People and Civilizations
	World History	Asian Civilizations
	World History	Ancient Greek and Roman Civilizations
	World History	The Arab World
	World History	From the Middle Ages to the Reformation
	World History	The Enlightenment and the French Revolution
	World History	The Age of Imperialism
	World History	World War II and After the War
Science	Life Science	Classifying Living Things
	Life Science	Cells and Heredity
	Life Science	Plant Growth
	Life Science	Ecosystems
	Life Science	The Human Body and the Immune System
	Earth Science	Earth's Surface
	Earth Science	Earth's Rocks and Fossils
	Earth Science	Oceans and Ocean Life
	Physical Science	Matter
	Physical Science	Light and Energy
Mathematics	Numbers and Number Sense	Numbers and Computation
	Probability and Statistics	Probability and Statistics
	Measurement	Measurement
	Geometry	Geometry
Language and Literature	Poetry and Stories	Poetry and Stories
	Language Arts	Grammar and Usage
	Language Arts	Common English Sayings and Expressions
Visual Arts	Visual Arts	Classical Art
	Visual Arts	From Baroque Art to Realism
Music	A World of Music	A World of Music

CHAPTER 1

Social Studies •
History and Geography ①

Key Words 🔊 001

01	**producer** [prəˈdjusɚ]	*(n.)* 生產者　*manufacturer (n.) 製造商　*capital goods 資本財 Producers are people who make goods or provide services. 生產者就是製造產品或是提供服務的人。
02	**consumer** [kənˈsjumɚ]	*(n.)* 消費者　*consumer price index 消費者物價指數 　　　　　　　*consumer goods 消費財 The people who buy goods and services are consumers. 購買商品與服務的人稱為消費者。
03	**investor** [ɪnˈvɛstɚ]	*(n.)* 投資人　*stockholder (n.) 股東（= shareholder） 　　　　　　*to invest in sth. 投資某物 An investor is a person or group that invests money in a business. 投資人為投資金錢在生意上的個人或群體。
04	**entrepreneur** [ˌɑntrəprəˈnɝ]	*(n.)* 企業家　*entrepreneurship (n.) 企業家精神；創業 Entrepreneurs are people who start and run their own businesses. 企業家為自行創業與做生意的人。
05	**marketplace** [ˈmɑrkɪtˌples]	*(n.)* 市場；市場機制　*mart (n.) 市場；購物中心　*market price 市場價格 A marketplace is a place where goods and services are bought and sold. 市場就是買賣商品與服務的地方。
06	**distribution** [ˌdɪstrəˈbjuʃən]	*(n.)* 物流；分配　*distribution cost 物流成本　*distribution center 物流中心 Distribution involves transporting or delivering goods to a number of people or places. 物流需要運輸或遞送商品給許多人或到許多地方。
07	**consumption** [kənˈsʌmpʃən]	*(n.)* 消費；消耗　*conspicuous consumption 炫耀性消費 　　　　　　　　*fit for human consumption 可供人食用 The using of goods and services is consumption. 使用商品與服務稱為消費。
08	**opportunity cost** [ˌɑpɚˈtjunətɪ kɔst]	*(n.)* 機會成本　*There is no such thing as a free lunch. 天下沒有白吃的午餐。 The value of something that is not chosen when choosing between two things is called the opportunity cost. 在兩者間做選擇，沒被選到者的價值稱作機會成本。
09	**demand** [dɪˈmænd]	*(n.)* 需求　*to make a demand for sth. 需求某物　*on-demand (a.) 需求的 The amount of a product or service that people want to buy is the demand. 民眾需要的產品或服務量就稱為需求。
10	**supply** [səˈplaɪ]	*(n.)* 供給　*supply chain 供給鏈　*in short supply 供給不足；短缺 If the supply of a product increases, the price usually goes down. 若產品的供給增加，價錢則下滑。

consumer
producer

entrepreneur

marketplace

distribution

Power Verbs 🔊 002

produce
生產
Factories produce all kinds of goods. 工廠生產各種物品。

manufacture
[ˌmænjəˈfæktʃə]
大量製造
Factories manufacture all kinds of goods. 工廠大量製造各種物品。

consume
消費；消耗
People consume many kinds of goods and services. 人們使用許多種類的商品與服務。

distribute
流通；分配
In a free market, goods and services are produced and distributed according to the law of supply and demand.
在自由市場中，產品與服務是根據供需法則來生產與流通的。

reap
獲得
The investors are hoping to reap huge profits. 投資人期盼獲得龐大的利潤。

make
獲得（= earn）
The investors are hoping to make huge profits. 投資人期盼賺取高額利潤。

Word Families 🔊 003

inflation
[ɪnˈfleʃən]
通貨膨脹
Inflation causes a continual increase in prices in an economy.
通貨膨脹會造成經濟上價格的持續增加。

deflation
[dɪˈfleʃən]
通貨緊縮
Deflation causes a reduction in economic activity. 通貨緊縮會造成經濟活動的蕭條。

scarcity
[ˈskɛrsətɪ]
不足；缺乏
When there is a scarcity of a product, the price often goes up.
當缺乏產品時，通常價格會上漲。

shortage
[ˈʃɔrtɪdʒ]
短缺
When there is a shortage of a product, the price often goes up.
當一種產品短缺時，通常價格會上漲。

Gross Domestic Product (GDP) 國內生產毛額
The GDP is the total value of all the goods and services produced within a country in a year, not including its income from foreign investments.
國內生產毛額值是一年內國內的產品與服務的總價值，不包含國外投資的收益。

Gross National Product (GNP) 國民生產毛額
The GNP is the total value of the goods and services produced by the residents of a nation in a year. 國民生產毛額為在一年內由國民生產的產品與服務的總值。

Kinds of Economies
經濟的種類

manufacturing economy 製造業經濟   **service economy** 服務業經濟

global economy 全球經濟   **national economy** 國家經濟

state economy 各州經濟   **local economy** 地方經濟

Checkup

Write | 請依提示寫出正確的英文單字和片語。

1	生產者	_____	9	需求	_____
2	消費者	_____	10	供給	_____
3	投資人	_____	11	生產	_____
4	企業家	_____	12	獲得	r_____
5	市場；市場機制	_____	13	通貨膨脹	_____
6	物流；分配 (n.)	_____	14	通貨緊縮	_____
7	消費；消耗 (n.)	_____	15	不足；缺乏	_____
8	機會成本	_____	16	國內生產總值	_____

B

Complete the Sentences | 請在空格中填入最適當的答案，並視情況做適當的變化。

entrepreneur	consumption	producer	demand	consumer
opportunity cost	distribution	marketplace	investor	supply

1 _____ are people who start and run their own businesses.
企業家為自行創業與做生意的人。

2 An _____ is a person or group that invests money in a business.
投資人為投資金錢在生意上的個人或群體。

3 A _____ is a place where goods and services are bought and sold.
市場就是買賣商品與服務的地方。

4 _____ involves transporting or delivering goods to a number of people or places. 物流需要運輸或遞送商品給許多人或到許多地方。

5 The using of goods and services is _____. 使用商品與服務稱為消費。

6 The value of something that is not chosen when choosing between two things is called the _____ _____.
在兩者間做選擇，沒被選到者的價值稱做機會成本。

7 If the _____ of a product increases, the price usually goes down.
若產品的供給增加，價錢則下滑。

8 The amount of a product or service that people want to buy is the _____.
民眾需要的產品或服務量就稱為需求。

C

Read and Choose | 閱讀下列句子，並且選出最適當的答案。

1 Factories (manufacture | invest) all kinds of goods.

2 Consumers (produce | consume) many kinds of goods and services.

3 Goods are produced and (distributed | reaped) according to the law of supply and demand.

4 (Deflation | Inflation) causes a continual increase in prices in an economy.

Look, Read, and Write | 看圖並且依照提示，在空格中填入正確答案。

1 ▸ someone that grows or makes particular goods or products

_____

3 ▸ a person who starts a business and is willing to risk loss to make money

_____

2 ▸ a person who buys goods and services

_____

4 ▸ the value of the action that you do not choose, when choosing between two possible options

_____

E

Read and Answer | 閱讀並且回答下列問題。 🔊 004

Basic Economics

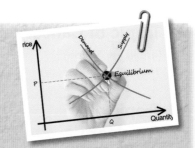

In free-market economies, companies decide what and how much of a product they will produce. However, they are interested in making profits. So they do not want to produce too much or too little of a product. They want to produce exactly the right amount necessary. So they often pay attention to the law of supply and demand.

This law states that when the supply of a product is low yet demand is high, then the price will be high. However, if the supply of a product is high yet demand is low, then the price will be low. Companies want to find a median. They want just the right amount of supply and just the right amount of demand.

But, there are often other factors that companies must consider. Once they make something, they must deliver it to the market. This way, people can purchase the product. This is called distribution. Distribution is often done by trucks, trains, ships, and airplanes. Without an effective distribution system, even in-demand products will not sell well.

Once products are at the market, they must be consumed. This means that people purchase them. The amount of consumption depends on many things. It depends on the supply and demand, of course. And the price is also another important factor.

What is true? Write T(true) or F(false).

1 Companies are interested in earning profits. _____
2 The law of supply and demand is important in economics. _____
3 A low demand and a high supply usually result in a high price. _____
4 Distribution is the selling of products to customers. _____

World Geography 世界地理

01 **topographic map**
[ˌtɑpəˈɡræfɪk mæp]

(n.) 地形圖　*terrain (n.) 地勢；地形　*scale (n.) 比例尺　*legend (n.) 圖例

A **topographic map** shows the features of the Earth's surface, including hills, mountains, and valleys.
地形圖顯示出地表的特徵，包含了山丘、山脈與溪谷。

02 **contour**
[ˈkɑntʊr]

(n.) 等高線（ **= contour line** ）　*contour map 等高線地圖

Contour lines are used to show something's elevation on a topographic map. 等高線在地形圖中用於指示高度。

03 **Arctic Circle**
[ˈɑrktɪk ˈsɝkḷ]

(n.) 北極圈　*Arctic (n.) 北極；北極地區（ = North Pole ）
*midnight sun 永晝　*polar night 永夜

The **Arctic Circle** lies at the line of latitude approximately 66 degrees north of the equator. 北極圈大約位於北緯 66 度。

04 **Antarctic Circle**
[ænˈtɑrktɪk ˈsɝkḷ]

(n.) 南極圈　*Antarctic (n.) 南極地區（ = South Pole ）　*Antarctica (n.) 南極洲

The **Antarctic Circle** lies at the line of latitude approximately 66 degrees south of the equator.　南極圈大約位於南緯 66 度。

05 **Tropic of Cancer**
[ˈtrɑpɪk ɔv ˈkænsɚ]

(n.) 北回歸線　*tropical zone 熱帶　*temperate zone 溫帶
*frigid/polar zone 寒帶

The **Tropic of Cancer** is found at the line of latitude 23.5 degrees north.
北回歸線位於北緯 23.5 度。

06 **Tropic of Capricorn**
[ˈtrɑpɪk ɔv ˈkæprɪkɔrn]

(n.) 南回歸線　*equator (n.) 赤道　*summer/winter solstice 夏／冬至

The **Tropic of Capricorn** is found at the line of latitude 23.5 degrees south.　南回歸線位於南緯 23.5 度。

07 **absolute location**
[ˈæbsəˌlut loˈkeʃən]

(n.) 絕對位置　*geographic coordinate 地理座標（經緯度）

Each spot on Earth has an **absolute location** identified by the lines of latitude and longitude. 地球上的每個地點都有一個依經緯度標示的絕對位置。

08 **relative location**
[ˈrɛlətɪv loˈkeʃən]

(n.) 相對位置　*cardinal direction 基本方位（東、西、南、北）

Relative location is the approximate location of a place in relation to other landmarks. 相對位置是一個相對於其他地點的大概位置。

09 **elevation**
[ˌɛləˈveʃən]

(n.) 海拔高度（ **= altitude** ）　*at an elevation of 在海拔高度……處

Something's **elevation** is how high or low it is compared to the level of the sea. 某地的海拔高度為與海平面比較起來的高低程度。

10 **desertification**
[ˌdɛzətɪfɪˈkeʃən]

(n.) 沙漠化　*salinization (n.) 土壤鹽鹼化

The process by which fertile land becomes desert is called **desertification.** 沃土轉變成沙漠的過程，稱為沙漠化。

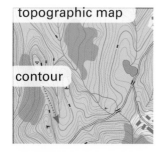

topographic map

contour

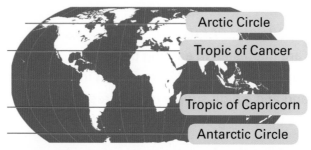

Arctic Circle

Tropic of Cancer

Tropic of Capricorn

Antarctic Circle

desertification

mark
標示；代表
Lines of latitude and longitude mark where in the world something is.
經線與緯線標示出地球上某地的位置。

denote
[dɪˋnot]
標示；代表
Lines of latitude and longitude denote where in the world something is.
經線與緯線標示出地球上某地的位置。

identify
[aɪˋdɛntəˏfaɪ]
識別
Lines of latitude and longitude are identified by degrees.
經線與緯線是以度數作為識別。

utilize
[ˋjutɪˏaɪz]
利用
Geography helps people learn how to utilize land and water wisely.
地理幫助人們學習如何聰明地利用土地與水資源。

make use of
利用
Geography helps people learn how to make use of land and water wisely.
地理幫助人們學習如何聰明地利用土地與水資源。

Reading Maps
閱讀地圖

lines of latitude 緯度線
lines of longitude 經度線
prime meridian 本初子午線
equator 赤道
Northern Hemisphere 北半球
Southern Hemisphere 南半球
map scale 比例尺
compass rose 羅盤玫瑰
（羅盤方位圖）

Geographic Terms
地理專用術語

basin 盆地
source 水源
bay （海或湖）灣
gulf 海灣
peninsula [pəˋnɪnsələ] 半島
mesa 臺地
plateau 高原
glacier [ˋgleʃɚ] 冰河

The World's Biggest Lakes
世界最大湖泊

Caspian Sea (Asia) 裏海
Lake Superior (North America)
蘇必略湖
Lake Victoria (Africa)
維多利亞湖
Lake Huron (North America)
休倫湖
Lake Michigan (North America)
密西根湖
Lake Tanganyika (Africa)
塔干依喀湖
Lake Baikal (Asia) 貝加爾湖

compass rose

glacier

bay

Checkup

Write | 請依提示寫出正確的英文單字和片語。

1	地形圖	_____	9	海拔高度	_____
2	等高線	_____	10	沙漠化	_____
3	北極圈	_____	11	標示；代表	d_____
4	南極圈	_____	12	識別	_____
5	北回歸線	_____	13	利用	u_____
6	南回歸線	_____	14	經度線	_____
7	絕對位置	_____	15	緯度線	_____
8	相對位置	_____	16	赤道	_____

B

Complete the Sentences | 請在空格中填入最適當的答案，並視情況做適當的變化。

Tropic of Capricorn	Antarctic Circle	relative location	topographic map
Tropic of Cancer	Arctic Circle	absolute location	elevation

1 A _____ _____ shows the features of the Earth's surface, including hills, mountains, and valleys. 地形圖顯示出地表的特徵，包含了山丘、山脈與溪谷。

2 The _____ _____ _____ is found at the line of latitude 23.5 degrees north. 北回歸線位於北緯 23.5 度。

3 The _____ _____ _____ is found at the line of latitude 23.5 degrees south. 南回歸線位於南緯 23.5 度。

4 The _____ _____ lies at the line of latitude approximately 66 degrees south of the equator. 南極圈大約位於南緯 66 度。

5 The _____ _____ lies at the line of latitude approximately 66 degrees north of the equator. 北極圈大約位於北緯 66 度。

6 _____ _____ is the approximate location of a place in relation to other landmarks. 相對位置是一個相對於其他地點的大概位置。

7 Each spot on Earth has an _____ _____ identified by the lines of latitude and longitude. 地球上的每個地點都有一個依經緯度標示的絕對位置。

8 Something's _____ is how high or low it is compared to the level of the sea. 某地的海拔高度為與海平面比較起來的高低程度。

C

Read and Choose | 閱讀下列句子，並且選出最適當的答案。

1 Lines of latitude and longitude (compare | mark) where in the world something is.

2 Geography helps people learn how to (denote | utilize) land and water wisely.

3 Lines of latitude and longitude are (identified | used) by degrees.

4 The Tropic of (Cancer | Capricorn) is found at the line of latitude 23.5 degrees north.

D

Look, Read, and Write | 看圖並且依照提示，在空格中填入正確答案。

▸ a line on a map that joins points of equal height or depth

_____

▸ the location of a place frequently expressed in degrees of longitude and latitude

_____

▸ an imaginary line that goes around the Earth near the North Pole

_____

▸ the process by which an area becomes a desert

_____

E

Read and Answer | 閱讀並且回答下列問題。 🔊 008

The Earth's Climate Zones

There are three main climate zones on the Earth. They are the tropical, temperate, and polar climate zones.

The tropical zones are found near the equator. Basically, they are found between the Tropic of Cancer and the Tropic of Capricorn. In general, the tropical zone has hot weather most of the year. Many areas in the tropical zone have very wet weather, but this is not always the case.

The temperate zones are the largest of the three main climate zones. One temperate zone lies between the Tropic of Cancer and the Arctic Circle. The other temperate zone lies between the Tropic of Capricorn and the Antarctic Circle. Most of the world's population lives in temperate zones. Temperate zones are neither too hot nor too cold. They experience changing seasons all year long. For the most part, the weather is not too extreme in these places.

The polar zones are found north of the Arctic Circle and south of the Antarctic Circle. The weather in these places is constantly cold. Few people live in these places. Few animals live in them as well.

Fill in the blanks.

1 The three main climate zones are the tropical, _____, and polar climate zones.

2 Tropical zones often have hot, _____ weather.

3 One of the temperate zones is between the Tropic of Capricorn and the _____ _____.

4 _____ people and animals live in the polar zones.

Early People and Civilizations 早期人民與文明

Key Words 🔊 009

01 Ice Age
[aɪs edʒ]
(n.) 冰河時代　*glacial period 冰期　*interglacial period 間冰期
During the Ice Age, it was so cold that much of the Earth's surface was covered by huge sheets of ice called glaciers.
在冰河時代時，嚴寒的天氣讓地表覆蓋了稱為冰河的巨大冰塊。

02 Stone Age
[ston edʒ]
(n.) 石器時代　*like something out of the Stone Age 形容某物過時、老派
People learned how to farm in the New Stone Age.
人類在新石器時代時學會如何耕作。

03 Bronze Age
[branz edʒ]
(n.) 青銅器時代　*Copper Age 銅石器並用時代（石器時代與青銅器時代的過渡）
Humans learned how to make things with bronze during the Bronze Age.
人類在青銅器時代學會如何用銅製造物品。

04 Iron Age
[ˈaɪɚn edʒ]
(n.) 鐵器時代
During the Iron Age, humans began to make weapons and tools from iron.
人類在鐵器時代時就開始利用鐵製造武器與工具。

05 Fertile Crescent
[ˈfɝtḷ ˈkrɛsṇt]
(n.) 肥沃月灣　*Tigris 底格里斯河　*Euphrates 幼發拉底河　*cuneiform (n.) 楔形文字
One of the world's first farming civilizations arose in the Fertile Crescent in Mesopotamia. 世界上最先有農業的文明之一，發源於美索不達米亞的肥沃月灣。

06 polytheism
[ˈpɑlɪθiˌɪzəm]
(n.) 多神教　*pantheism (n.) 泛神信仰（神存在於自然萬物，自然萬物中皆有神）
Believing in and worshipping multiple gods is polytheism.
多神教信仰與崇拜多種神祇。

07 monotheism
[ˈmɑnoθiˌɪzəm]
(n.) 一神教　*atheist (n.) 無神論者　*agnostic (n.) 不可知論者（不肯定神是否存在）
Believing in and worshipping only one god is monotheism.
一神教信仰與崇拜唯一真神。

08 Code of Hammurabi
[kod ɔv ˈhæmurabɪ]
(n.) 漢摩拉比法典　*An eye for an eye, a tooth for a tooth. 以牙還牙，以眼還眼。
The Code of Hammurabi is the oldest set of laws and was created by the Babylonian king Hammurabi.
漢摩拉比法典是由巴比倫國王漢摩拉比所創立最古老的一套法律。

09 Hebrew
[ˈhibru]
(n.) 希伯來文　*Judaism (n.) 猶太教　*Jewish (n.) 猶太人
The Israelites spoke a language called Hebrew.
古以色列人所說的語言稱為希伯來文。

10 covenant
[ˈkʌvɪnənt]
(n.) 誓約　*Ark of the Covenant 約櫃（聖經中放置《十誡》的法櫃）
According to the Hebrew Bible, God made a covenant with a man named Abraham. 根據希伯來聖經上所述，上帝與一名叫做亞伯拉罕的男子訂定誓約。

Ice Age 　Fertile Crescent 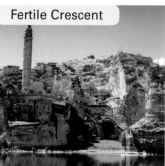　Code of Hammurabi 　Hebrew

domesticate
[də`mɛstə,ket]

馴養；馴化

Early farmers learned how to domesticate wild animals and plants.
早期的農夫學會如何馴養野生動物與種植植物。

tame

馴養

Dogs were among the first animals to be tamed. 狗是最早被馴養的動物之一。

raise

飼養

Mesopotamian farmers raised dogs, pigs, and sheep.
美索不達米亞的農夫飼養狗、豬還有羊。

worship
[`wɜʃɪp]

崇拜

The Israelites were among the first people in the world to worship only one god.
古以色列人是世界上最早崇拜一神的民族之一。

practice

實行

The Israelites were among the first people in the world to practice monotheism.
古以色列人是世界上最早遵從一神教的民族之一。

wander

流浪；閒逛

The Israelites wandered in the desert for forty years on their way
to Canaan. 古以色列人在前往迦南的路上，在大漠中流浪了 40 年之久。

establish
[ə`stæblɪʃ]

創立；確立

Jehovah established a covenant with the Israelites.
耶和華與古以色列人們建立誓約。

Word Families ⊙ 011

Old Stone Age	舊石器時代（= Paleolithic Period）
	The Old Stone Age was the first part of the Stone Age and began around 2,000,000 B.C. 舊石器時代是石器時代的第一期，約始於西元前 200 萬年前。
New Stone Age	新石器時代（= Neolithic Period）
	The New Stone Age was the last part of the Stone Age and began around 10,000 B.C. 新石器時代是石器時代的終期，約始於西元前 1 萬年前。

Early Civilizations and People
早期文明與人類

Mesopotamia 美索不達米亞		**Mesopotamian** 美索不達米亞人的	
Sumer 蘇美		**Sumerian** 蘇美人的	
Babylonia 巴比倫尼亞		**Babylonian** 巴比倫帝國的；巴比倫人	
Israel 以色列		**Israelite** 古以色列人的	
Assyria 亞述		**Assyrian** 亞述的；亞述人	

Checkup

A

Write | 請依提示寫出正確的英文單字和片語。

1	冰河時代	_____	9	漢摩拉比法典 _____
2	石器時代	_____	10	肥沃月灣 _____
3	銅器時代	_____	11	馴養；馴化 d_____
4	鐵器時代	_____	12	馴養 t_____
5	誓約	_____	13	崇拜 _____
6	多神教	_____	14	實行 _____
7	一神教	_____	15	流浪；閒逛 _____
8	希伯來文	_____	16	創立；確立 _____

B

Complete the Sentences | 請在空格中填入最適當的答案，並視情況做適當的變化。

monotheism	New Stone Age	Bronze Age	Ice Age	Hebrew
polytheism	Fertile Crescent	Code of Hammurabi	Iron Age	covenant

1 People learned how to farm in the _____ _____ _____.
人類在新石器時代時學會如何耕作。

2 Humans learned how to make things with bronze during the _____ _____. 人類在青銅器時代學會如何用銅製造物品。

3 One of the world's first farming civilizations arose in the _____ _____ in Mesopotamia. 世界上最先有農業的文明之一，發源於美索不達米亞的肥沃月灣。

4 Believing in and worshipping only one god is _____.
一神教信仰與崇拜唯一真神。

5 Believing in and worshipping multiple gods is _____.
多神教信仰與崇拜多種神祇。

6 The _____ _____ _____ is the oldest set of laws and was created by the Babylonian king Hammurabi.
漢摩拉比法典是由巴比倫國王漢摩拉比所創立最古老的一套法律。

7 The Israelites spoke a language called _____.
古以色列人所說的語言稱為希伯來文。

8 According to the Hebrew Bible, God made a _____ with a man named Abraham. 根據希伯來聖經上所述，神與一名叫做亞伯拉罕的男子訂定誓約。

C

Read and Choose | 閱讀下列句子，並且選出最適當的答案。

1 Early farmers learned how to (domesticate | practice) wild animals and plants.

2 Dogs were among the first animals to be (covered | tamed).

3 The Israelites (established | wandered) in the desert for forty years on their way to Canaan.

4 The (New | Old) Stone Age was the first part of the Stone Age.

Look, Read, and Write | 看圖並且依照提示，在空格中填入正確答案。

 ▸ a time when a large part of the world was covered with ice

_____

 ▸ a period of time when people used iron to make weapons and tools

_____

 ▸ the belief that there is more than one god

_____

 ▸ the belief that there is only one God

_____

E

Read and Answer | 閱讀並且回答下列問題。012

The Story of Israel

In the past in the Middle East, there were many different religions. People often prayed to many gods. There were mountain gods. There were gods of rivers, lakes, and seas. There were all kinds of gods. However, one religion began that worshipped only one god.

Abraham and Isaac

There was a man named Abram. He was said to be a descendant of both Noah and Adam. He lived in a land called Canaan. There, the god Yahweh made a covenant with Abram. Yahweh promised Abram many descendants and said that the land he was living on would forever be theirs. In return, Abram had to worship only Yahweh. Abram agreed. His name changed to Abraham, which means "father of many nations."

Abraham's descendants through his son Isaac became the Israelites. Isaac and his wife Rebecca later had twins: Jacob and Esau. Jacob's descendants founded the twelve tribes of the Israelites. They made the city Jerusalem the center of their political power. For a time, they were powerful. Later, they were made slaves and taken to Egypt. It was in Egypt that Moses would later free the Israelites and return them to their land many years later.

What is NOT true?

1 Most people in the Middle East worshipped only one god.
2 Abram only worshipped Yahweh.
3 Isaac was the son of Abraham.
4 The Israelites made their capital at Jerusalem.

Unit 04 Asian Civilizations 亞洲文明

01	**Indus Valley civilization** [ˈɪndəs ˈvælɪ ˌsɪvḷəˈzeʃən]	*(n.)* 印度河文明（= Harappan civilization） The Indus Valley civilization was based on irrigation farming. 印度河文明建立於灌溉農業的基礎上。
02	**reincarnation** [ˌriɪnkɑrˈneʃən]	*(n.)* 輪迴說　*a reincarnation of sb. 某人的轉世化身 Hindus believe in reincarnation, which is rebirth in a new body. 印度教徒相信輪迴一說，也就是在新的軀體中重生。
03	**Veda** [ˈvedə]	*(n.)*《吠陀經》　*Sanskrit (n.) 梵文 The four Vedas are the oldest sacred texts of Hinduism. 四部《吠陀經》是印度教最古老的經文。
04	**raja** [ˈrɑdʒə]	*(n.)*（印度）王公；首領　*rani (n.)（印度）王后；女爵 The Indian raja Chandragupta Maurya founded the first Indian empire in about 321 B.C. 印度國王旃陀羅笈多・孔雀，約於西元前 321 年創立了第一個印度帝國。
05	**dynasty** [ˈdaɪnəstɪ]	*(n.)* 朝代　*to establish/overthrow a dynasty 建立／推翻一個王朝 The Shang dynasty began in 1750 B.C. in the Huang He Valley. 商朝在西元前 1750 年發跡於黃河流域。
06	**Middle Kingdom** [ˈmɪdḷ ˈkɪŋdəm]	*(n.)* 中國　*Celestial Empire 天朝　*Son of Heaven 天子 *Mandate of Heaven 天命 The Chinese Empire was often referred to as the Middle Kingdom. 中國的帝國常被稱作中國。
07	**warlord** [ˈwɔrˌlɔrd]	*(n.)* 軍閥　*Warring States period 戰國時代 Warlords were military leaders who had their own armies in ancient China. 在中國古代擁有自己軍隊的軍事領袖為軍閥。
08	**pictograph** [ˈpɪktəˌgræf]	*(n.)* 象形文字　*ideogram (n.) 表意符號 The Chinese language is made up of thousands of pictographs. 中國文字是由數千個象形文字所組成的。
09	**czar** [zɑr]	*(n.)* 沙皇（= tsar）　*dictator (n.) 獨裁者（= autocrat = despot） *tyrant (n.) 暴君 The czar was the ruler of Russia.　沙皇是俄羅斯的統治者。
10	**Shinto** [ˈʃɪnto]	*(n.)* 神道教　*Shinto shrine 神社　*torii (n.) 鳥居 Shinto, Japan's oldest religion, is based on nature. 日本最古老的宗教神道教，以崇拜自然為主。

warlord

pictograph

czar

Shinto shrine

Power Verbs 🔊 014

reincarnate
[ˌriɪm`kɑr͵net]

投胎；轉世

Some people believe that they are reincarnated after death.
有些人相信人死後會投胎轉世。

be restricted to

受限於……

People in India are restricted to the caste in which they were born.
印度人民受限於他們出生所屬的種姓制度。

centralize
[`sɛntrəl͵aɪz]

集權中央

The first Indian emperor, Maurya, centralized the government so that he could rule his vast empire. 首任印度皇帝月護王集權中央，以統治他的龐大帝國。

unify

統一

Qin Shi Huang unified China into one empire. 秦始皇一統中國，使之成為一大帝國。

unite

統一

Qin Shi Huang united China into one empire. 秦始皇一統中國，使之成為一大帝國。

Word Families 🔊 015

Indus River
印度河（= the Indus）
The Indus civilization developed along the Indus River region.
印度河文明發展於印度河沿岸。

Ganges River
恆河（= the Ganges）
The Ganges River begins in the Himalayan peaks. 恆河源於喜馬拉雅的山峰上。

Huang He
黃河（= the Yellow River）
Chinese civilization began in the Huang He Valley. 中國文化開始於黃河流域。

shogun
[`ʃo͵gun]
幕府將軍
Shoguns were warlords in feudal Japan. 幕府將軍是日本封建時代時的軍閥。

daimyo
[`daɪm͵jo]
大名（諸侯）
The vassals of a shogun were called daimyos. 幕府將軍的封臣稱為大名。

samurai
[`sæmu͵raɪ]
武士
Warriors in medieval Japan were called samurais.
日本中世紀的戰士稱為武士。

Famous Chinese Dynasties
著名的中國朝代

Shang dynasty 商朝（= Yin dynasty）	**Qin dynasty** 秦朝	**Han dynasty** 漢朝
Sui dynasty 隋朝	**Tang dynasty** 唐朝	**Song dynasty** 宋朝
Ming dynasty 明朝	**Qing dynasty** 清朝（= Manchu dynasty）	

Checkup

A

Write | 請依提示寫出正確的英文單字和片語。

1	印度河文明	_____	9	軍閥	_____
2	輪迴說	_____	10	神道教	_____
3	《吠陀經》	_____	11	投胎；轉世	_____
4	（印度）王公；首領	_____	12	受限於……	_____
5	朝代	_____	13	集權中央	_____
6	中國	_____	14	統一	_____
7	象形文字	_____	15	幕府將軍	_____
8	沙皇	_____	16	武士	_____

B

Complete the Sentences | 請在空格中填入最適當的答案，並視情況做適當的變化。

raja	pictograph	Indus Valley	dynasty	warlord
Veda	reincarnation	Middle Kingdom	Shinto	czar

1 The _____ _____ civilization was based on irrigation farming.
印度河文明建立於灌溉農業的基礎上。

2 Hindus believe in _____, which is rebirth in a new body.
印度人相信輪迴一說，也就是在新的軀體中重生。

3 The Indian _____ Chandragupta Maurya founded the first Indian empire in about 321 B.C. 印度首領旃陀羅笈多 · 孔雀，約於西元前 321 年創立了第一個印度帝國。

4 The Shang _____ began in 1750 B.C. in the Huang He Valley.
商朝在西元前 1750 年發跡於黃河流域。

5 The Chinese Empire was often referred to as the _____ _____.
中國的帝國常被稱作中國。

6 _____ were military leaders who had their own armies in ancient China.
在中國古代擁有自己軍隊的軍事領袖為軍閥。

7 The Chinese language is made up of thousands of _____.
中國文字是由數千個象形文字所組成的。

8 The _____ was the ruler of Russia. 沙皇是俄羅斯的統治者。

C

Read and Choose | 閱讀下列句子，並且選出最適當的答案。

1 Some people believe that they are (restricted | reincarnated) after death.

2 People in India are (restricted | reincarnated) to the caste in which they were born.

3 The first Indian emperor, Maurya, (based | centralized) the government so that he could rule his vast empire.

4 Qin Shi Huang (founded | unified) China into one empire.

D

1 ▸ an early civilization formed in the Indus Valley around 2500 B.C.

_____

3 ▸ one or all of the holy books of writings of Hinduism

_____

2 ▸ the belief that people are born again with a different body after death

_____

4 ▸ a Japanese religion that people worship various gods that represent nature

_____

E

Read and Answer | 閱讀並且回答下列問題。 🔊 016

Early Indus Civilization

In the Indus Valley, which is in modern-day India and Pakistan, an early civilization formed long ago. It lasted from around 2500 B.C. to 1500 B.C. It is also known as the Harappan civilization.

The people in the Indus Valley civilization mostly farmed the land. So they knew the secret of agriculture. This let them stop living as nomads. But they were not just farmers. They also built many cities. Archaeologists have found several settlements where there were cities. They built palaces, temples, baths, and other buildings. They also planned their cities on a grid pattern. So they were laid out in squares.

The people of the Indus Valley were advanced in other ways, too. They made pottery. They made objects from both copper and bronze. And they even had their own writing system. It was based on pictographs. But it has not yet been translated.

The Indus Valley was one of the world's first civilized areas. Little is known about it. But researchers are learning more and more every year.

Answer the questions.

1 What is the name of the civilization in the Indus Valley?

_____

2 What was in the cities in the Indus Valley?

_____

3 What did the people of the Indus Valley use to make objects from?

_____

4 What kind of writing system did the people of the Indus Valley use?

_____

Ancient Greek and Roman Civilizations 古希臘與羅馬文明

Key Words 🔊 017

01	**Minoan** [mɪˈnoən]	(a.) 邁諾安的　(n.) 邁諾安人　*Knossos 克諾索斯（邁諾安文明最壯觀的遺址） The Minoans lived on the island of Create. 邁諾安人住在克里特島上。

01 **Minoan** [mɪˈnoən]
(a.) 邁諾安的　(n.) 邁諾安人　*Knossos 克諾索斯（邁諾安文明最壯觀的遺址）
The Minoans lived on the island of Create.
邁諾安人住在克里特島上。

02 **Mycenaean** [ˌmaɪsəˈnɪən]
(a.) 邁錫尼的　(n.) 邁錫尼人　*Homeric Hymns《荷馬史詩》
The Mycenaeans conquered the Minoans.
邁錫尼人征服了邁諾安人。

03 **Phoenician** [fəˈnɪʃən]
(a.) 腓尼基的　(n.) 腓尼基人　*Phoenician alphabet 腓尼基字母
The Phoenicians invented an alphabet that is the basis for the alphabet we use today. 腓尼基人發明了字母，而這正是我們目前使用字母的根源。

04 **city-state** [ˈsɪtɪstet]
(n.) 城邦（= polis）　*autonomy (n.) 自治權；自主權
Greek city-states had different values and cultures.
希臘的城邦有許多不同的價值與文化。

05 **acropolis** [əˈkrɑpəlɪs]
(n.) 衛城　*the Acropolis 雅典衛城　*citadel (n.) 城堡；要塞
Greek city-states were built around an acropolis.
希臘的城邦建在衛城附近。

06 **Hellenistic** [ˌhɛlɪˈnɪstɪk]
(a.) 希臘化的　*Hellenistic period 希臘化時期　*Alexander the Great 亞歷山大帝
During the Hellenistic Era, Greek culture spread around the Mediterranean region. 希臘文化在希臘化時期傳播至地中海地區。

07 **monarchy** [ˈmɑnəkɪ]
(n.) 君主政體　*constitutional monarchy 君主立憲
A king or queen rules a land in a monarchy.
由國王或皇后統治一個國家，稱為君主政體。

08 **oligarchy** [ˈɑlɪˌgɑrkɪ]
(n.) 寡頭政治　*meritocracy (n.) 菁英統治（= elitism）
An oligarchy is ruled by only a few wealthy and powerful people.
由一群富裕且有權勢的人所治理，稱為寡頭政治。

09 **Pax Romana** [pæks roˈmenə]
(n.) 羅馬和平　*Pax Americana/Britannica 美利堅／大英帝國和平
The Pax Romana began under Augustus's rule, and it lasted nearly 200 years. 羅馬和平從奧古斯都的統治下開始，持續近 200 年。

10 **Edict of Milan** [ˈidɪkt ɔv mɪˈlæn]
(n.) 米蘭敕令　*Diocletianic Persecution（戴克里先對於基督徒的）大迫害
Constantine I issued the Edict of Milan and made Christianity legal.
君士坦丁一世頒布米蘭敕令，將基督教合法化。

Minoan ruins

acropolis

Alexander the Great

monarchy

Power Verbs ● 018

reign
[ren]

統治

Tyrants sometimes **reigned** in parts of ancient Greece.
古希臘的某些時期由暴君統治。

rule

統治

Tyrants sometimes **ruled** in parts of ancient Greece. 古希臘的某些時期由暴君統治。

oppress
[ə`prɛs]

壓迫

The people were often **oppressed** by various tyrants. 人民常受到多位暴君的壓迫。

grant

授予

The Romans often **granted** citizenship to conquered people.
羅馬人常授予戰俘公民權。

confer

賦予

The Romans often **conferred** citizenship on conquered people.
羅馬人常賦予戰俘公民權。

spread

擴展；傳播

The Pax Romana **spread** to much of the area around the Mediterranean Sea.
羅馬和平擴展至地中海多處的地區。

expand

擴展；擴張

The Pax Romana **expanded** to much of the area around the Mediterranean Sea.
羅馬和平擴展至地中海多處的地區。

Word Families ● 019

patrician
[pə`trɪʃən]

（古羅馬）貴族

The **patricians** were the aristocrats in the Roman Empire.
羅馬貴族是羅馬帝國中的貴族。

plebeian
[plɪ`biən]

庶民

The common people in the Roman Empire were called **plebeians**.
羅馬帝國中的普通人稱為庶民。

consul
[`kɑnsḷ]

執政官

Rome had two elected leaders, who were called **consuls**.
羅馬有兩位選出來的領袖，稱為執政官。

democracy
[dɪ`mɑkrəsɪ]

民主政體；民主國家

Greek **democracy** influenced many later nations.
希臘的民主政體影響許多後來的國家。

republic
[rɪ`pʌblɪk]

共和政體；共和國

The Roman **Republic** was founded in 510 B.C.
羅馬共和國創立於西元前 510 年。

tyrant
[`taɪrənt]

暴君；專制君主

A **tyrant** is a ruler who oppresses the people. 壓迫人民的統治者就是暴君。

dictator
[`dɪk,tetɚ]

獨裁者

A **dictator** is an oppressive ruler. 獨裁者就是暴虐的統治者。

Checkup

Write | 請依提示寫出正確的英文單字和片語。

1	邁諾安人	_____	9	羅馬和平	_____
2	邁錫尼人	_____	10	米蘭敕令	_____
3	腓尼基人	_____	11	統治	_____
4	城邦	_____	12	壓迫	_____
5	衛城	_____	13	賦予	c_____
6	希臘化的	_____	14	執政官	_____
7	君主政體	_____	15	暴君	_____
8	寡頭政治	_____	16	獨裁者	_____

B

Complete the Sentences | 請在空格中填入最適當的答案，並視情況做適當的變化。

Edict of Milan Minoan	Hellenistic city-state	oligarchy monarchy	Pax Romana Mycenaean	Phoenician acropolis

1 The _____ conquered the Minoans.
邁錫尼人征服了邁諾安人。

2 The _____ lived on the island of Create.
邁諾安人住在克里特島上。

3 Greek _____ had different values and cultures.
希臘的城邦有許多不同的價值與文化。

4 Greek city-states were built around an _____.
希臘的城邦建在衛城附近。

5 During the _____ era, Greek culture spread around the Mediterranean region. 希臘文化在希臘化時期傳播至地中海地區。

6 A king or queen rules a land in a _____.
由國王或皇后統治一個國家，稱為君主政體。

7 An _____ is ruled by only a few wealthy and powerful people.
由一群富裕且有權勢的人所治理，稱為寡頭政治。

8 The _____ _____ began under Augustus's rule, and it lasted nearly 200 years. 羅馬和平從奧古斯都的統治下開始，持續近 200 年。

C

Read and Choose | 閱讀下列句子，並且選出最適當的答案。

1 Tyrants sometimes (issued | reigned) in parts of ancient Greece.

2 The people were often (expanded | oppressed) by various tyrants.

3 The Romans often (ruled | granted) citizenship to conquered people.

4 The Pax Romana (spread | conferred) to much of the area around the Mediterranean Sea.

D

Look, Read, and Write | 看圖並且依照提示，在空格中填入正確答案。

1
▸ people who invented an alphabet that is the basis for the alphabet we use today

_____

3
▸ a fortified part of an ancient Greek city, usually built on a hill

_____

2
▸ a form of government in which a country is ruled by a monarch

_____

4
▸ an edict issued by Constantine I that made Christianity legal

_____

E

Read and Answer | 閱讀並且回答下列問題。 ◉ 020

Romulus and Remus

Rome: From Republic to Empire

According to legend, the brothers Romulus and Remus founded Rome in 753 B.C. Rome grew larger until around 620 B.C., when a group of people called the Etruscans conquered it. The Etruscans ruled Rome for 111 years. In 509 B.C., the Roman people overthrew King Tarquin the Proud. They were free again.

The Romans made a new kind of government. It was called a republic. Under the republic, they elected a small number of people to be their leaders. These leaders were called patricians. Up to 300 of them could be elected to the Senate. For the next 500 years, Rome remained a republic.

The assassination of Julius Caesar

Rome began to grow more powerful. It soon controlled all of the Italian Peninsula. From 264 B.C. to 146 B.C., it fought the Punic Wars against Carthage. The Romans won and became the masters of the Mediterranean Sea. Soon, the republic was enormous. But it became corrupt. A general—Julius Caesar—challenged the rule of the Senate and became a dictator. Yet he was murdered in 44 B.C., and the republic was ruled by three leaders. Eventually, those three men fought each other. Octavian won and became the first Roman emperor. The republic was gone. Now it was the Roman Empire.

What is true? Write T(true) or F(false).

1   Rome was conquered by the Etruscans in 753 B.C.   _____
2   There were 300 members of the Roman Senate.   _____
3   Rome fought the Punic Wars against Carthage.   _____
4   Julius Caesar became the first Roman emperor.   _____

Review Test 1

A

Write | 請依提示寫出正確的英文單字和片語。

1	物流；分配 (n.)	_____	11	大量製造	_____
2	消費；消耗 (n.)	_____	12	不足；缺乏	_____
3	地形圖	_____	13	標示；代表	d_____
4	南極圈	_____	14	利用	u_____
5	冰河時代	_____	15	馴養；馴化	d_____
6	銅器時代	_____	16	漢摩拉比法典	_____
7	印度流域文明	_____	17	投胎；轉世	_____
8	朝代	_____	18	受限於……	_____
9	希臘化的	_____	19	統治	_____
10	寡頭政治	_____	20	壓迫	_____

B

Choose the Correct Word | 請選出與鋪底字意思相近的答案。

1 Early farmers learned how to domesticate wild animals and plants.

   a. demand   b. tame   c. denote

2 The Pax Romana spread to much of the area around the Mediterranean Sea.

   a. expanded   b. conferred   c. granted

3 Tyrants sometimes reigned in parts of ancient Greece.

   a. oppressed   b. ruled   c. expanded

4 Qin Shi Huang unified China into one empire.

   a. utilized   b. founded   c. united

C

Complete the Sentences | 請在空格中填入最適當的答案，並視情況做適當的變化。

monotheism	demand	absolute location	pictograph

1 The amount of a product or service that people want to buy is the _____.
民眾需要的產品或服務量就稱為需求。

2 Each spot on Earth has an _____ _____ identified by the lines of latitude and longitude. 地球上的每個地點都有一個依經緯度標示的絕對位置。

3 Believing in and worshipping only one god is _____.
一神教信仰與崇拜唯一真神。

4 The Chinese language is made up of thousands of _____.
中國文字是由數千個象形文字所組成的。

2

Social Studies •
History and Geography ②

Key Words

🔊 021

01	**caravan** [ˈkærəˌvæn]	*(n.)*（來往於沙漠）商隊　*caravansary (n.)（商隊）旅館　*convoy (n.)（護衛）車隊 A caravan is a group of traders who travel along trading routes by camel. 一群商人騎著駱駝通行於通商路線稱為商隊。
02	**Bedouin** [ˈbɛdʊɪn]	*(n.)* 貝都因人　*nomad (n.) 流浪者；遊牧民族 The Bedouins lived in the desert and traveled in caravans. 貝都因人居住在沙漠，成群結隊而行。
03	**Muhammad** [mʊˈhæməd]	*(n.)* 穆罕默德（= Mohammed）　*Koran (n.)《可蘭經》 Muhammad was the founder of the religion of Islam. 穆罕默德是伊斯蘭教的創立者。
04	**prophet** [ˈprɑfɪt]	*(n.)* 先知　*the Prophet 穆罕默德　*prophetess (n.) 女先知　*oracle (n.) 神諭 Muhammad is regarded as a prophet of Allah by Muslims. 穆罕默德被穆斯林視為是真主阿拉的先知。
05	**Ramadan** [ˌræməˈdɑn]	*(n.)* 齋戒月（伊斯蘭曆的第九個月）　*fast (n.) (v.) 齋戒；禁食 Muslims must fast during daylight hours during the month of Ramadan. 齋戒月期間，穆斯林必定於白天禁食。
06	**Mecca** [ˈmɛkə]	*(n.)* 麥加　*pilgrimage (n.) 朝聖；朝覲 　　　　*to make/go on a pilgrimage to Mecca 去麥加朝聖 Mecca is the holiest city in Islam because the prophet Muhammad was born there. 先知穆罕默德在麥加出生，因此那裡是伊斯蘭教的聖地。
07	**caliph** [ˈkælɪf]	*(n.)* 哈里發（伊斯蘭教領袖）　*Sunni Islam 遜尼派　*Shia Islam 什葉派 A caliph was a Muslim political and religious leader who was selected as a successor of Muhammad. 哈里發被挑選出來作為穆罕默德的繼承者，是伊斯蘭教的政治與宗教領袖。
08	**bazaar** [bəˈzɑr]	*(n.)*（尤指中東和印度的）市集　*bazaar (n.) 義賣　*fair (n.) 集市；露天遊樂場 A bazaar is a large market in the Middle East. 市集是中東的大型市場。
09	**Ottoman Empire** [ˈɑtəmən ˈɛmpaɪr]	*(n.)* 鄂圖曼帝國 The Ottoman Empire was the greatest Islamic Empire and was located in the area of modern-day Turkey. 鄂圖曼帝國是最大的伊斯蘭教帝國，位於現今的土耳其。
10	**sultan** [ˈsʌltən]	*(n.)* 蘇丹　*sultana (n.) 蘇丹娜（女性的統治者） A sultan is a ruler of an Islamic country. 蘇丹是伊斯蘭教國家的統治者。

caravan

Bedouin

Mecca

bazaar

flourish
[ˈflɝɪʃ]

繁榮；興旺

Early Arab civilizations flourished in harsh desert regions.
早期的阿拉伯文明在嚴酷的大漠地區繁榮興盛起來。

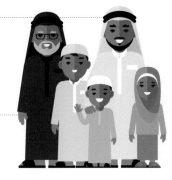

forbid

禁止

Muslims are forbidden from eating pork. 穆斯林禁食豬肉。

prohibit

禁止

Muslims are prohibited from eating pork. 穆斯林禁食豬肉。

dedicate
[ˈdɛdəˌket]

奉獻

Muhammad dedicated the Kaaba shrine to Allah.
穆罕默德將卡巴天房獻給真主阿拉。

devote

奉獻

Muhammad devoted himself to religion. 穆罕默德對宗教全心奉獻。

reveal

顯露出；洩漏

Muslims believe that the angel Gabriel revealed himself to Muhammad.
穆斯林相信天使加百利曾向穆罕默德表明身分。

expand

擴展；擴張

The Ottoman Empire expanded into North Africa and Eastern Europe.
鄂圖曼帝國擴張到北非與東歐。

decline

衰落

The Ottoman Empire declined after the death of Suleiman the Magnificent.
蘇萊曼大帝死後，鄂圖曼帝國便衰敗了。

Word Families 🔊 023

Islam

伊斯蘭教（回教）

Islam is the name of the religion that was founded by Muhammad.
伊斯蘭教是由穆罕默德所創立的宗教名稱。

Muslim

穆斯林（伊斯蘭教徒）

Muslims are followers of Islam. 穆斯林是伊斯蘭教的信徒。

Allah

真主阿拉

Allah, the Arabic word for God, is the god of Islam.
阿拉是伊斯蘭教的神，在阿拉伯語中有上帝之意。

Koran

《可蘭經》

The *Koran* is the holy book of Islam. 《可蘭經》是伊斯蘭教的聖典。

Hajj
[hædʒ]

朝覲

The Hajj is a pilgrimage to Mecca that all Muslims are supposed to make once in their lives. 朝覲即為前往麥加朝聖，是所有穆斯林一生中都應該做一次的事。

Checkup

Write | 請依提示寫出正確的英文單字和片語。

1	商隊	_____	9	鄂圖曼帝國	_____
2	貝都因人	_____	10	蘇丹	_____
3	穆罕默德	_____	11	繁榮；興旺	_____
4	先知	_____	12	禁止	p_____
5	齋戒月	_____	13	奉獻	_____
6	麥加	_____	14	顯露出；洩漏	_____
7	哈里發	_____	15	衰落	_____
8	市集	_____	16	穆斯林	_____

B

Complete the Sentences | 請在空格中填入最適當的答案，並視情況做適當的變化。

Ramadan	prophet	caliph	Ottoman Empire	Mecca
Bedouin	caravan	sultan	Muhammad	bazaar

1 A _____ is a group of traders who travel along trading routes by camel.
一群商人騎著駱駝通行於通商路線稱為商隊。

2 The _____ lived in the desert and traveled in caravans.
貝都因人居住在沙漠，成群結隊而行。

3 _____ is the holiest city in Islam because the prophet Muhammad was born there. 由於先知穆罕默德在麥加出生，因此那裡是伊斯蘭教的聖地。

4 Muhammad is regarded as a _____ of Allah by Muslims.
穆罕默德被穆斯林視為是真主阿拉的先知。

5 A _____ was a Muslim political and religious leader who was selected as a successor of Muhammad.
哈里發被挑選出來作為穆罕默德的繼承者，是伊斯蘭教的政治與宗教領袖。

6 A _____ is a large market in the Middle East. 市集是中東的大型市場。

7 The _____ _____ was the greatest Islamic Empire and was located in the area of modern-day Turkey.
鄂圖曼帝國是最大的伊斯蘭教帝國，所在位於現今的土耳其。

C

8 A _____ is a ruler of an Islamic country. 蘇丹是伊斯蘭教國家的統治者。

Read and Choose | 閱讀下列句子，並且選出最適當的答案。

1 Muhammad (prohibited | devoted) himself to religion.

2 Muslims are (flourished | forbidden) from eating pork.

3 Muhammad (dedicated | declined) the Kaaba shrine to Allah.

4 Muslims believe that the angel Gabriel (revealed | regarded) himself to Muhammad.

Look, Read, and Write | 看圖並且依照提示，在空格中填入正確答案。

1

▸ a group of people traveling together on a long journey especially through the desert

_____

3

▸ a person who delivers messages that are believed to have come from God

_____

2

▸ the ninth month of the Islamic year when Muslims do not eat or drink anything

_____

4

▸ a journey to Mecca that is a religious duty for Muslims

_____

E

Read and Answer | 閱讀並且回答下列問題。 ⊙ 024

The Spread of Islam

In 632, Muhammad died. He was the founder of Islam. At his death, there were few Muslims. And they had very little land. But after Muhammad's death, Islam began to spread rapidly.

Soon after Muhammad's death, Muslim leaders selected caliphs to govern the Muslim community. During the reigns of the first four caliphs (from 632 to 661), Islam spread throughout the Arabian Peninsula. By 661, Islam conquered land from Persia in the Near East to Egypt in Africa. From 661 to 750, the Umayyad dynasty ruled the Islamic world. They spread Islam throughout northern Africa. In 711, an Islamic army crossed the Mediterranean Sea and entered Spain. In a few years, they had captured Spain. The Muslims went north and entered France. But, in 732, Charles Martel defeated an Islamic army near Tours. The Muslim advance to the north was stopped.

Meanwhile, the Muslims could not defeat the Byzantine Empire in the east. They advanced on Constantinople several times. But they always lost. Later, however, the Ottoman Empire arose in the east. It challenged the Byzantines. By the fifteenth century, the Byzantine Empire was weak. In 1453, the Ottomans conquered it. They made Constantinople their capital. From there, they would rule a vast Islamic empire until the twentieth century.

Fill in the blanks.

1   The founder of Islam was _____.
2   The first four caliphs ruled from _____ to 661.
3   _____ _____ defeated the Muslims near Tours.
4   The _____ Empire defeated the Byzantine Empire.

Key Words 🔊 025

01	**feudalism** [ˈfjudl̩ɪzəm]	(n.) 封建制度 *feudal lord 封建領主 *manor (n.) 莊園；領地 Feudalism was the most prominent social system in Europe during the Middle Ages. 封建制度是中世紀歐洲最重要的社會體制。
02	**Catholic Church** [ˈkæθəlɪk tʃɜtʃ]	(n.) 天主教會 *Roman Catholic Church 羅馬公教教會 *Eastern Orthodox Church 東正教教會 In the Middle Age, most Europeans were Christians, and the Catholic Church had great power. 中世紀的歐洲人多為基督徒，天主教會擁有極大的權力。
03	**Magna Carta** [ˈmægnə ˈkɑrtə]	(n.) 大憲章 *separation of church and state 政教分離 The Magna Carta, also called the Great Charter, was originally issued in the year 1215 by King John of England. 大憲章也稱作 Great Charter，起初是在 1215 年由英國的約翰王所頒布的。
04	**Black Death** [blæk dɛθ]	(n.) 黑死病 *plague (n.) 瘟疫；鼠疫 *bubonic plague 腺鼠疫（黑死病即屬此） A plague called the Black Death killed millions of people in Europe in the fourteenth century. 14 世紀時，一種叫做黑死病的瘟疫於歐洲肆虐，造成數百萬人的死亡。
05	**guild** [gɪld]	(n.) 同業公會 *Freemasonry (n.) 共濟會 Guilds were associations of craft workers such as masons, bakers, and blacksmiths. 同業公會是如石匠、糕點師傅或鐵匠等工匠們的組織。
06	**Reformation** [ˌrɛfəˈmeʃən]	(n.) 宗教改革 *justification by faith alone 因信稱義 The Reformation began in the sixteenth century as an attempt to reform the Roman Catholic Church. 宗教改革是為了要革新羅馬天主教會，始於 16 世紀。
07	**Counter-Reformation** [ˈkaʊntə ˌrɛfəˈmeʃən]	(n.) 反宗教改革 *indulgence (n.)（宗教）大赦；贖罪券 Roman Catholics began a reform movement called the Counter-Reformation. 羅馬的天主教徒開始一項稱為反宗教改革的運動。
08	**Protestant** [ˈprɑtɪstənt]	(n.) 新教徒 *Catholic (n.) 天主教徒 *Christian (n.) 基督教徒 Martin Luther's followers were called Protestants. 馬丁・路德的信徒叫做新教徒。
09	**Inquisition** [ˌɪnkwəˈzɪʃən]	(n.) 宗教法庭 *heresy (n.) 異端；邪說 *heretic (n.) 異教徒 *cult (n.) 邪教；異端 The Inquisition investigated people suspected of heresy and of not being Christians. 宗教法庭調查有異端嫌疑者與非基督教徒者。
10	**execution** [ˌɛksɪˈkjuʃən]	(n.) 處決 *stay of execution 緩期執行死刑 *to carry sth. into execution 執行某事 Public executions were common during the Inquisition. 當眾處決在宗教法庭中很常見。

Black Death

guild

Reformation

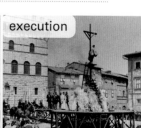
execution

infect
感染；傳染
The bubonic plague **infected** and killed millions of people and caused the Black Death. 數百萬人感染並死於腺鼠疫，造成黑死病。

clash
衝突；牴觸
The popes of Rome **clashed** with the Christian leaders of the Byzantine Empire. 羅馬教皇與拜占庭帝國的基督教領袖意見相左。

reform
改革；革新
Martin Luther wanted to **reform** the Roman Catholic Church.
馬丁・路德想要改革羅馬天主教會。

split
分裂
As the result of the Reformation, Christianity **split** into a number of different groups, including Catholics, Lutherans, and Calvinists.
宗教改革的結果就是基督教分裂成多個教派，包含天主教派、路德教派與喀爾文教派。

declare
[dɪˋklɛr]
宣告；聲明
England's King Henry VIII **declared** himself the head of the Anglican Church and left the Catholic Church. 英國國王亨利八世脫離天主教會，宣布自己為英國國教的領袖。

Word Families
🔊 027

monastery
[ˋmɑnəsˏtɛrɪ]
修道院
A **monastery** is a religious community where monks live.
修道院是修道士所居住的宗教場所。

convent
[kənˋvɛnt]
女修道院
A **convent** is a religious community where nuns live.
女修道院是修女所居住的宗教場所。

pope
教皇；教宗
The **pope** is the head of the Catholic Church. 教皇是天主教會的領神。

bishop
[ˋbɪʃəp]
主教
A **bishop** is a priest with a high rank who is in charge of many churches and priests. 掌管多所教堂與神父的高階神父叫做主教。

The System of Feudalism
封建制度

Important Figures in the Reformation
宗教改革的重要人物

manor 領地
lord 領主
vassal 家臣；封臣
serf/peasant 農奴／農民
knight 騎士

Martin Luther 馬丁・路德
John Calvin 約翰・喀爾文
John Knox 約翰・諾克斯
Ulrich Zwingli 烏利希・慈運理

Checkup

A

Write | 請依提示寫出正確的英文單字和片語。

1	封建制度	_____	9	宗教法庭	_____
2	天主教會	_____	10	處決	_____
3	大憲章	_____	11	感染；傳染	_____
4	黑死病	_____	12	衝突；牴觸	_____
5	同業公會	_____	13	改革；革新	_____
6	宗教改革	_____	14	分裂	_____
7	反宗教改革	_____	15	宣告；聲明	_____
8	新教徒	_____	16	主教	_____

B

Complete the Sentences | 請在空格中填入最適當的答案，並視情況做適當的變化。

Catholic Church	Magna Carta	Protestant	Inquisition	feudalism
Counter-Reformation	Black Death	guild	Reformation	execution

1 _____ was the most prominent social system in Europe during the Middle Ages. 封建制度是中世紀歐洲最重要的社會體制。

2 In the Middle Age, most Europeans were Christians, and the _____ _____ had great power. 中世紀的歐洲人多為基督徒，天主教會擁有極大的權力。

3 _____ were associations of craft workers such as masons, bakers, and blacksmiths. 同業公會是如石匠、糕點師傅或鐵匠等手工藝者們的組織。

4 The _____ investigated people suspected of heresy and of not being Christians. 宗教法庭調查有異端嫌疑者與非基督教徒者。

5 The _____ began in the sixteenth century as an attempt to reform the Roman Catholic Church. 宗教改革是為了要革新羅馬天主教會，始於 16 世紀。

6 Roman Catholics began a reform movement called the _____. 羅馬的天主教徒開始一項稱為反宗教改革的運動。

7 Martin Luther's followers were called _____. 馬丁・路德的信徒叫做新教徒。

8 Public _____ were common during the Inquisition. 當眾處決在宗教法庭中很常見。

C

Read and Choose | 閱讀下列句子，並且選出最適當的答案。

1 The bubonic plague (infected｜attempted) and killed millions of people and caused the Black Death.

2 The popes of Rome (clashed｜crashed) with the Christian leaders of the Byzantine Empire.

3 Martin Luther wanted to (split｜reform) the Roman Catholic Church.

4 England's King Henry VIII (investigated｜declared) himself the head of the Anglican Church and left the Catholic Church.

Look, Read, and Write | 看圖並且依照提示，在空格中填入正確答案。

1 ▸ a document signed in 1215 by King John of England that gave people certain rights

_____

3 ▸ the sixteenth century movement led to the Protestant churches being established

_____

2 ▸ a deadly disease that spread through Asia and Europe in the fourteenth century

_____

4 ▸ a place where monks live and work together

_____

E

Read and Answer | 閱讀並且回答下列問題。 028

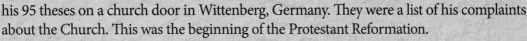

The Reformation

For centuries, the Catholic Church dominated life in Europe. But many priests in the Church were corrupt. They were more interested in money and living a good life than in religion. Some people were upset about that. One of them was Martin Luther. In 1517, he posted his 95 theses on a church door in Wittenberg, Germany. They were a list of his complaints about the Church. This was the beginning of the Protestant Reformation.

Martin Luther

Luther did not intend to form a new church. He only wanted to reform the Roman Catholic Church. But the Church called him a heretic and excommunicated him. This caused a split in Germany. Many of the German people disliked the Church. But they wanted to remain Christians. The Reformation soon turned violent. In Germany, Catholics and Protestants fought against each other. This happened until 1555. That year, the Peace of Augsburg allowed every German prince to choose to be Catholic or Protestant.

At the same time as the problems in Germany, the Reformation quickly moved across Europe. Men like Jean Calvin and Ulrich Zwingli led their own protests against the Church. Soon, new Protestant sects were founded. There was the Lutheran sect. There were Presbyterians and Baptists. There were also Calvinists. And, in England, the Anglican Church was founded when Henry VIII broke away from the Roman Catholic Church.

What is NOT true?

1   Martin Luther started the Protestant Reformation.
2   Martin Luther remained a Catholic for his entire life.
3   Jean Calvin was another leader of the Protestant Reformation.
4   The Anglican Church was founded in England.

The Enlightenment and the French Revolution 啟蒙運動與法國大革命

Key Words 🔊 029

01	**Enlightenment** [ɪnˈlaɪtn̩mən]	(n.) 啟蒙運動　*natural and legal rights 天賦人權 The eighteenth century is called the age of **Enlightenment**. 18 世紀被稱為啟蒙時代。
02	**rationalism** [ˈræʃənəlˌɪzəm]	(n.) 理性主義　*empiricism (n.) 經驗主義　*Romanticism (n.) 浪漫主義 The Enlightenment was an age of **rationalism**. 啟蒙時代是理性主義的時代。
03	**geocentric** [ˌdʒioˈsɛntrɪk]	(a.) 以地球為中心的　*geocentric theory 地球中心說 The **geocentric** theory is the theory that the sun and the stars revolve around the Earth. 地球中心說表示太陽與星星繞著地球轉。
04	**heliocentric** [ˌhilɪoˈsɛntrɪk]	(a.) 以太陽為中心的　*heliocentric theory 太陽中心說 Galileo Galilei believed in Copernicus's **heliocentric** theory. 伽利略相信哥白尼的太陽中心說。
05	**divine right** [dəˈvaɪn raɪt]	(n.) 君權神授　*enlightened despotism 開明專制 The **divine right** of kings states that kings have been chosen to rule by God. 君權神授闡明了國王是由上帝選擇來治理國家的。
06	**French Revolution** [frɛntʃ ˌrɛvəˈluʃən]	(n.) 法國大革命　*Glorious Revolution 光榮革命（1688年的英國政變） Liberty, equality, and brotherhood became the slogan of the **French Revolution**. 自由、平等、博愛是法國大革命的口號。
07	**Estates-General** [ɪsˈtets ˈdʒɛnərəl]	(n.) 三級會議　*clergy (n.) 神職人員　*noble (n.) 貴族　*commoner (n.) 平民 King Louis XVI called a meeting of the **Estates-General** in 1789. 路易十六於 1789 年召開三級會議。
08	**Bastille** [bæsˈtil]	(n.) 巴士底獄　*Bastille Day 法國國慶日　*Tennis Court Oath 網球場宣言 The **Bastille** was a prison in Paris and was an important symbol in the French Revolution. 巴士底獄是巴黎的一座監獄，而且是法國大革命中一個重要的象徵。
09	**Napoleon** [nəˈpoljən]	(n.) 拿破崙　*Napoleonic Code《拿破崙法典》　*Napoleonic Wars 拿破崙戰爭 **Napoleon** Bonaparte became the emperor of France following the French Revolution. 拿破崙‧波拿巴於法國大革命後，成為了法國的君王。
10	**Waterloo** [ˌwɔtɚˈlu]	(n.) 滑鐵盧　*to meet one's Waterloo 遭遇最終的失敗 Napoleon was defeated by the Duke of Wellington at the Battle of **Waterloo** in 1815. 拿破崙在 1815 年的滑鐵盧一役中，遭威靈頓公爵擊敗。

French Revolution

Bastille

Napoleon

Battle of Waterloo

Power Verbs

🔊 030

execute
[ˈɛksɪ͵kjut]

處決

Queen Marie Antoinette was **executed** during the French Revolution.
皇后瑪麗 · 安東尼在法國大革命期間遭到處決。

behead

斬首

King Louis XVI was **beheaded** during the French Revolution.
國王路易十六在法國大革命期間遭到斬首。

overcome

戰勝；克服

The people of France rose up in rebellion and **overcame** the monarchy.
法國人民起義推翻王權。

seize

掌握；抓住

In 1799, Napoleon **seized** power in France. 拿破崙在 1799 年掌握法國大權。

exile
[ˈɛksaɪl]

流放

Napoleon was **exiled** to the island of Saint Helena after his final defeat.
拿破崙在他最後戰役失敗後，被流放到聖海倫娜島。

banish

流放

Napoleon was **banished** to the island of Saint Helena after his final defeat.
拿破崙在他最後戰役失敗後，被流放到聖海倫娜島。

Word Families

🔊 031

three estates 三種階級

France was divided into **three estates**: the clergy of the Catholic Church, the nobles, and the other 98%, most of whom were poor peasants.
法國分成三種階級：天主教會神職人員、貴族以及佔百分之九十八的大多數窮苦農民。

guillotine
[ˈgɪlə͵tin]

斷頭台

The **guillotine** was a device used to behead and execute people during the French Revolution. 斷頭台是法國大革命期間，用來斬首與處決民眾的刑具。

Important Figures in the Enlightenment
啟蒙運動的重要人物

Rene Descartes 勒內 · 笛卡兒
Sir Isaac Newton 艾薩克 · 牛頓爵士
Denis Diderot 德尼 · 狄德羅
Voltaire 伏爾泰
Jean-Jacques Rousseau 尚-雅克 · 盧梭

Important Figures in the French Revolution
法國大革命的重要人物

Louis XVI 路易十六
Marie Antoinette 瑪麗 · 安東尼
Robespierre 羅伯斯皮爾

Checkup

A

Write | 請依提示寫出正確的英文單字和片語。

1	啟蒙運動 _____	9	拿破崙 _____
2	理性主義 _____	10	滑鐵盧 _____
3	以地球為中心的 _____	11	處決 _____
4	以太陽為中心的 _____	12	斬首 _____
5	君權神授 _____	13	戰勝；克服 _____
6	法國大革命 _____	14	掌握；抓住 _____
7	三級會議 _____	15	流放 e _____
8	巴士底獄 _____	16	斷頭台 _____

B

Complete the Sentences | 請在空格中填入最適當的答案，並視情況做適當的變化。

Estates-General	geocentric	Enlightenment	rationalism	Napoleon
French Revolution	heliocentric	divine right	Bastille	Waterloo

1 The eighteenth century is called the age of _____.
18 世紀被稱為啟蒙時代。

2 The Enlightenment was an age of _____.
啟蒙時代是理性主義的時代。

3 Galileo Galilei believed in Copernicus's _____ theory.
伽利略相信哥白尼的太陽中心說。

4 The _____ _____ of kings states that kings have been chosen to rule by God. 君權神授闡明了國王是由神選擇來治理國家的。

5 Liberty, equality, and brotherhood became the slogan of the _____ _____. 自由、平等、博愛是法國大革命的口號。

6 King Louis XVI called a meeting of the _____ in 1789.
路易十六於 1789 年召開三級會議。

7 _____ Bonaparte became the emperor of France following the French Revolution. 拿破崙・波拿巴於法國大革命後，成為了法國的君王。

8 Napoleon was defeated by the Duke of Wellington at the Battle of _____ in 1815. 拿破崙在 1815 年的滑鐵盧一役中，遭威靈頓公爵擊敗。

C

Read and Choose | 閱讀下列句子，並且選出最適當的答案。

1 King Louis XVI was (headed | beheaded) during the French Revolution.

2 Queen Marie Antoinette was (executed | chosen) during the French Revolution.

3 In 1799, Napoleon (banished | seized) power in France.

4 Napoleon was (exiled | beheaded) to the island of Saint Helena after his final defeat.

Look, Read, and Write | 看圖並且依照提示，在空格中填入正確答案。

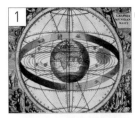
1 ▸ having or relating to the Earth as the center

_____

3 ▸ the right that is supposedly given to a king or queen by God to rule

_____

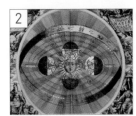
2 ▸ having or relating to the sun as the center

_____

4 ▸ a prison in Paris that was an important symbol in the French Revolution

_____

E

Read and Answer | 閱讀並且回答下列問題。 🔊 032

The French Revolution

In France in the eighteenth century, life was difficult for most people. The ruler of France was the king. He ruled by divine right. This was the idea that God had chosen the king to be the ruler. This meant that the king could do anything he wanted. There were also nobles with great power in France. The clergy mostly lived good lives, too. But the rest of the people had difficult lives. They were poor, had little or no land, and had no freedom.

In the 1780s, the world was changing. The Americans had won their revolution with England and become free. The French people wanted the same thing. King Louis XVI and his wife, Marie Antoinette, were oppressive rulers. They taxed the people. But the people became tired of their poor lives. So, on July 14, 1789, they rebelled. They stormed the Bastille on that day. It was a prison in Paris. They freed the prisoners and took the weapons that were there. The French Revolution had begun.

The French Revolution was very violent. Louis XVI was beheaded during the revolution. More nobles and clergy were killed, too. Thousands of people died during the revolution. In the end, the monarchy was destroyed. But France did not become a democracy like the people had hoped. Instead, Napoleon Bonaparte, a general, became the emperor of France. He would then lead France to war with many European nations until he was finally defeated in 1815.

Answer the questions.

1 What two groups of people in France had good lives?_____

2 Who ruled France when the French Revolution began?

_____

3 When did the French Revolution begin? _____

4 Who ruled France after the French Revolution ended? _____

The Age of Imperialism

帝國主義的年代

Key Words
🔊 033

01	**imperialism** [ɪmˈpɪriəlɪzəm]	*(n.)* 帝國主義　*economic/cultural imperialism 經濟／文化擴張主義 During the Age of **Imperialism**, European nations competed to establish colonies in Asia. 在帝國主義的時代裡，歐洲國家爭相在亞洲建立殖民地。
02	**nationalism** [ˈnæʃənlɪzəm]	*(n.)* 國家主義；民族主義　*patriotism (n.) 愛國主義　*patriot (n.) 愛國者 *ethnocentrism (n.) 民族優越主義 **Nationalism** is excessive devotion to one's country. 國家主義對祖國有一種過度的熱愛。
03	**Great Power** [gret ˈpaʊɚ]	*(n.)* 強國　*superpower (n.) 超級大國；超級強權　*hegemony (n.) 霸權 The **Great Powers** in Europe dominated much of the world in the nineteenth and twentieth centuries. 歐洲列強於 19 與 20 世紀主宰世界多國。
04	**rivalry** [ˈvaɪvlrɪ]	*(n.)* 競爭　*rivalry with sb./sth. 與某人／某物的競爭 *rivalry to/for sb./sth. 為某人／某物競爭 *rivalry between/among sb./sth. 某人／某物之間的競爭 Many European countries had **rivalries** with one another. 許多歐洲國家互相競爭。
05	**alliance** [əˈlaɪəns]	*(n.)* 聯盟；結盟　*in alliance with sb. 與某人結盟　*to form an alliance 結盟 Countries often establish **alliances** with one another so that they can work together. 國家間經常互相結盟，以共同合作。
06	**armistice** [ˈɑrməstɪs]	*(n.)* 休戰協議　*Armistice Day 第一次世界大戰停戰日　*truce (n.) 講和；休戰 In 1918, the Germans and the Allied Powers signed an **armistice** to end World War I. 德國與協約國於 1918 年簽署休戰協議，結束第一次世界大戰。
07	**Russian Revolution** [ˈrʌʃən ˌrɛvəˈluʃən]	*(n.)* 俄國革命　*palace revolution 宮廷政變 The **Russian Revolution** led to the downfall of the czar and the onset of communism in Russia. 俄國革命導致沙皇垮臺，開始了俄國的共產主義。
08	**communism** [ˈkɑmjʊˌnɪzəm]	*(n.)* 共產主義　*capitalism (n.) 資本主義　*socialism (n.) 社會主義 **Communism** is based on communal ownership of all property. 共產主義是以共有所有財產為根本。
09	**civil war** [ˈsvl wɔr]	*(n.)* 內戰　*disorder (n.) 動亂；騷亂　*coup (n.) 政變 Russia became the world's first communist nation after the Russian civil war. 俄國在俄國內戰後，成為世界上第一個共產國家。
10	**totalitarianism** [ˌtotæləˈtɛrɪənˌɪzəm]	*(n.)* 極權主義　*Fascism (n.) 法西斯主義　*secret police 祕密警察 **Totalitarianism** is an oppressive form of government. 極權主義是一種壓迫專制的政府型態。

Lenin

Karl Marx, the founder of modern communism

Mussolini　Hitler

Stalin

take control of 控制；掌控

The British **took control of** India's economy and government.
英國掌控了印度的經濟與政治。

take over 掌管

Many Chinese ports were **taken over** by European traders.
中國的多處港口受到歐洲商人的掌控。

adopt 接受；採取

The Meiji government of Japan encouraged the Japanese to **adopt** Western customs. 日本的明治政府鼓勵人民吸取西方文化。

modernize 現代化
[ˈmɑdən͵aɪz]

Japan began to **modernize** and developed a powerful army.
日本開始進行維新，訓練戰力堅強的軍隊。

tyrannize 施行暴政；欺壓
[ˈtɪrə͵naɪz]

The communists **tyrannized** the people of Russia. 共產主義者對俄國人民施行暴政。

oppress 壓迫
[əˈprɛs]

The communist governments have **oppressed** their own people.
共產主義政府壓迫自己國家的人民。

ally 同盟（國） *to ally with 結為盟友

Allies are people or countries that work together as friends.
人或國家像朋友一樣合作，叫做同盟（國）。

alliance 聯盟；結盟

An alliance is a group of people or countries that work together.
一群人或國家共同合作，叫做聯盟。

confederation 聯盟；聯合
[kən͵fɛdəˈreʃən]

A confederation is a group of people or countries that work together.
一群人或國家共同合作，叫做聯盟。

Central Powers 同盟國

The Central Powers, which were led by Germany, lost World War I.
由德國主導的同盟國輸掉了第一次世界大戰。

Allied Powers 協約國（= the Allies）

The Allied Powers, which were led by England and France, won World War I.
由英國與法國主導的協約國，贏得第一次世界大戰。

World War I
第一次世界大戰

Central Powers 同盟國
Austria-Hungary / Austrian-Hungarian Empire 奧匈帝國
Germany / German Empire 德國 **Ottoman Empire** 鄂圖曼帝國
Bulgaria / Kingdom of Bulgaria 保加利亞

Allied Powers 協約國
Great Britain 大英帝國 **France** 法國 **Russia / Russian Empire** 俄國

Checkup

A

Write | 請依提示寫出正確的英文單字和片語。

1	帝國主義	_____	9	內戰	_____
2	國家主義；民族主義	_____	10	極權主義	_____
3	強國	_____	11	控制；掌控	_____
4	競爭	_____	12	接受；採取	_____
5	聯盟；結盟	_____	13	現代化	_____
6	休戰協議	_____	14	施行暴政；欺壓	_____
7	俄國革命	_____	15	壓迫	_____
8	共產主義	_____	16	聯盟；聯合 c_____

B

Complete the Sentences | 請在空格中填入最適當的答案，並視情況做適當的變化。

Great Power	civil war	armistice	imperialism	communism
Russian Revolution	rivalry	alliance	nationalism	totalitarianism

1 During the Age of _____, European nations competed to establish colonies in Asia. 在帝國主義的時代裡，歐洲國家爭相在亞洲建立殖民地。

2 _____ is excessive devotion to one's country.
國家主義對祖國有一種激進的熱愛。

3 The _____ _____ in Europe dominated much of the world in the nineteenth and twentieth centuries. 歐洲列強於 19 與 20 世紀主宰世界多國。

4 Many European countries had _____ with one another.
許多歐洲國家互相競爭。

5 Countries often establish _____ with one another so that they can work together. 國家間經常互相結盟，以共同合作。

6 In 1918, the Germans and the Allied Powers signed an _____ to end World War I. 德國與協約國於 1918 年簽署休戰協議，結束第一次世界大戰。

7 The _____ _____ led to the downfall of the tsar and the onset of communism in Russia. 俄國革命導致沙皇垮臺，開始了俄國的共產主義。

8 Russia became the world's first communist nation after the Russian _____ _____. 俄國在俄國內戰後，成為世界上第一個共產國家。

C

Read and Choose | 閱讀下列句子，並且選出最適當的答案。

1 The British (took | taken) control of India's economy and government.
2 Many Chinese ports were (took | taken) over by European traders.
3 The Meiji government of Japan encouraged the Japanese to (adopt | compete) Western customs.
4 The communists (tyrannized | allied) the people of Russia.

D

Look, Read, and Write | 看圖並且依照提示，在空格中填入正確答案。

 ▸ an agreement to stop
fighting a war

_____

 ▸ a war between
groups of people in
the same country

_____

 ▸ the belief in a society
without different social
classes and privately
owned property

_____

 ▸ the belief that a
government should
have total power
over its citizens

_____

E

Read and Answer | 閱讀並且回答下列問題。 ⊙ 036

The Great War

For centuries, European countries had fought each other. But,
from 1914 to 1918, there was a different kind of war. It was a
world war. At that time, people called it the Great War. Later,
it was called World War I (WWI). At first, people thought it
would just be another war. By the time it ended, millions were
dead. And many people were horrified by the carnage of war.

Before WWI began, many European countries had alliances with each other. They
promised to defend other countries if they were in trouble. On June 28, 1914,
Archduke Francis Ferdinand of Austria-Hungary was assassinated in Sarajevo. The
Austrians quickly declared war on Serbia. However, because of the different alliances,
what should have been a small war became an enormous one. The Central Powers led
by Germany, Austria-Hungary, and the Ottoman Empire were on one side. The Allied
Powers led by England, France, and Russia were on the other side.

The Germans swiftly attacked France. However, the German advance was stopped.
Neither side could move against the other. Thus trench warfare began. For four years,
each side succeeded in killing many of the other's soldiers. Tanks and airplanes were
used in war for the first time. So were chemical weapons. Finally, the war ended. But
it didn't end war. Around two decades later, World War II began. It was an even worse
war than WWI had been.

What is true? Write T(true) or F(false).

1   Very few people died in World War I.   _____
2   Archduke Francis Ferdinand was from Germany.   _____
3   England was a member of the Allied Powers.   _____
4   The first tanks were used in World War I.   _____

World War II and After the War 第二次世界大戰與戰後

Unit **10**

Key Words

🔊 037

01	**independence** [ˌɪndɪˈpɛndəns]	*(n.)* 獨立　*to achieve/gain/win independence from sth. 從某處取得／獲得／贏得獨立 After World War II, many nations demanded **independence** from colonial rule. 許多國家在第二次世界大戰後，要求脫離殖民統治而獨立。
02	**NATO** [ˈneto]	*(n.)* 北大西洋公約組織（= Atlantic Alliance） **NATO** stands for the North Atlantic Treaty Organization. NATO 四字母代表著北大西洋公約組織。
03	**Warsaw Pact** [ˈwɔrsɔ pækt]	*(n.)* 華沙公約組織（= Warsaw Treaty Organization） The **Warsaw Pact** was a group of communist countries founded to counter NATO. 華沙公約組織由一群共產主義國家創立，用來制衡北大西洋公約組織。
04	**arms race** [ɑrmz res]	*(n.)* 軍備競賽　*nuclear arms race 核軍備競賽　*space race 太空競賽 The USA and the USSR were in an **arms race** after World War II ended. 美國與蘇聯在第二次世界大戰結束後，互相進行軍備競賽。
05	**civil disobedience** [ˈsɪvl̩ ˌdɪsəˈbidiəns]	*(n.)* 公民不服從；不合作主義　*Non-Cooperation Movement 不合作運動 Mohandas Gandhi taught **civil disobedience** and nonviolent refusal to British rule in India. 莫罕達斯·甘地對於英國在印度的統治，教導了公民不服從與非暴力抗議。
06	**anti-Semitism** [ˌæntɪˈsɛməˌtɪzəm]	*(n.)* 反猶太主義　*the Holocaust 納粹大屠殺　*the Gestapo 蓋世太保 　　　　　　　　　*concentration camp 集中營　*pogrom (n.)（種族或宗教）迫害 **Anti-Semitism** is discrimination against Jews. 反猶太主義是一種對猶太人的歧視。
07	**apartheid** [əˈpɑrtˌhet]	*(n.)*（尤指南非的）種族隔離政策　*genocide (n.)（尤指對整個民族的）種族滅絕 **Apartheid** was the segregation policy of the government of South Africa. 種族隔離政策是南非政府的隔離政策。
08	**refugee** [ˌrɛfjʊˈdʒi]	*(n.)* 難民　*refugee camp 難民營　*asylum (n.)（尤指政治）避難；庇護 **Refugees** are people who are displaced from their homes, often because of wars or natural disasters. 因為戰爭或自然災害而搬離家園的人叫做難民。
09	**globalization** [ˈɡloʊbəlaɪˈzeʃən]	*(n.)* 全球化　*localization (n.) 在地化　*glocalization (n.) 全球在地化 **Globalization** includes the spread of economies, technology, and culture among countries. 全球化包含了經濟、科技與文化的傳播。
10	**terrorism** [ˈtɛrəˌrɪzəm]	*(n.)* 恐怖主義　*counterterrorism (n.) 反恐怖主義　*mujahideen (n.) 穆斯林聖戰者 **Terrorism** is the attacking of civilians to achieve political purposes. 恐怖主義是以攻擊民眾來達到政治上的目的。

NATO

Warsaw Pact

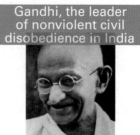

Gandhi, the leader of nonviolent civil disobedience in India

refugee

suppress

壓制；阻止

The British government **suppressed** Indian protests for decades.
英國政府壓制印度的反對意見數十年。

convince

說服；使相信

Adolf Hitler used propaganda to **convince** Germans his ideas were correct.
阿道夫‧希特勒利用宣傳來使德國人相信他的想法是正確的。

persuade
[pəˋswed]

說服

Adolf Hitler used propaganda to **persuade** Germans his ideas were correct.
阿道夫‧希特勒利用宣傳來說服德國人他的想法是正確的。

race

競賽

The USA and the USSR **raced** to reach the moon first.
美國與蘇聯互相比賽誰先登上月球。

have a rivalry with 與……競賽（= compete with）

The USA and the USSR **had a rivalry with** one another. 美國與蘇聯相互競爭。

discriminate
[dɪˌskrɪməˋneʃən]

歧視

Blacks were **discriminated** against in the USA for a long time.
在美國的黑人長期遭到歧視。

terrorize
[ˋtɛrəˌraɪz]

使……害怕；恐嚇

Many terrorist groups try to **terrorize** as many people as they can.
許多恐怖主義組織盡其所能恐嚇人。

Anne Frank's memorial
in Amsterdam

Holocaust
[ˋhɑləˌkɔst]

（納粹）大屠殺

The Nazis killed around six million Jews during the Holocaust.
納粹分子在大屠殺中殺害了約六百萬的猶太人。

genocide
[ˋdʒɛnəˌsaɪd]

種族屠殺

The Nazis committed genocide against the Jews.
納粹分子對猶太人進行種族屠殺。

coup

政變

A coup is a military takeover of a government.
政變就是以武力奪取政權。

guerrilla
[kənˌfɛdəˋreʃən]

游擊隊員

Guerrillas are rebels who fight against the government.
游擊隊員是反政府的抗爭者。

Jewish Holocaust Monument in Berlin

martial law

戒嚴

Martial law is the control of a country by the military.
戒嚴是由軍隊來掌管國家。

Checkup

A

Write | 請依提示寫出正確的英文單字和片語。

1	獨立	_____	9	全球化	_____
2	北大西洋公約組織	_____	10	恐怖主義	_____
3	華沙公約組織	_____	11	壓制；阻止	_____
4	軍備競賽	_____	12	說服；使相信	_____
5	公民不服從	_____	13	與……競賽	_____
6	反猶太主義	_____	14	使……害怕；恐嚇	_____
7	種族隔離政策	_____	15	種族屠殺	_____
8	難民	_____	16	戒嚴	_____

B

Complete the Sentences | 請在空格中填入最適當的答案，並視情況做適當的變化。

anti-Semitism	globalization	independence	refugee	apartheid
civil disobedience	arms race	Warsaw Pact	NATO	terrorism

1 After World War II, many nations demanded _____ from colonial rule. 許多國家在第二次世界大戰後，要求脫離殖民統治而獨立。

2 The _____ _____ was a group of communist countries founded to counter NATO. 華沙公約組織由一群共產主義國家創立，用來制衡北大西洋公約組織。

3 The USA and the USSR were in an _____ _____ after World War II ended. 美國與蘇聯在第二次世界大戰結束後，互相進行軍備競賽。

4 Mohandas Gandhi taught _____ _____ and nonviolent refusal to British rule in India. 莫罕達斯‧甘地對於英國在印度的統治，教導了公民不服從與非暴力抗議。

5 _____ is discrimination against Jews.
反猶太主義是一種對猶太人的歧視。

6 _____ are people who are displaced from their homes, often because of wars or natural disasters. 因為戰爭或自然災害而搬離家園的叫做難民。

7 _____ includes the spread of economies, technology, and culture among countries. 全球化包含了經濟、科技與文化的傳播。

8 _____ is the attacking of civilians to achieve political purposes.
恐怖主義是以攻擊民眾來達到政治上的目的。

C

Read and Choose | 閱讀下列句子，並且選出最適當的答案。

1 The British government (suppressed | obeyed) Indian protests for decades.
2 Adolf Hitler used propaganda to (convince | compete) Germans his ideas were correct.
3 The USA and the USSR (raced | refused) to reach the moon first.
4 Many terrorist groups try to (discriminate | terrorize) as many people as they can.

Look, Read, and Write | 看圖並且依照提示，在空格中填入正確答案。

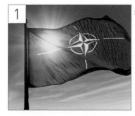 ► an military organization consisting of the US and many European countries

_____

 ► refusal to obey laws as a way of forcing the government to do or change something

Gandhi

_____

 ► a political system that people of different races are separated in South Africa

Nelson Mandela

_____

 ► the killing of millions of Jews and other people by the Nazis during World War II

_____

E

Read and Answer | 閱讀並且回答下列問題。 ● 040

Globalization

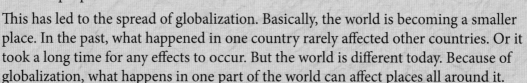

In the years after World War II, the world greatly changed. Much of this was due to new technology. For instance, the jet was developed. This increased the speed that people could travel. There were also advances in telecommunications. Computers and the Internet were invented. It became much easier for people to communicate with others all around the world.

This has led to the spread of globalization. Basically, the world is becoming a smaller place. In the past, what happened in one country rarely affected other countries. Or it took a long time for any effects to occur. But the world is different today. Because of globalization, what happens in one part of the world can affect places all around it.

Thanks to globalization, people can now do business more easily with those in other countries. When you go to the supermarket, you can see various foods from all of the different countries.

This happens because of globalization. Also, people are learning more about other countries these days. This leads to more understanding about other countries. In the age of globalization, there has not been a single world war. And the world is becoming richer. Globalization has surely been good for the world.

Fill in the blanks.

1   There was much new technology developed after _____ _____ ____.
2   Because of globalization, the _____ is becoming smaller.
3   It is _____ to do business with people in other countries these days.
4   Since the age of globalization, the world is becoming _____.

A

Write | 請依提示寫出正確的英文單字和片語。

1	（來往於沙漠）商隊	_____	11	禁止	p_____
2	先知	_____	12	奉獻	_____
3	宗教改革	_____	13	處決 (n.)	_____
4	新教徒	_____	14	宗教法庭	_____
5	啟蒙運動	_____	15	斬首 (v.)	_____
6	巴士底獄	_____	16	流放	b_____
7	帝國主義	_____	17	壓迫	_____
8	內戰	_____	18	掌管	t_____
9	難民	_____	19	與……競賽	_____
10	全球化	_____	20	說服	p_____

B

Choose the Correct Word | 請選出與鋪底字意思相近的答案。

1 Muslims are prohibited from eating pork.

   a. forbidden   b. persuaded   c. suppressed

2 Adolf Hitler used propaganda to convince Germans his ideas were correct.

   a. oppress   b. persuade   c. execute

3 The communists tyrannized the people of Russia.

   a. oppressed   b. took over   c. terrorized

4 Napoleon was exiled to the island of Saint Helena after his final defeat.

   a. raced   b. seized   c. banished

C

Complete the Sentences | 請在空格中填入最適當的答案，並視情況做適當的變化。

French Revolution	Great Power	prophet	Catholic Church

1 Muhammad is regarded as a _____ of Allah by Muslims.
   穆罕默德被穆斯林視為是阿拉真主的先知。

2 In the Middle Age, most Europeans were Christians, and the _____
   _____ had great power. 中世紀的歐洲人多為基督徒，天主教會擁有極大的權力。

3 Liberty, equality, and brotherhood became the slogan of the _____
   _____. 自由、平等、博愛是法國大革命的口號。

4 The _____ _____ in Europe dominated much of the world in the
   nineteenth and twentieth centuries. 歐洲列強於 19 與 20 世紀主宰世界多國。

3

Science ①

Classifying Living Things 生物的分類

Unit 11

Key Words

🔊 041

01	**taxonomy** [tækˈsɑnəmɪ]	*(n.)* 分類法　*binomial nomenclature 二名法 Taxonomy is the science of classifying living things. 分類法是一種分類生物的科學。
02	**classification** [ˌklæsəfəˈkeʃən]	*(n.)* 分類；類別　*classification (of sth.) under sth.（將某物）歸入某物的分類 The sorting of things or organisms into groups of similar things is called **classification**. 將相似的物件或生物分門別類，叫做分類。
03	**Monera kingdom** [məˈnirə ˈkɪŋdəm]	*(n.)* 原核生物界　*prokaryote (n.) 原核生物　*blue-green algae 藍綠菌（藻） The **Monera** kingdom, also called prokaryotes, includes very simple single-celled organisms like bacteria. 又稱為 prokaryotes 的原核生物界，包含了如細菌般簡單的單細胞生物。
04	**Protista kingdom** [proˈtɪstə ˈkɪŋdəm]	*(n.)* 原生生物界　*protist (n.) 原生生物　*eukaryote (n.) 真核生物 Organisms in the **Protista** kingdom are protists such as amoebas, algae, and some slime molds. 原生生物界中的生物，就是像變形蟲、水藻與一些黏菌的單細胞生物。
05	**Fungi kingdom** [ˈfʌŋgaɪ ˈkɪŋdəm]	*(n.)* 真菌界　*fungus (n.) 真菌（複數：fungi）　*mold (n.) 黴；黴菌 Organisms in the **Fungi** kingdom include various mushrooms and yeasts. 真菌界的生物包含了各種菌類與酵母。
06	**Plantae kingdom** [plænti ˈkɪŋdəm]	*(n.)* 植物界（= plant kingdom）　*vascular plant 維管束植物　*seed plant 種子植物 The **Plantae** kingdom includes a wide variety of organisms from tiny mosses to ferns and flowering plants. 植物界涵蓋了眾多生物，從微小的苔蘚、蕨類到開花植物。
07	**Animalia kingdom** [ˌænəˈmeliə ˈkɪŋdəm]	*(n.)* 動物界（= animal kingdom）　*metamorphosis (n.) 變態 Organisms in the **Animalia** kingdom include over one million different kinds of animals. 動物界中的生物涵蓋逾一百萬種的動物。
08	**Arthropoda** [arˈθrɑpədə]	*(n.)* 節肢動物門　*invertebrate (n.) 無脊椎動物　*exoskeleton (n.) 外骨骼 **Arthropoda**, the largest phylum of the Animalia kingdom, include insects, spiders, and crabs. 節肢動物門包含了昆蟲、蜘蛛與螃蟹，是動物界中最大的一門。
09	**Mollusca** [məˈlʌskə]	*(n.)* 軟體動物門　*protostome (n.) 原口生物　*deuterostome (n.) 後口生物 **Mollusca**, the second largest phylum in the Animalia kingdom, include oysters, snails, and squids. 軟體動物門包含了牡蠣、蝸牛與烏賊，是動物界中次大的一門。
10	**Chordata** [ˈkɔrˈdetə]	*(n.)* 脊索動物門　*vertebrate (n.) 脊椎動物　*notochord (n.) 脊索 Fish, birds, reptiles, amphibians, and mammals are all **Chordata** with backbones. 魚、鳥類、爬蟲類、兩棲動物與哺乳類動物，都是有脊骨的脊索動物。

Monera

Protist
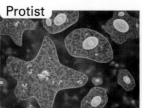

Fungi

Arthropoda

be based on

根據

The classification system used today **is based on** the method of Linnaeus, the Swedish scientist. 目前所使用的分類系統，是根據瑞典科學家林奈烏斯的方式。

come from

起源於……

The classification system used today **comes from** the method of Linnaeus, the Swedish scientist. 目前所使用的分類系統，起源於瑞典科學家林奈烏斯的方式。

classify

分類

Living things are **classified** into seven levels. 生物被分類成七大層級。

divide

劃分

Living things are **divided** into seven levels. 生物被劃分成七大層級。

sort

分類

Organisms are **sorted** according to their characteristics.
生物的分類是根據牠們的特性。

group

歸類；分組

Organisms are **grouped** according to their characteristics.
生物的歸類是根據牠們的特性。

categorize
[ˋkætəgəˏraɪz]

分類

Organisms are **categorized** according to their characteristics.
生物的分類是根據牠們的特性。

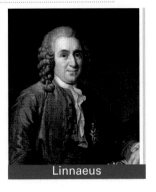
Linnaeus

Word Families
🔊 043

Animal Phyla
動物門

Arthropoda – insects, spiders, and crabs
節肢動物門——昆蟲、蜘蛛還有螃蟹

Mollusca – oysters, snails, and squids
軟體動物門——牡蠣、蝸牛與烏賊

Chordata – fish, mammals, and birds
脊索動物門——魚、哺乳動物與鳥類

Annelid – earthworms and leeches
環節動物門——蚯蚓與水蛭

Echinodermata – starfish and sea urchins
棘皮動物門——海星與海膽

Platyhelminthes – flatworms
扁形動物門——扁蟲

The Seven Levels of Classification
分類的七大層級

kingdom
界

phylum
門
* 複數 phyla

division
門

class
綱

order
目

family
科

genus
屬
* 複數 genera

species
種
* variety 變種

Mollusca　Annelid　Echinodermata　Platyhelminthes

Checkup

Write | 請依提示寫出正確的英文單字和片語。

1	分類法	_____	9	分類；類別	_____
2	原核生物界	_____	10	脊索動物門	_____
3	原生生物界	_____	11	根據	_____
4	真菌界	_____	12	起源於……	_____
5	植物界	_____	13	分類 (v.)	c_____
6	動物界	_____	14	環節動物門	_____
7	節肢動物門	_____	15	棘皮動物門	_____
8	軟體動物門	_____	16	扁形動物門	_____

B

Complete the Sentences | 請在空格中填入最適當的答案，並視情況做適當的變化。

Mollusca	Monera	Animalia	taxonomy	Plantae
Fungi	Arthropoda	Chordata	classification	Protista

1　_____ is the science of classifying living things.
分類法是一種分類生物的科學。

2　The sorting of things or organisms into groups of similar things is called
_____. 將相似的物件或生物分門別類，叫做分類。

3　Organisms in the _____ kingdom are protists such as amoebas, algae, and
some slime molds. 原生生物界中的生物，就是像變形蟲、水藻與一些黏菌的單細胞生物。

4　The _____ kingdom, also called prokaryotes, includes very simple single-
celled organisms like bacteria.
又稱為「prokaryotes」的原核生物界，包含了如細菌般簡單的單細胞生物。

5　Organisms in the _____ kingdom include over one million different kinds
of animals. 動物界中的生物涵蓋逾一百萬種的動物。

6　The _____ kingdom includes a wide variety of organisms from tiny mosses
to ferns and flowering plants. 植物界涵蓋了眾多生物，從微小的苔蘚、蕨類到開花植物。

7　_____, the largest phylum of the Animalia kingdom, include insects,
spiders, and crabs. 節肢動物門包含了昆蟲、蜘蛛與螃蟹，是動物界中最大的一門。

8　Fish, birds, reptiles, amphibians, and mammals are all _____ with
backbones. 魚、鳥類、爬蟲類、兩棲動物與哺乳類動物，都是有脊骨的脊索動物。

C

Read and Choose | 閱讀下列句子，並且選出最適當的答案。

1　The classification system used today is (based | sorted) on the method of Linnaeus.

2　Living things are (group | classified) into seven levels.

3　Organisms are (included | categorized) according to their characteristics.

4　Organisms in the (Protista | prokaryotes) kingdom are protists such as amoebas
and algae.

D

Look, Read, and Write | 看圖並且依照提示，在空格中填入正確答案。

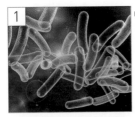
1 ► a kingdom that contains single-celled organisms, such as bacteria

_____

3 ► the largest phylum of the Animalia kingdom, which includes insects, spiders, and crabs

_____

2 ► a kingdom that contains various mushrooms, molds, and yeasts

_____

4 ► the second largest phylum in the Animalia kingdom, which includes oysters, snails, and squids

_____

E

Read and Answer | 閱讀並且回答下列問題。 🔊 044

The Five Kingdoms of Life

There is an amazing variety of life on the Earth. Scientists have classified all forms of life into five different kingdoms. Each kingdom has its own characteristics.

The first is the Monera kingdom. There are about 10,000 species in it. The members of this kingdom are prokaryotes that are unicellular. Its members include various kinds of bacteria and some algae.

The second is the Protista kingdom. There are around 250,000 species in it. The members of this kingdom include protozoans and some kinds of algae.

The third is the Fungi kingdom. There are around 100,000 species in it. Members of this kingdom are similar to plants. But they do not use photosynthesis to create nutrients. Mushrooms are members of this kingdom.

The fourth is the Plantae kingdom. There are around 250,000 species in it. Plants, trees, flowers, and bushes all belong to this kingdom.

The fifth is the Animalia kingdom. It is the biggest with over 1,000,000 species in it. It is formed by multicellular animals.

What is true? Write T(true) or F(false).

1 There are five different kingdoms of life.   _____
2 There are around 250,000 species in the Monera kingdom.   _____
3 Mushrooms belong to the Fungi kingdom.   _____
4 The Plantae kingdom has the greatest number of species.   _____

Cells and Heredity 細胞與遺傳

Key Words 🔊 045

01	**genetics** [dʒəˋnɛtɪks]	(n.) 遺傳學　*genetic code 遺傳密碼　*genetically modified 基因改造的 The study of heredity is **genetics**. 遺傳的研究稱為遺傳學。
02	**chromosome** [ˋkromə͵som]	(n.) 染色體　*X/Y chromosomes X／Y染色體 　　　　　　*chromosomal crossover 染色體互換 Humans have 23 pairs of **chromosomes**, all of which carry genetic information. 人類有 23 對染色體，每一個染色體都帶有基因的訊息。
03	**DNA** [͵dienˋe]	(n.) **DNA**　*DNA fingerprint DNA指紋鑑定　*DNA replication DNA複製 **DNA**, which stands for deoxyribonucleic acid, is the primary material that comprises chromosomes. DNA 代表「去氧核糖核酸」，是構成染色體的主要物質。
04	**cell division** [sɛl dəˋvɪʒən]	(n.) 細胞分裂　*cell cycle 細胞週期　*cell count 細胞數 **Cell division** is what causes organisms to grow. 細胞分裂是造成生物生長的原因。
05	**mitosis** [mɪˋtosɪs]	(n.) 有絲分裂　*amitosis (n.) 無絲分裂　*asexual reproduction 無性生殖 Body cells make more body cells by **mitosis**. 體細胞藉由有絲分裂來製造更多的體細胞。
06	**meiosis** [maɪˋosɪs]	(n.) 減數分裂　*gamete (n.) 配子（精子或卵子） 　　　　　　*sexual reproduction 有性生殖 Reproductive cells are produced by **meiosis**. 生殖細胞是由減數分裂而來。
07	**dominant** [ˋdɑmənənt]	(a.) 顯性的（= **stronger**）　*trait (n.) 性狀；特徵　*co-dominance (n.) 共顯性 A **dominant** gene is one that is expressed physically or visually. 顯性基因會從身體或視覺上顯現出來。
08	**recessive** [rɪˋsɛsɪv]	(a.) 隱性的（= **weaker**）　*Punnett square 旁氏表；棋盤法 A **recessive** gene is present in the body but is overshadowed by a dominant gene. 隱性基因存於人體，但顯性基因會蓋過它。
09	**mutation** [mjuˋteʃən]	(n.) 突變　*genetic mutation 基因突變　*hybrid (n.) 雜交種；混種 A **mutation** is a random change in a gene. 基因無規則的改變叫做突變。
10	**natural selection** [ˋnætʃərəl səˋlɛkʃən]	(n.) 物競天擇　*survival of the fittest 適者生存 **Natural selection** is the process by which species that are best adapted to their environment survive and reproduce. 最能適應環境的物種生存下來並繁衍後代的過程，稱為物競天擇。

Cell
Nucleus
Chromosome
DNA
Gene

AA　　　　Aa　　　　aa

A → dominant gene
a → recessive gene

regulate	管理；規範 Chromosomes regulate a cell's activities. 染色體管理細胞的活動。
control	管理；支配 Chromosomes control a cell's activities. 染色體管理細胞的活動。
duplicate [ˈdjupləkɪt]	複製（= copy） In the first stage of mitosis, each chromosome duplicates itself. 每個染色體在有絲分裂的第一階段會自行複製。
take place	發生 All life processes take place in cells. 所有生命的過程都在細胞中發生。
mutate	突變 Some organisms mutate and develop different genetic structures than their parents. 有些生物突變而生成與父母不同的遺傳結構。
comprise	包含（= be comprised of） A chromosome is comprised of genes. 一個染色體包含多個基因。
consist of	由……構成 A chromosome consists of genes. 一個染色體是由多個基因所構成的。

Word Families 🔊 047

heredity	遺傳 The passing on of genetic traits from one generation to another is called heredity. 遺傳特徵的世代流傳叫做遺傳。
inheritance [ɪnˈhɛrɪtəns]	遺傳；繼承 Genes affect the inheritance of traits. 基因影響特徵的遺傳。
tissue	組織 Tissues are a group of similar cells that share the same function in an organism. 組織是在一生物中一組具有相同機能的細胞。
organ	器官 Organs are a group of tissues, such as the heart and liver, that work together to perform a specific function. 器官是如心臟與肝臟的一組組織，共同運作以執行特定的功能。

Four Types of Tissues
組織的四大類型

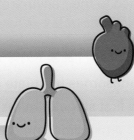

epithelial tissue 上皮組織

connective tissue 結締組織

muscle tissue 肌肉組織

nerve tissue 神經組織

Checkup

Write | 請依提示寫出正確的英文單字和片語。

1	遺傳學	_____	9	物競天擇
2	染色體	_____	10	管理；規範 r_____
3	細胞分裂	_____	11	複製
4	有絲分裂	_____	12	發生
5	減數分裂	_____	13	突變 (v.)
6	顯性的	_____	14	包含
7	隱性的	_____	15	遺傳；繼承
8	突變 (n.)	_____	16	上皮組織

B

Complete the Sentences | 請在空格中填入最適當的答案，並視情況做適當的變化。

meiosis	DNA	chromosome	mutation	natural selection
dominant	recessive	cell division	mitosis	genetics

1 Humans have 23 pairs of _____, all of which carry genetic information. 人類有 23 對染色體，每一個染色體都有基因的訊息。

2 _____, which stands for deoxyribonucleic acid, is the primary material that comprises chromosomes. DNA 代表「去氧核糖核酸」，是構成染色體的主要物質。

3 _____ _____ is what causes organisms to grow.
細胞分裂是造成生物生長的原因。

4 Body cells make more body cells by _____.
體細胞藉由有絲分裂來製造更多的體細胞。

5 Reproductive cells are produced by _____.
生殖細胞是由減數分裂而來。

6 A _____ gene is present in the body but is overshadowed by a dominant gene. 隱性基因存於人體，但顯性基因會蓋過它。

7 A _____ is a random change in a gene.
基因無規則的改變叫做突變。

8 _____ _____ is the process by which species that are best adapted to their environment survive and reproduce.
最能適應環境的物種生存下來並繁衍後代的過程，稱為物競天擇。

C

Read and Choose | 閱讀下列句子，並且選出最適當的答案。

1 Chromosomes (regulate | mutate) a cell's activities.

2 In the first stage of mitosis, each chromosome (duplicates | controls) itself.

3 Some organisms (mutate | cause) and develop different genetic structures than their parents.

4 A chromosome is (carried | comprised) of genes.

Look, Read, and Write | 看圖並且依照提示，在空格中填入正確答案。

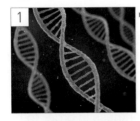 ▸ the part of a cell that contains the genes which control how organisms grow

_____

 ▸ a substance that carries genetic information in the cells of organisms

_____

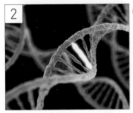 ▸ the stronger gene that is expressed physically or visually

_____

 ▸ the scientific study of how genes control the characteristics of organisms

_____

E

Read and Answer | 閱讀並且回答下列問題。 🔊 048

Gregor Mendel

These days, scientists can do amazing things with genetics. They can modify the genetic structure of plants. This can let them produce more fruit or grain. Some are even resistant to diseases. But the field of genetics is very young. It is barely over 100 years old. And it was all started by a monk called Gregor Mendel.

Gregor Mendel enjoyed gardening. He especially liked to grow peas in his garden. While doing that, he noticed that some pea plants had different characteristics. He saw that some were tall while others were short. The colors of their flowers were different. And there were other differences, too. He wanted to know why. So he started experimenting with them.

Mendel started crossbreeding plants with one another. He learned about dominant and recessive genes this way. He created hybrids, which are plants that carry the genes of different plants. He grew many generations of peas and learned a lot about them. What Mendel learned became the basis for modern genetics.

Mendel did most of his work with peas in the 1850s and 1860s. But, at first, people ignored his work. It was not until the early twentieth century that people began to study his research. Then they realized how much he had really accomplished.

Fill in the blanks.

1 Gregor Mendel is the father of _____.
2 Gregor Mendel conducted experiments on _____ plants.
3 Gregor Mendel learned about _____ and recessive genes.
4 Gregor Mendel's work was not discovered until the _____ century.

Key Words 🔊 049

| 01 | **long-day plant** [ˈlɔŋˈde plænt] | (n.) 長日照植物　　*phototropism (n.) 向光性　　*photoperiod (n.) 光週期 |
| | | Long-day plants need many hours of daylight in order to bloom. 長日照植物需要數小時的日光才能開花。 |

| 02 | **short-day plant** [ˈʃɔrtˈde plænt] | (n.) 短日照植物　　*photosynthesis (n.) 光合作用　　*geotropism (n.) 向地性 |
| | | Short-day plants need long periods of darkness in order to bloom. 短日照植物需要長時間的黑暗才能開花。 |

| 03 | **angiosperm** [ˈændʒioˌspɝm] | (n.) 被子植物（= flowering plant） |
| | | Angiosperms are flowering plants whose seeds are surrounded by a fruit. 被子植物是種子被果實包住的開花植物。 |

| 04 | **gymnosperm** [ˈdʒɪmnəˌspɝm] | (n.) 裸子植物 |
| | | Gymnosperms like conifers produce seeds that are not surrounded by a fruit. 如針葉樹的裸子植物，所產的種子不為果實所包覆。 |

| 05 | **seed leaf** [sid lif] | (n.) 子葉（= cotyledon）　　*monocotyledon (n.) 單子葉植物 *dicotyledon (n.) 雙子葉植物 |
| | | The seed leaf is the main leaf in an embryo. 子葉是在胚芽中的主要葉片。 |

| 06 | **self-pollination** [ˌsɛlfpɑləˈneʃən] | (n.) 自花授粉　　*pollination (n.) 授粉　　*fertilization (n.) 受精 |
| | | The transfer of pollen within the same flower is called self-pollination. 在同朵花上傳遞花粉稱為自花授粉。 |

| 07 | **cross-pollination** [ˈkrɔsˌpɑləˈneʃən] | (n.) 異花授粉　　*cross-fertilization 異花授粉；雜交受精 *in vitro fertilization 體外受精 |
| | | The transfer of pollen from one flower to another is called cross-pollination. 從一朵花傳遞花粉到另一朵稱為異花授粉。 |

| 08 | **wind-pollinated** [ˈwɪndˌpɑləˈnetɪd] | (a.) 風力授粉的　　*abiotic-pollination (n.) 非生物授粉 *pollen vector 授粉媒介 |
| | | Wind-pollinated flowers are pollinated by the wind. 風力授粉的花朵倚賴風力傳授花粉。 |

| 09 | **animal-pollinated** [ˈænəmlˌpɑləˈnetɪd] | (a.) 動物授粉的　　*biotic-pollination (n.) 生物授粉 |
| | | Animal-pollinated flowers are pollinated by animals. 動物授粉的花朵倚賴動物傳授花粉。 |

| 10 | **germination** [ˌdʒɝməˈneʃən] | (n.) 發芽　　*sprout (v.) 發芽　　*embryo (n.) 胚；胚胎 *in embryo 在胚胎階段 |
| | | An embryo inside a seed is protected by a tough outer coat for germination. 種子內的胚芽受到外層的堅韌外皮保護，以利發芽。 |

angiosperm

gymnosperm

wind-pollinated

animal-pollinated

self-pollinate　自花授粉
Some plants **self-pollinate** in order to reproduce. 有些植物藉由自花授粉來繁殖。

cross-pollinate　異花授粉
Bees help **cross-pollinate** flowers when they fly from flower to flower.
蜜蜂穿梭於花叢間幫助了花朵異花授粉。

fertilize　使⋯⋯受精
Once the egg cells are **fertilized**, the fertilized egg cells develop into seeds.
卵細胞一旦受精，受精卵便會發育成種子。

thrive
[θraɪv]　茂盛生長
Many nonvascular plants **thrive** in moist places such as forests and swamps.
許多無維管束植物，在像是森林與沼澤的潮濕地方茂盛生長。

Word Families ● 051

tropism
[ˈtropɪzəm]　向性
Tropism is the response of a plant toward or away from a stimulus.
植物對刺激的趨近或遠離反應稱為向性。

phototropism　向光性
The response of plants to light is called **phototropism**.
植物對光線的反應稱為向光性。

gravitropism
[ˈɡrævəˌtropɪzəm]　向地性（= geotropism）
The response of plants to gravity is called **gravitropism**.
植物對地心引力的反應稱為向地性。

annual　一年生的
Annual plants complete their life cycle within one growing season.
一年生植物在一個生長期中結束它們的生命周期。

perennial
[pəˈrɛnɪəl]　多年生的
Perennial plants live for many years. 多年生植物生長許多年。

Roots 根

taproots 主根	rhizomes 根莖；根狀莖	fibrous roots 鬚根	aerial roots 氣根；氣生根	prop roots 支持根；支柱根

Checkup

A

Write | 請依提示寫出正確的英文單字和片語。

1	長日照植物 _____	9	動物授粉的 _____
2	短日照植物 _____	10	發芽 _____
3	被子植物 _____	11	自花授粉 (v.) _____
4	裸子植物 _____	12	異花授粉 (v.) _____
5	子葉 _____	13	使……受精 _____
6	自花授粉 (n.) _____	14	茂盛生長 _____
7	異花授粉 (n.) _____	15	向性 _____
8	風力授粉的 _____	16	多年生的 _____

B

Complete the Sentences | 請在空格中填入最適當的答案，並視情況做適當的變化。

cross-pollination	animal-pollinated	short-day	seed leaf	angiosperm
self-pollination	wind-pollinated	long-day	germination	gymnosperm

1 _____ plants need long periods of darkness in order to bloom.
短日照植物需要長時間的黑暗才能開花。

2 _____ are flowering plants whose seeds are surrounded by a fruit.
被子植物是種子被果實包住的開花植物。

3 _____ like conifers produce seeds that are not surrounded by a
fruit. 如松柏科植物的裸子植物，所產的種子不為果實所包覆。

4 The _____ _____ is the main leaf in an embryo. 子葉是在胚芽中的主要葉片。

5 The transfer of pollen from one flower to another is called _____.
從一朵花傳遞花粉到另一朵稱為異花授粉。

6 _____ flowers are pollinated by the wind.
風力授粉的花朵倚賴風力傳授花粉。

7 _____ flowers are pollinated by animals.
動物授粉的花朵倚賴動物傳授花粉。

8 An embryo inside a seed is protected by a tough outer coat for _____.
種子內的胚芽受到外層的堅韌外皮保護，以利發芽。

C

Read and Choose | 閱讀下列句子，並且選出最適當的答案。

1 Bees help (cross-pollinate | self-pollinate) flowers when they fly from flower to
flower.

2 Once the egg cells are (fertilized | germinated), the fertilized egg cells develop
into seeds.

3 Many nonvascular plants (pollinate | thrive) in moist places such as forests and
swamps.

4 The response of plants to light is called (gravitropism | phototropism).

Look, Read, and Write | 看圖並且依照提示，在空格中填入正確答案。

1 ▸ a plant that needs many hours of daylight in order to bloom

_____

3 ▸ a seed begins to grow

_____

2 ▸ the process by which pollen from the male part is carried to the female part of the same flower

_____

4 ▸ a plant living for only one year or season, having a life cycle that is one year or season long

_____

E

Read and Answer | 閱讀並且回答下列問題。 052

Pollination and Germination

All plants reproduce somehow. This allows them to produce offspring that will grow into mature plants. There are two important steps in plant reproduction. The first is pollination. The second is germination.

Most plants have both male and female reproductive organs. However, they must come into contact with each other in order for the plant to reproduce. This happens through pollination. Pollen from the male part of a plant must reach the female part of the plant. This can happen in many ways. The wind may sometimes blow the pollen from one part to the other. But this is very ineffective. Many times, animals such as bees, butterflies, and other insects pollinate plants. As they go from plant to plant, pollen gets stuck to their bodies. When they land on a new plant, some of it rubs off. Many times, this pollinates the plant. Once the pollen goes from the anther (the male part) to the stigma (the female part), the plant has been pollinated and can start to reproduce.

The other important step is germination. Germination happens after a plant's seeds have been formed. At first, the plant's seeds are dormant. However, when they germinate, they come to life and begin to grow. If the conditions are good, then the seed will become a seedling. Eventually, it will mature and become a plant.

What is NOT true?

1   Pollination happens before germination.
2   Most plants have both male and female parts.
3   Insects frequently pollinate plants.
4   Germination is what forms a plant's seeds.

Key Words
🔊 053

01	**diversity** [daɪˈvɝsətɪ]	*(n.)* 多樣性　*biodiversity (n.) 生物多樣性　*species diversity 物種多樣性 Diversity in ecosystems refers to the variety of species in an ecosystem. 生態系統的多樣性，指的是生態系統中物種的多樣化。
02	**interaction** [ˌɪntəˈrækʃən]	*(n.)* 互相影響　*interaction of sth. with sth. 某物與某物的相互影響 The interaction of species helps create balance in an ecosystem. 物種間的互相影響有助於生態的平衡。
03	**keystone species** [ˈkiˌston ˈspiʃiz]	*(n.)* 關鍵物種　*pioneer species 先鋒物種　*exotic species 外來種 *flagship species 旗艦物種（能夠吸引公眾關注的物種） A keystone species is an organism whose absence would dramatically alter an ecosystem. 該物種的存在與否，會對生態系統造成劇烈影響的生物，叫做關鍵物種。
04	**carbon cycle** [ˈkɑrbən ˈsaɪkl̩]	*(n.)* 碳循環（生物之間或與環境間的碳物質交換，主要途徑有光合作用和呼吸作用） Carbon constantly circulates as solids, liquids, and gases in the carbon cycle. 碳恆以固體、液體與氣體的型態，流通於碳循環中。
05	**nitrogen cycle** [ˈnaɪtrədʒən ˈsaɪkl̩]	*(n.)* 氮循環　*oxygen cycle 氧循環 The circulation of nitrogen from living organisms to the nonliving parts of the ecosystem is the nitrogen cycle. 生態系統中從生物到非生物的氮流通，稱為氮循環。
06	**symbiotic** [ˌsɪmbaɪˈɑtɪk]	*(a.)* 共生的　*to live in symbiosis with sth. 與某物共生 Symbiotic relationships involve two organisms living together. 共生關係是指兩種生物共同生活。
07	**parasitic** [ˌpærəˈsɪtɪk]	*(a.)* 寄生的　*to be parasitic on sb./sth. 依賴某人／事物生活 Parasitic relationships harm one of the organisms. 寄生關係會傷害到其中一方的生物。
08	**mutual** [ˈmjutʃʊəl]	*(a.)* 相互的；共同的　*mutual friends/enemies 共同朋友／敵人 Mutual relationships benefit both organisms. 互利共生的關係使雙方互惠。
09	**commensalism** [kəˈmɛnsəlɪzəm]	*(n.)* 片利共生　*predation (n.) 掠食　*competition (n.) 競爭 The relationship in which one organism benefits and the other organism is neither helped nor harmed is called commensalism. 一方得利但對另一方無利害關係，叫做片利共生。
10	**succession** [səkˈsɛʃən]	*(n.)* 演替　*biomass (n.) 生物量 There are two major types of ecological succession: primary and secondary succession. 生態演替主要有兩種：初級演替與次級演替。

keystone species

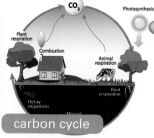
carbon cycle

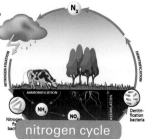
nitrogen cycle

succession

Power Verbs 🔊 054

interact
[ˌɪntəˈrækt]

互相影響；互動
Organisms **interact** with one another in their ecosystems.
生物在他們的生態系統中相互影響。

circulate
[ˈsɝkjəˌlet]

循環；流通
Nitrogen **circulates** through the living and nonliving parts of ecosystems.
氮在生態系統中的生物到非生物間循環。

move through

穿行；穿越
Nitrogen **moves through** the living and nonliving parts of ecosystems.
氮在生態系統中的生物到非生物間穿行。

go through

歷經
Ecosystems **go through** cycles called succession. 生態系統歷經循環，稱做演替。

undergo

經歷（= experience）
Ecosystems **undergo** cycles called succession. 生態系統經歷循環，稱做演替。

take root in

生根
Primary succession occurs when plants first **take root in** a barren area.
初級演替於植物首次在不毛之地落地生根時發生。

Word Families 🔊 055

diverse

不同的；多種的
Some ecosystems are more **diverse** than others.
有些生態系統與其他生態系統比起來更多變。

varied

不同的；多變的
Some ecosystems are more **varied** than others.
有些生態系統與其他生態系統比起來更多變。

various

各種的；許多的
There are **various** ecosystems throughout the regions of the world.
世界上各區域有各種不同的生態系統。

parasite
[ˈpærəˌsaɪt]

寄生生物；寄生蟲
Parasites are organisms that live on other organisms and benefit from them.
寄居於其他生物上，並從中得利的生物稱為寄生蟲。

host

宿主
The **host** is the organism that a parasite lives in or on.
有寄生蟲寄居在身上或體內的生物稱為宿主。

Types of Symbiosis 共生關係的類型	**mutualism** 互利共生	**parasitism** 寄生	**commensalism** 片利共生

Checkup

Write | 請依提示寫出正確的英文單字和片語。

1	多樣性	_____	9	片利共生 _____
2	互相影響 (n.)	_____	10	演替 _____
3	關鍵物種	_____	11	互相影響；互動 (v.) _____
4	碳循環	_____	12	循環；流通 _____
5	氮循環	_____	13	經歷 u_____
6	共生的	_____	14	生根 _____
7	寄生的	_____	15	寄生物 _____
8	相互的；共同的	_____	16	互利共生 _____

B

Complete the Sentences | 請在空格中填入最適當的答案，並視情況做適當的變化。

diversity	carbon cycle	symbiotic	interaction	commensalism
mutual	nitrogen cycle	parasitic	succession	keystone species

1. _____ in ecosystems refers to the variety of species in an ecosystem.
   生態系統的多樣性，指的是生態系統中物種的多樣化。

2. The _____ of species helps create balance in an ecosystem.
   物種間的互相影響有助於生態的平衡。

3. Carbon constantly circulates as solids, liquids, and gases in the _____
   _____. 碳恆以固體、液體與氣體的型態，流通於碳循環中。

4. The circulation of nitrogen from living organisms to the nonliving parts of the
   ecosystem is the _____ _____.
   生態系統中從生物到非生物的氮流通，稱為氮循環。

5. _____ relationships involve two organisms living together.
   共生關係是指兩種生物共同生活。

6. _____ relationships harm one of the organisms.
   寄生關係會傷害到其中一方的生物。

7. _____ relationships benefit both organisms. 互利共生的關係使雙方互惠。

8. There are two major types of ecological _____: primary and secondary
   succession. 生態演替主要有兩種：初級演替與次級演替。

C

Read and Choose | 閱讀下列句子，並且選出最適當的答案。

1. Organisms (interact | alter) with one another in their ecosystems.
2. Nitrogen (goes | circulates) through the living and nonliving parts of ecosystems.
3. Ecosystems (benefit | undergo) cycles called succession.
4. Primary succession occurs when plants first take (root | stem) in a barren area.

Look, Read, and Write | 看圖並且依照提示，在空格中填入正確答案。

1

▸ a species has a large effect on its environment

_____

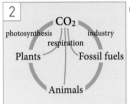

3

nitrogen in **Plant** proteins

nitrogen in **Animal** proteins

Decomposers (Bacteria)

▸ the circulation of nitrogen between living organisms and the environment

_____

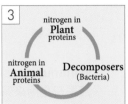

2

CO₂

photosynthesis   industry
respiration
Plants   Fossil fuels
Animals

▸ the circulation of carbon between living organisms and the environment

_____

4

▸ a relationship between two species that one gets an advantage and the other is not affected by it

_____

E

Read and Answer | 閱讀並且回答下列問題。 ◉ 056

The Carbon and Nitrogen Cycles

Carbon is one of the most important elements. All living things are made from carbon. But it is constantly changing forms. This is called the carbon cycle. In the atmosphere, carbon is often present in the form of carbon dioxide. This is a compound that has one carbon atom and two oxygen atoms. Plants breathe in the carbon dioxide and use it to produce nutrients. The carbon then becomes part of the plants. These plants die and then often get buried. Over time, these plants may turn into fossil fuels like coal or petroleum. People later burn these fossil fuels, which releases carbon dioxide into the atmosphere.

Another important element is nitrogen. There is also a nitrogen cycle. Nitrogen is actually the most common element in the atmosphere. Around 80% of the air we breathe is nitrogen. We don't need nitrogen like we need oxygen. But nitrogen is still important.

There is often nitrogen in the soil. Plants absorb the nitrogen from the soil. When people and animals eat the plants, they release the nitrogen into their bodies. Bacteria in people's and animals' bodies can fix the nitrogen so that the bodies can use it. Later, when the people and animals die and decompose, the nitrogen returns to the soil or the atmosphere. Then it can be reused again.

Answer the questions.

1 What is all life made from?   _____

2 What do some plants turn into?   _____

3 How much of the atmosphere is nitrogen?   _____

4 What fixes nitrogen in the body so that people can use it? _____

The Human Body and the Immune System 人體與免疫系統

Key Words

🔊 057

01	**immune system** [ɪˈmjun ˈsɪstəm]	(n.) 免疫系統　*immune response 免疫反應 *innate/adaptive immunity 先天／後天免疫 The **immune system** is the part of the body that protects it from infections. 免疫系統是用來保護人體免於感染的部位。
02	**lymphatic system** [lɪmˈfætɪk ˈsɪstəm]	(n.) 淋巴系統　*lymph (n.) 淋巴液　*lymph gland 淋巴結　*lymph vessel 淋巴管 The **lymphatic system** helps protect the body from diseases by producing white blood cells. 淋巴系統藉由製造白血球來保護身體免於疾病。
03	**antibiotic** [ˌæntɪbaɪˈɑtɪk]	(a.) 抗生的　(n.) 抗生素　*to take / be on antibiotic 服用抗生素 **Antibiotics** are medicines that kill bacteria. 抗生素是用來消滅細菌的藥。
04	**infection** [ɪnˈfɛkʃən]	(n.) 感染　*to be exposed to infection 暴露於易受感染的環境 *sexually transmitted infection 性傳染病 *secondary infection 二度感染 An **infection** is caused by germs or bacteria. 感染是由病菌或細菌所引起的。
05	**contagious** [kənˈtedʒəs]	(a.) 傳染性的（= communicable）　*highly contagious 高度傳染性的 A **contagious** disease may be transmitted from one person to another. 傳染病能由人傳到另一人身上。
06	**epidemic** [ˌɛpɪˈdɛmɪk]	(n.) 流行病　(a.) 流行性的　*an epidemic of influenza 流感的流行 An **epidemic** is a disease that spreads rapidly and makes many people sick. 流行病是一種迅速傳播，並讓許多人生病的疾病。
07	**communicable disease** [kəˈmjunəkəbļ dɪˈziz]	(n.) 傳染性疾病　*droplet infection 飛沫傳染　*contagion (n.) 接觸傳染 A **communicable disease**, like the flu or smallpox, is one that can be communicated from person to person. 如同流行性感冒或天花的傳染性疾病，是一種會感染於人與人之間的疾病。
08	**vaccination** [ˌvæksņˈeʃən]	(n.) 疫苗　*a vaccination against/for sth. 接種疫苗 *inoculate (n.) 接種；預防注射 A **vaccination** makes a person immune to a certain virus. 疫苗使人對特定的疾病免疫。
09	**bacterial** [bækˈtɪrɪəl]	(a.) 細菌的　*bacterial infection/contamination/growth 細菌感染／污染／生長 Penicillin destroys many types of **bacterial** infections. 盤尼西林能消滅多種的細菌感染。
10	**viral** [ˈvaɪrəl]	(a.) 病毒的　*viral infection/marketing 病毒感染／病毒式傳銷 *to go viral （透過網路傳播而）非常受歡迎 **Viral** infections are those caused by viruses. 病毒感染是由病毒所引起的感染。

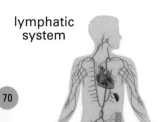

lymphatic system

antibiotic

communicable disease

vaccination

Power Verbs 🔊 058

clog
阻塞
If the arteries become clogged up, the result can be high blood pressure.
如果動脈變得堵塞的話，可能會造成高血壓。

communicate
[kə`mjunə͵ket]
傳染；感染
A communicable disease can be communicated. 傳染性疾病會被傳染。

spread
散播
Some viruses can spread through the air. 有些病毒能散播於空氣中。

infect
感染；傳染
Many viruses can infect people. 許多病毒能傳染給民眾。

vaccinate
[`væksn͵et]
注射疫苗
People can get vaccinated for many different viruses.
人們能注射許多種不同病毒的疫苗。

immunize
[`ɪmjə͵naɪz]
使……免疫
Getting a vaccination will immunize the body from a certain virus.
注射疫苗能使人體對特定的病毒免疫。

paralyze
[`pærə͵laɪz]
使……癱瘓（麻痺）
Some viruses, like polio, can paralyze people.
像是小兒麻痺症的病毒能讓人們癱瘓。

disable
使……殘障
Some viruses, like polio, can disable people.
像是小兒麻痺症的病毒能讓人們殘障。

Word Families 🔊 059

antibody
[`æntɪ͵bɑdɪ]
抗體
The immune system creates antibodies to help fight invading viruses.
免疫系統製造抗體來對抗侵襲的病毒。

antigen
[`æntɪ͵dʒən]
抗原
Antigens in the body cause the immune system to begin creating antibodies.
人體中的抗原能讓免疫系統開始製造抗體。

bacterial disease
細菌性疾病
Bacterial diseases are caused by bacteria invading the body.
細菌性疾病是由侵襲人體的細菌所引起的。

viral disease
病毒性疾病（= virus disease）
Viral diseases are caused by viruses invading the body.
病毒性疾病是由侵襲人體的病毒所引起的。

COLD VIRUS

VIRUS INFLUENZA
DNA VIRUS

COMPUTER VIRUS
H.I.V. VIRUS

BLOOD VIRUS

Checkup

A

Write | 請依提示寫出正確的英文單字和片語。

1	免疫系統	_____	9	細菌的	_____
2	淋巴系統	_____	10	病毒的	_____
3	抗生素	_____	11	阻塞	_____
4	感染	_____	12	傳染；感染 c	_____
5	傳染性的	_____	13	使……免疫	_____
6	流行性的	_____	14	使……癱瘓（麻痺）	_____
7	傳染性疾病	_____	15	使……殘廢	_____
8	疫苗	_____	16	抗體	_____

B

Complete the Sentences | 請在空格中填入最適當的答案，並視情況做適當的變化。

bacterial	immune system	viral	vaccination	infection
lymphatic	communicable	antibiotic	epidemic	contagious

1 The _____ _____ is the part of the body that protects it from infections. 免疫系統是用來保護人體免於感染的部位。

2 The _____ system helps protect the body from diseases by producing white blood cells. 淋巴系統藉由製造白血球來保護身體免於疾病。

3 _____ are medicines that kill bacteria.
抗生素是用來消滅細菌的藥。

4 An _____ is caused by germs or bacteria.
感染是由病菌或細菌所引起的。

5 A _____ disease may be transmitted from one person to another.
傳染病能由人傳到另一人身上。

6 Penicillin destroys many types of _____ infections.
盤尼西林能消滅多種的細菌性感染。

7 _____ infections are those caused by viruses.
病毒感染是由病毒所引起的感染。

8 A _____ makes a person immune to a certain virus.
疫苗使人對特定的疾病免疫。

C

Read and Choose | 閱讀下列句子，並且選出最適當的答案。

1 If the arteries become (caused | clogged) up, the result can be high blood pressure.

2 Getting a vaccination will (infect | immunize) the body from a certain virus.

3 Some viruses, like polio, can (paralyze | protect) people.

4 The immune system creates (antibodies | antigens) to help fight invading viruses.

Look, Read, and Write | 看圖並且依照提示，在空格中填入正確答案。

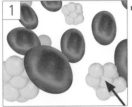 1

▸ the cells and tissues in the body that make it able to protect itself against infection

_____

 3

▸ a disease spreads very quickly and affects a large number of people

_____

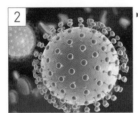 2

▸ a disease caused by viruses invading the body

_____

 4

▸ a disease that is transmitted through infected individuals or through a vector

_____

E

Read and Answer | 閱讀並且回答下列問題。 ⓞ 060

The Immune System

Every day, the body is attacked by bacteria, viruses, and other invaders. It is the body's immune system that fights these invaders. It helps keep the person healthy. The immune system is made up of various cells, tissues, and organs.

White blood cells are very important. They are also called leukocytes. They move through the body in lymphatic vessels. There are two types of leukocytes. The first try to destroy invading organisms. These are phagocytes. The second are lymphocytes. They help the body remember various invaders. This way, it can destroy them in the future.

Antigens often invade the body. The body then produces antibodies. They fight the antigens. If the antibodies succeed, they will always remain in the body. This lets the body fight the disease again in the future. This is very effective against viruses.

People are often born immune to certain diseases. This is called innate immunity. But there is adaptive immunity, too. This happens when the body recognizes threats to it. It then learns how to defeat them. Also, thanks to vaccinations, people can become immune to many diseases. Vaccinations help improve the strength of the immune system.

What is true? Write T(true) or F(false).

1   The immune system can make people sick.   _____

2   Leukocytes are red blood cells.   _____

3   The body sometimes produces antibodies.   _____

4   People are often born with innate immunity.   _____

Review Test 3

A

Write | 請依提示寫出正確的英文單字和片語。

1	節肢動物門 _____	11	根據 _____
2	軟體動物門 _____	12	分類 s_____
3	遺傳學 _____	13	物競天擇 _____
4	染色體 _____	14	管理；規範 _____
5	異花授粉 (n.) _____	15	自花授粉 (v.) _____
6	風力授粉的 _____	16	使……受精 _____
7	碳循環 _____	17	片利共生 _____
8	氮循環 _____	18	演替 _____
9	免疫系統 _____	19	傳染 (v.) i_____
10	傳染性的 _____	20	使……癱瘓（麻痺） _____

B

Choose the Correct Word | 請選出與鋪底字意思相近的答案。

1　Organisms are categorized according to their characteristics.
　　a. germinated　　　　b. regulated　　　　c. sorted

2　Ecosystems undergo cycles called succession.
　　a. sort　　　　b. go through　　　　c. circle

3　Some viruses, like polio, can paralyze people.
　　a. disable　　　　b. move　　　　c. spread

4　All life processes take place in cells.
　　a. occur　　　　b. involve　　　　c. comprise

C

Complete the Sentences | 請在空格中填入最適當的答案，並視情況做適當的變化。

Protista	germination	cell division	symbiotic

1　Organisms in the _____ kingdom are protists such as amoebas, algae, and some slime molds. 原生生物界中的生物，就是像變形蟲、水藻與一些黏菌的單細胞生物。

2　_____ _____ is what causes organisms to grow.
細胞分裂是造成生物生長的原因。

3　An embryo inside a seed is protected by a tough outer coat for _____.
種子內的胚芽受到外層的堅韌外皮保護，以利發芽。

4　_____ relationships involve two organisms living together.
共生關係是指兩種生物共同生活。

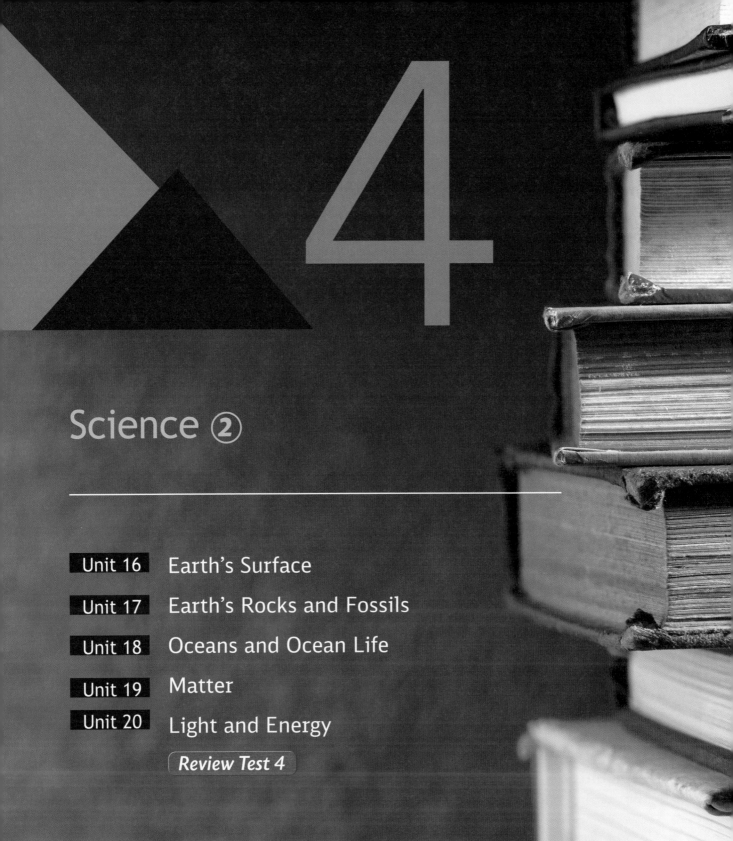

4

Science ②

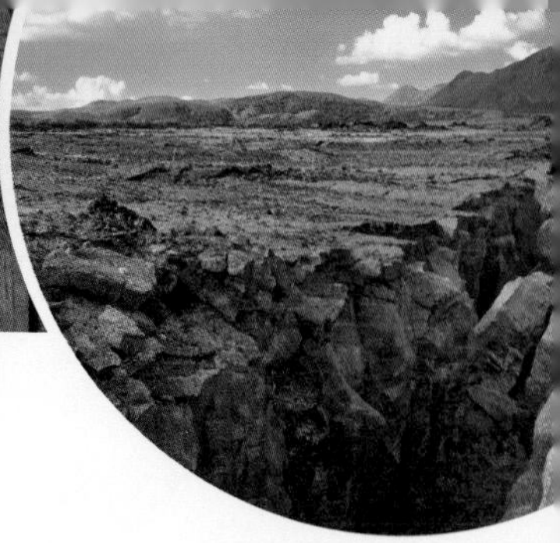

Unit 16 Earth's Surface 地球表面

Key Words

061

01 **mantle** [ˋmæntl̩]
(*n.*) 地函 *upper/lower mantle 上／下部地函 *crust (n.) 地殼 *core (n.) 地核
The **mantle** is the part of the Earth between the crust and the core.
位於地殼與地核之間的是地函。

02 **lithosphere** [ˋlɪθə͵sfɪr]
(*n.*) 岩石圈 *tectonic plate 板塊 *pedosphere (n.) 土壤圈
The **lithosphere** is made up of the crust and the upper mantle.
岩石圈是由地殼和上部地函所組成的。

03 **asthenosphere** [æsˋθinə͵sfɪr]
(*n.*) 軟流圈 *magma (n.)（地表下逕流的）岩漿 *lava (n.)（火山噴出的）岩漿
The **asthenosphere** is right below the lithosphere, but it is less rigid.
軟流圈在岩石圈正下方，但物質較軟。

04 **Pangaea** [pændʒiə]
(*n.*) 盤古大陸 *continental drift 板塊飄移
Millions of years ago, all of the landmasses on Earth formed one giant continent called **Pangaea**.
數百萬年前，地球上的大陸形成一塊巨大的陸地，稱為盤古大陸。

05 **plate tectonics** [plet tɛkˋtɑnɪks]
(*n.*) 板塊構造學說 *fault (n.) 斷層 *graben (n.) 地塹 *oceanic trench 海溝
Plate tectonics is the theory that the Earth's crust is made of moving plates. 板塊構造學說主張地殼是由漂移的板塊所組成的。

06 **Moho** [ˋmoho]
(*n.*) 莫氏不連續面 *core-mantle boundary 古氏不連續面（地函與地核的交界）
The boundary between the Earth's crust and mantle is called the **Moho**.
地殼與地函的交界稱為莫氏不連續面。

07 **seismograph** [ˋsaɪzmə͵græf]
(*n.*) 地震儀 *seismogram (n.)（地震儀所記錄的）震動圖
A **seismograph** detects earthquakes and volcanic activity.
地震儀偵測地震與火山的活動。

08 **seismic wave** [ˋsaɪzmɪk wev]
(*n.*) 震波 *primary wave P波（= P-wave） *secondary wave S波（= S-wave）
Seismic waves are underground waves that are caused by earthquakes.
由地震引起地底下的波動為震波。

09 **focus** [ˋfokəs]
(*n.*) 震源（= **hypocenter**）
*shallow-focus/deep-focus earthquake 淺層／深層地震
The **focus** is the point where an earthquake begins.
震源是地震起始之處。

10 **epicenter** [ˋɛpɪ͵sɛntɚ]
(*n.*) 震央 *Richter magnitude scale 芮氏規模
The **epicenter** is directly above the earthquake's focus.
震央就位於震源正上方。

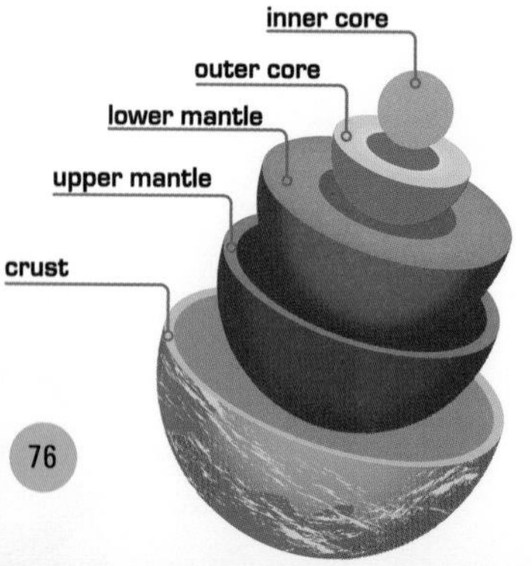

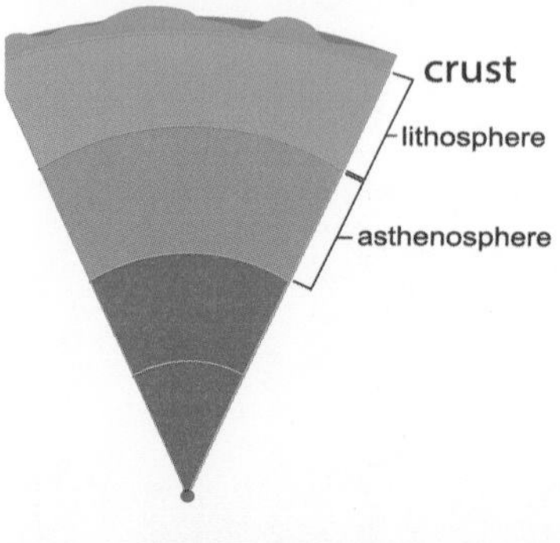

Pangaea

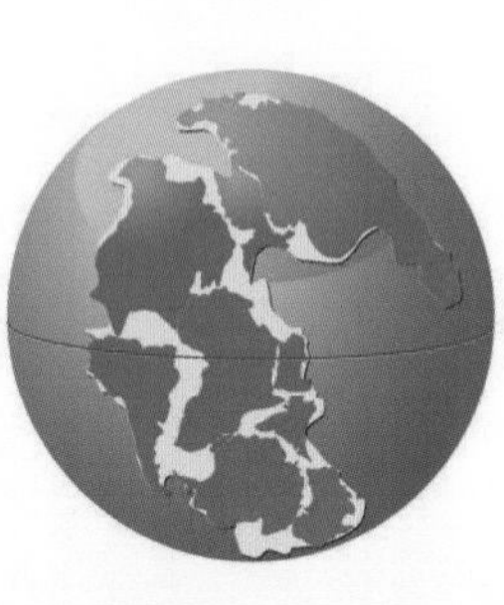

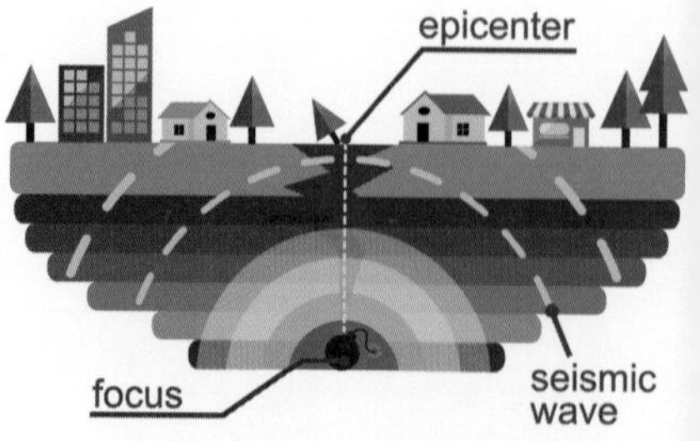

drift　漂移
The continents are slowly **drifting** to different places. 陸地緩慢地漂移至其他地方。

shift　移動
The continents are slowly **shifting** positions.　陸地緩慢地移動位置。

separate　分離
The Earth's plates sometimes **separate** from one another. 地球板塊有時會彼此分離。

connect　連接
The Earth's plates sometimes **connect** with one another. 地球板塊有時會互相連結起來。

collide　相撞
The Earth's plates sometimes **collide** with one another. 地球板塊有時會相撞。

erupt　爆發
Volcanoes can **erupt** and spew ash and gas into the air.
火山會爆發並且噴出灰燼與氣體到空氣中。

shake　搖動
Earthquakes cause the ground to **shake** violently. 地震造成地面劇烈地搖晃。

Word Families
🔊 063

continental drift　大陸漂移
The theory of continental drift states that the continents are in constant, yet slow, motion. 大陸漂移理論說明了陸地持續而緩慢地移動。

Alfred Wegener　阿爾弗雷德・魏格納
Alfred Wegener was the first scientist to propose the theory of continental drift. 阿爾弗雷德・魏格納是首位提出大陸漂移學說的科學家。

Earth's Plates　地球板塊

Eurasian Plate
歐亞大陸板塊

Pacific Plate
太平洋板塊

North American Plate
北美洲板塊

African Plate
非洲板塊

Australian-Indian Plate
印澳板塊

Antarctic Plate
南極板塊

Earth's Layers　地層

crust 地殼

mantle 地函

upper mantle 上部地函

lower mantle 下部地函

core 地核

outer core 外地核

inner core 內地核

Types of Volcanoes　火山類型

shield volcano
盾狀火山

cinder cone volcano
火山渣錐

composite volcano
複式火山；成層火山

Checkup

Write | 請依提示寫出正確的英文單字和片語。

1	地函 _____	9	震源 _____
2	岩石圈 _____	10	震央 _____
3	軟流圈 _____	11	漂移 _____
4	磐石大陸 _____	12	移動 _____
5	板塊構造學說 _____	13	分離 _____
6	莫氏不連續面 _____	14	相撞 _____
7	地震儀 _____	15	爆發 _____
8	震波 _____	16	大陸漂移 _____

Complete the Sentences | 請在空格中填入最適當的答案，並視情況做適當的變化。

asthenosphere	mantle	seismic wave	Moho	epicenter
lithosphere	focus	plate tectonics	Pangaea	seismograph

1 The _____ is the part of the Earth between the crust and the core.
位於地殼與地核之間的是地函。

2 The _____ is made up of the crust and the upper mantle.
岩石圈是由地殼和上部地函所組成的。

3 The _____ is right below the lithosphere, but it is less rigid.
軟流圈在岩石圈正下方，但物質較軟。

4 Millions of years ago, all of the landmasses on Earth formed one giant continent called _____. 數百萬年前，地球上的大陸形成一塊巨大的陸地，稱為盤古大陸。

5 A _____ detects earthquakes and volcanic activity.
地震儀偵測地震與火山的活動。

6 _____ _____ are underground waves that are caused by earthquakes. 由地震引起地底下的波動為震波。

7 The boundary between the Earth's crust and mantle is called the _____.
地殼與地函的介面稱為莫氏不連續面。

8 The _____ is the point where an earthquake begins. 震源是地震起始之處。

Read and Choose | 閱讀下列句子，並且選出最適當的答案。

1 The continents are slowly (drifting | erupting) to different places.
2 Volcanoes can (erupt | connect) and spew ash and gas into the air.
3 The Earth's plates sometimes (collide | move) with one another.
4 The continents are slowly (shifting | spewing) positions.

D

Look, Read, and Write | 看圖並且依照提示，在空格中填入正確答案。

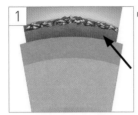
1

▸ the solid outer layer of the earth

_____

3

▸ underground waves that are caused by earthquakes

_____

2

▸ the study of how the surface of the earth is formed, how the separate pieces of it move

_____

4

▸ the part of the earth's surface that is directly above the place where an earthquake starts

_____

E

Read and Answer | 閱讀並且回答下列問題。 🔊064

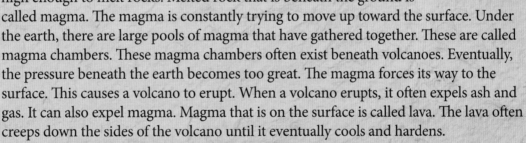

Volcanic Eruptions

Sometimes, volcanoes suddenly erupt. They spew tons of ash, gas, and lava. They might even kill large numbers of people. What is it that makes a volcano erupt?

Deep in the Earth, there is usually a lot of pressure. Also, the temperature deep underground can be very high. In fact, it is often high enough to melt rocks. Melted rock that is beneath the ground is called magma. The magma is constantly trying to move up toward the surface. Under the earth, there are large pools of magma that have gathered together. These are called magma chambers. These magma chambers often exist beneath volcanoes. Eventually, the pressure beneath the earth becomes too great. The magma forces its way to the surface. This causes a volcano to erupt. When a volcano erupts, it often expels ash and gas. It can also expel magma. Magma that is on the surface is called lava. The lava often creeps down the sides of the volcano until it eventually cools and hardens.

The size of the eruption depends on the amount of pressure that is released. Some volcanoes release a steady amount of lava. These have a low amount of pressure. Other volcanoes erupt explosively. They can shoot ash miles into the air. They can expel lava and gas very far in the area. These are the most dangerous eruptions. Mt. Vesuvius, Krakatoa, and Mt. St. Helens all had explosive eruptions that killed many people.

Fill in the blanks.

1 Melted rock that is underground is called _____.

2 Magma gathers in pools called _____ _____.

3 Volcanoes can expel lots of _____, gas, and lava when they erupt.

4 Mt. Vesuvius, Krakatoa and Mt. St. Helens were three powerful _____ that exploded explosively.

Key Words

🔊 065

01	**rock cycle** [rɑk `saɪkl̩]	(n.) 岩石循環　*water cycle 水循環　*geological time scale 地質年代表 The **rock cycle** is the process by which a rock changes from one type to another over thousands of years. 岩石在千年後從原本的型態轉換成另一種的過程，稱為岩石循環。
02	**plate boundary** [plet `baʊndrɪ]	(n.) 板塊邊界　*divergent boundary 張裂型板塊邊界 　　　　　　　*convergent boundary 聚合型板塊邊界 The place where two or more plates meet is the **plate boundary**. 兩塊以上的板塊交接處為板塊邊界。
03	**composition** [ˌkɑmpə`zɪʃən]	(n.) 成分；構成　*metallic/similar in composition 金屬成分的／成分相似的 The **composition** of soil varies depending on its location. 土壤的成分因所在地點而異。
04	**crystallization** [`krɪstəlɪˌzeʃən]	(n.) 結晶化　*nucleation (n.) 成核（現象）　*crystal growth 晶體生長 The process by which crystals are formed is called **crystallization**. 形成水晶的過程稱為結晶化。
05	**metamorphism** [ˌmɛtə`mɔrfɪzm̩]	(n.) 變質作用　*metamorphic rock 變質岩　*diagenesis (n.) 成岩作用 **Metamorphism** refers to the process by which metamorphic rock forms. 變質作用指的是岩石變質的形成。
06	**igneous rock** [`ɪgnɪəs rɑk]	(n.) 火成岩　*volcanic rock 火山岩　*granite (n.) 花崗岩　*basalt (n.) 玄武岩 **Igneous rocks** are formed through volcanic activity. 火成岩是從火山活動中形成的。
07	**sedimentary rock** [ˌsɛdə`mɛntərɪ rɑk]	(n.) 沉積岩　*limestone (n.) 石灰岩　*sandstone (n.) 砂岩　*shale (n.) 頁岩 **Sedimentary rocks** are formed through the buildup of sediment. 沉積岩是從沉積物的累積而來。
08	**index fossil** [`ɪndɛks `fɑsl̩]	(n.) 指標化石　*fossil (n.) 老頑固；思想僵化的人　*living fossil 活化石 **Index fossils** are fossils of organisms that are found in many places and lived during a relatively short period of time. 多處可見且相對生存時間較短的生物化石，為指標化石。
09	**fossil record** [`fɑsl̩ `rɛkəd]	(n.) 化石紀錄　*fossil fuel 化石燃料　*radiocarbon dating 放射性碳定年法 The **fossil record** is used to study the Earth's history. 化石記錄用於研究地球的歷史。
10	**mass extinction** [mæs ɪk`stɪŋkʃən]	(n.) 大滅絕　*Cretaceous-Tertiary extinction event 白堊紀－第三紀滅絕事件 A **mass extinction** occurs when a large number of species are suddenly killed. 大滅絕發生在大量物種突然死亡之時。

igneous rock

sedimentary rock

metamorphic rock

fossil record

crystallize　結晶化
Soil sometimes crystallizes and becomes hard. 土壤有時會結晶化並轉硬。

fossilize　使……成化石
It can take a very long time for bones to fossilize.
要使骨頭變成化石需要非常長的時間。

petrify　使……石化
[ˋpɛtrəˏfaɪ]
It can take a very long time for bones to petrify.
要使骨頭石化需要非常長的時間。

date　確定年代
Scientists can date the ages of fossils by using different methods.
科學家能利用不同的方法去確認化石的年代。

die out　逐漸消失；滅絕
The dinosaurs died out millions of years ago. 幾百萬年前，恐龍滅絕。

go extinct　絕種
The dinosaurs went extinct millions of years ago. 恐龍於幾百萬年前絕種。

Word Families 🔊 067

extrusive rock　噴出岩
Extrusive rocks are igneous rocks formed by the crystallization of magma on the Earth's surface.
噴出岩是由岩漿在地表結晶所形成的火成岩。

intrusive rock　侵入岩
Intrusive rocks are igneous rocks formed by the crystallization of magma below the Earth's surface.
侵入岩是由岩漿在地底下結晶所形成的火成岩。

Index Fossils
指標化石

mastodon
乳齒象

ammonite
菊石

trilobite
三葉蟲

Checkup

A

Write | 請依提示寫出正確的英文單字和片語。

1	岩石循環	_____	
2	板塊邊界	_____	
3	成分；構成	_____	
4	結晶化 (n.)	_____	
5	變質作用	_____	
6	火成岩	_____	
7	沉積岩	_____	
8	指標化石	_____	

9 化石紀錄 _____
10 大滅絕 _____
11 結晶化 (v.) _____
12 使……成化石 _____
13 使……石化 _____
14 確定年代 _____
15 絕種 _____
16 噴出岩 _____

B

Complete the Sentences | 請在空格中填入最適當的答案，並視情況做適當的變化。

| index fossil | metamorphism | sedimentary rock | rock cycle | fossil record |
| crystallization | composition | igneous rock | plate boundary | mass extinction |

1 The place where two or more plates meet is the _____ _____.
兩塊或許多板塊的交接處為板塊邊界。

2 The _____ of soil varies depending on its location.
土壤的成分因所在地點而異。

3 A _____ _____ occurs when a large number of species are suddenly killed. 大滅絕發生在大量物種突然死亡之時。

4 _____ refers to the process by which metamorphic rock forms.
變質作用指的是岩石變質的形成。

5 _____ _____ are formed through volcanic activity.
火成岩是從火山活動中形成的。

6 _____ _____ are formed through the buildup of sediment.
沉積岩是從沉積物的累積而來。

7 The _____ _____ is used to study the Earth's history.
化石記錄用於研究地球的歷史。

8 _____ _____ are fossils of organisms that are found in many places and lived during a relatively short period of time.
多處可見且相對生存時間較短的生物化石，為指標化石。

C

Read and Choose | 閱讀下列句子，並且選出最適當的答案。

1 Soil sometimes (fossilizes | crystallizes) and becomes hard.

2 It can take a very long time for bones to (fossilize | form).

3 Scientists can (refer | date) the ages of fossils by using different methods.

4 (Extrusive | Intrusive) rocks are formed by the crystallization of magma on the Earth's surface.

D

Look, Read, and Write | 看圖並且依照提示，在空格中填入正確答案。

1  ▸ the way that rock is broken down into pieces, then pressed together to form rock again

_____

3  ▸ a fossil that is found in many places and comes from the same time in history

_____

2  ▸ the process that something turns into crystal

_____

4 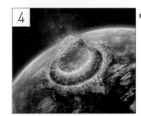 ▸ a widespread and rapid decrease in the biodiversity on Earth

_____

E

Read and Answer | 閱讀並且回答下列問題。 068

Mass Extinctions

Every once in a while, a mass extinction occurs on Earth. When this happens, large numbers of species all go extinct at once. Scientists have identified at least five mass extinctions during Earth's history. During these mass extinctions, up to 95% of all life on the planet was killed. The last mass extinction happened about 65 million years ago. Scientists refer to it as the K-T Extinction.

65 million years ago, the Earth looked very different. There were no humans. Instead, dinosaurs ruled the land and the seas. This was a time called the Cretaceous Period. Then, suddenly, there was a mass extinction. Scientists are not exactly sure what happened. But most of them believe that an asteroid or comet struck the Earth. This caused a tremendous change in the planet. Large amounts of dust were thrown into the atmosphere. This blocked the sun. No sunlight could reach the Earth, so many plants died. The animals that ate the plants then died. And the animals that ate those animals died, too.

The K-T Extinction killed all of the dinosaurs. And about half of the other species on the planet died, too. Of course, all life did not die. In fact, some life flourished. After the K-T Extinction, mammals began to increase in number. Eventually, humans evolved. So, without the K-T Extinction, humans might not ever have existed.

What is NOT true?

1 There have been at least five mass extinctions on the Earth.
2 The K-T Extinction happened about 65 million years ago.
3 All of the dinosaurs died during the K-T Extinction.
4 Most mammals were killed during the K-T Extinction.

Oceans and Ocean Life

Unit 18 海洋與海洋生物

01	**current** [ˈkɝənt]	*(n.)* 洋流（= ocean current） *warm/cold current 暖／寒流 Currents are caused by many factors, like wind, gravity, and heat from the sun. 許多因素會影響到洋流，像是風、引力與太陽的溫度。
02	**ocean floor** [ˈoʃən flor]	*(n.)* 海床（= seabed） *ocean basin 海盆 *mid-ocean ridge 中洋脊 Ocean floors can be divided into three major regions: the continental shelf, the continental slope, and the abyssal plain. 海床分為三種主要區域：大陸棚、大陸斜坡與深海平原。
03	**continental shelf** [ˌkɑntəˈnɛntl̩ ʃɛlf]	*(n.)* 大陸棚 *fishing ground 魚場 The continental shelf extends from the shore to a depth of about 200m and has a gentle slope. 大陸棚自海岸延伸至海底深度 200 公尺，包含一個緩坡。
04	**continental slope** [ˌkɑntəˈnɛntl̩ slop]	*(n.)* 大陸斜坡 *to slope up/down 傾斜向上／下 *to slope off 溜走 The continental slope is found between the continental shelf and the abyssal plain. 大陸斜坡位於大陸棚與深海平原之間。
05	**abyssal plain** [əˈbɪsl̩ plen]	*(n.)* 深海平原 *abyssal hill 深海丘陵 *abyssal fan 深海（沖積）扇 An abyssal plain is the flat and vast floor on the bottom of the ocean. 深海平原是海底平坦而廣大之處。
06	**trench** [trɛntʃ]	*(n.)* 海溝 *Mariana Trench 馬里亞納海溝 *Challenger Deep 挑戰者深淵 A trench is a deep V-shaped valley in the sea floor. 海溝是海床一處深 V 型的凹谷。
07	**tsunami** [tsuˈnɑmi]	*(n.)* 海嘯（= tidal wave） A tsunami is a very large wave that is often caused by an earthquake. 海嘯是常由地震所引起的巨大波浪。
08	**tide** [taɪd]	*(n.)* 潮汐 *The tide is out/in. 退／漲潮了。 *(at) high/low tide （處於）高／低潮 *time and tide wait for no man 時不我待 *tidal energy 潮汐能 The tide is the periodic rising and falling of the water level. 潮汐是週期性水面的漲退。
09	**coral reef** [ˈkɔrəl rif]	*(n.)* 珊瑚礁 *coral island 珊瑚礁島 *coral bleaching 珊瑚白化 Coral reefs are formed by small animals called corals. 珊瑚礁是由稱為珊瑚蟲的小生物所形成的。
10	**atoll** [ˈætɔl]	*(n.)* 環礁 *fringing reef 裙礁 *barrier reef 堡礁 An atoll is a ring of coral reefs that surround a lagoon. 環礁是圍繞潟湖的環狀珊瑚礁。

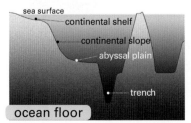

sea surface
continental shelf
continental slope
abyssal plain
trench
ocean floor

tsunami

coral reef

atoll

○ 070

ebb
退潮
Low tide occurs when the water **ebbs**. 當水退潮時則出現了低潮。

recede
後退
Low tide occurs when the water **recedes**. 當水退時則出現了低潮。

flood
湧進；氾濫
High tide occurs when the water **floods**. 當水湧入時則出現了高潮。

trigger
引起
An underwater earthquake can often **trigger** a tsunami.
水面下的地震常能引起海嘯。

devastate
[ˈdɛvəsˌtet]
破壞
Tsunamis can **devastate** the coastal areas that they strike.
海嘯來襲能破壞整個沿岸地區。

wipe out
摧毀
Tsunamis can **wipe out** the coastal areas that they strike.
海嘯來襲能摧毀整個沿岸地區。

Word Families

○ 071

high tide
高潮（= flood tide）
High tide is the time when the sea is at its highest level.
海平面處於最高的時期稱為高潮。

low tide
低潮（= ebb tide）
Low tide is the time when the sea is at its lowest level.
海平面處於最低的時期稱為低潮。

Ocean Life
海洋生物

benthos
[ˈbɛθɑs]
底棲生物
Benthos are organisms living on or near the seabed, like seaweed, corals, and snails. 如海藻、珊瑚蟲和螺類般居住在海底，或海底附近的生物，稱為底棲生物。

nekton
[ˈnɛkˌtɑn]
游泳生物
Nektons are free-swimming animals, such as fish and whales. 如魚和鯨魚般可在水中悠游的動物，稱為游行動物。

plankton
[ˈplæŋktən]
浮游生物
Planktons are tiny, drifting organisms in the water.
微小並漂浮於水上的生物，稱為浮游生物。

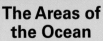
The Areas of the Ocean
海洋生態區

near-shore zone 近岸區

open-ocean zone 遠洋區

intertidal zone 潮間帶

Checkup

A

Write | 請依提示寫出正確的英文單字和片語。

1	洋流	_____	9	珊瑚礁	_____
2	海床	_____	10	環礁	_____
3	大陸棚	_____	11	退潮	_____
4	大陸斜坡	_____	12	後退	_____
5	深海平原	_____	13	湧進；氾濫	_____
6	海溝	_____	14	引起	_____
7	海嘯	_____	15	破壞	d_____
8	潮汐	_____	16	浮游生物	_____

B

Complete the Sentences | 請在空格中填入最適當的答案，並視情況做適當的變化。

coral reef	current	atoll	continental slope	trench
ocean floor	tsunami	tide	continental shelf	abyssal plain

1 _____ are caused by many factors, like wind, gravity, and heat from the sun. 許多因素會影響到洋流，像是風、引力與太陽的溫度。

2 _____ _____ can be divided into three major regions: the continental shelf, the continental slope, and the abyssal plain.
海床分為三種主要區域：大陸棚、大陸斜坡與深海平原。

3 The _____ _____ is found between the continental shelf and the abyssal plain. 大陸斜坡位於大陸棚與深海平原之間。

4 An _____ _____ is the flat and vast floor on the bottom of the ocean.
深海平原是海底平坦而廣大之處。

5 A _____ is a deep V-shaped valley in the sea floor.
海溝是海床一處深 V 型的凹谷。

6 The _____ is the periodic rising and falling of the water level.
潮汐是週期性水面的漲退。

7 An _____ is a ring of coral reefs that surround a lagoon.
環礁是圍繞潟湖的環狀珊瑚礁。

8 _____ _____ are formed by small animals called corals.
珊瑚礁是由稱為珊瑚蟲的小生物所形成的。

C

Read and Choose | 閱讀下列句子，並且選出最適當的答案。

1 Low tide occurs when the water (floods | ebbs).

2 High tide occurs when the water (floods | ebbs).

3 An underwater earthquake can often (trigger | recede) a tsunami.

4 Tsunamis can (cause | devastate) the coastal areas that they strike.

D

Look, Read, and Write | 看圖並且依照提示，在空格中填入正確答案。

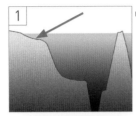

1 ▸ the part of a continent that lies under the ocean and slopes down to the ocean floor

_____

3 ▸ the very small animal and plant life in an ocean, lake, etc.

_____

2 ▸ a very large wave in the ocean that is usually caused by an earthquake

_____

4 ▸ an island that is made of coral and shaped like a ring

_____

E

Read and Answer | 閱讀並且回答下列問題。 ◉072

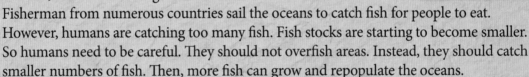

Ocean Resources and Conservation

Oceans cover around 71% of the Earth's surface. And they are full of many different resources that can benefit humanity.

For one, the oceans are a great source of fish and seafood. Fisherman from numerous countries sail the oceans to catch fish for people to eat. However, humans are catching too many fish. Fish stocks are starting to become smaller. So humans need to be careful. They should not overfish areas. Instead, they should catch smaller numbers of fish. Then, more fish can grow and repopulate the oceans.

The oceans also have many valuable resources beneath their floors. For instance, oil and natural gas are pumped from beneath the seafloor in many places. But, again, humans need to be careful. Sometimes, oil spills release large amounts of oil into the water. This can kill many fish, birds, and other sea creatures.

There are even large amounts of certain ores beneath the ocean. Gold, silver, and other valuable metals could be mined in the future. And people can even use the oceans for energy. Tidal energy could provide cheap and abundant energy in the future. But we need to take good care of our oceans. They have many resources, but we need to conserve them, too.

Answer the questions.

1 How much of the Earth's surface do the oceans cover? _____

2 What is happening to fish stocks nowadays? _____

3 What happens when there is an oil spill in the ocean?

_____

4 What might tidal energy be able to do?

_____

Matter 物質

Key Words

🎧 073

01	**physical property** [ˈfɪzɪkl̩ ˈprɑpətɪ]	*(n.)* 物理性質　*physical change 物理變化 The **physical properties** of a substance are its physical characteristics, such as its color, shape, or hardness. 物質的物理性質是如顏色、形狀或是硬度的物理特徵。
02	**chemical property** [ˈkɛmɪkl̩ ˈprɑpətɪ]	*(n.)* 化學性質　*chemical reaction 化學反應 A characteristic of a substance that reacts with other materials and forms new substances is its **chemical property**. 某物質與其他材料反應並生成新物質的特性，稱為化學性質。
03	**atomic number** [əˈtɑmɪk ˈnʌmbɚ]	*(n.)* 原子序　*proton (n.) 質子　*electron (n.) 電子　*neutron (n.) 中子 The number of protons in an atom is its **atomic number**. 原子內的質子數量叫做原子序。
04	**atomic mass** [əˈtɑmɪk mæs]	*(n.)* 原子質量　*dalton (n.) 道爾頓（原子質量單位）　*mass number 質量數 Fundamental properties of atoms include atomic number and **atomic mass**. 原子的基礎性質包含原子序和原子質量。
05	**isotope** [ˈaɪsəˌtop]	*(n.)* 同位素　*radioisotope (n.) 放射性同位素　*isotope separation 同位素分離 **Isotopes** are atoms that have the same number of protons but different numbers of neutrons. 具有相同的質子數，中子數卻不同的原子稱為同位素。
06	**periodic table** [ˌpɪrɪˈadɪk ˈtebl̩]	*(n.)* 元素週期表　*chemical element 化學元素 The **periodic table** is the table that shows the chemical elements arranged by their atomic numbers. 以原子序排列的化學元素表，稱為元素週期表。
07	**plasma** [ˈplæzəmə]	*(n.)* 電漿　*plasma screen 電漿顯示器　*solar plasma 太陽電漿　*ion (n.) 離子 **Plasma** is not a solid, liquid, or gas but is the fourth state of matter. 電漿為非固體、液體或氣體的第四類物質。
08	**reactivity** [ˌriækˈtɪvətɪ]	*(n.)* 反應性　*reversible/irreversible reaction 可逆／不可逆反應 A substance's **reactivity** refers to the property that enables it to go through chemical changes more easily than others. 物質的反應性指的是更能幫助化學變化發生的特色。
09	**stability** [stəˈbɪlətɪ]	*(n.)* 穩定性　*chemical equilibrium 化學平衡 A substance's **stability** refers to the property that enables it to resist going through chemical changes. 物質的穩定性是指能幫助避免起化學變化的特色。
10	**litmus paper** [ˈlɪtməs ˈpepɚ]	*(n.)* 石蕊試紙　*pH indicator pH值　*acid (n.) 酸　*base (n.) 鹼 **Litmus paper** is used to test if something is an acid or a base. 石蕊試紙用來檢測某物為酸或鹼。

isotope

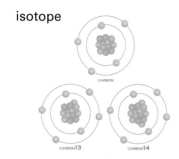

periodic table

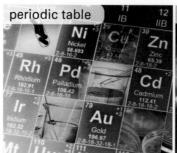

plasma

litmus paper

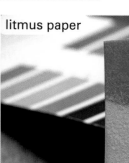

be composed of
由……組成
What is matter composed of? 物質由什麼所組成？

be made of
以……製／組合
All matter is made of elements. 所有物質皆是以元素所組合而成。

react
反應；起作用
Many elements react with one another to form compounds.
許多元素與其他元素互相反應，形成化合物。

stabilize
穩定
Many compounds stabilize after they have been formed.
許多化合物形成後便穩定下來。

determine
[dɪˋtɝmɪn]
確定；決定
Litmus paper lets a person determine if something is an acid or a base.
石蕊試紙幫助人確認某物為酸或鹼。

indicate
指出
Litmus paper indicates if something is an acid or a base.
石蕊試紙指出某物為酸或鹼。

Word Families 🔊 075

Physical Properties
物理性質

mass 質量
volume 體積
density 密度

Chemical Properties
化學性質

reactivity 反應性
stability 穩定性

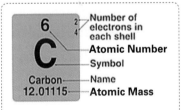

Number of electrons in each shell
Atomic Number
Symbol
Name
Atomic Mass

Types of Reactions
反應類型

synthesis reaction
合成反應

decomposition reaction
分解反應

single replacement reaction
單置換反應

double replacement reaction
雙置換反應

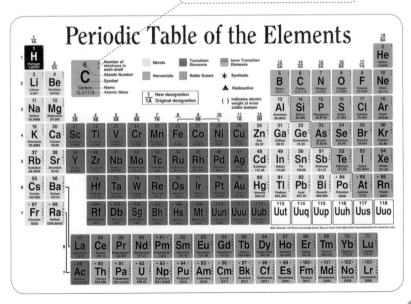

Periodic Table of the Elements

Checkup

Write | 請依提示寫出正確的英文單字和片語。

1	物理性質	9	穩定性
2	化學性質	10	石蕊試紙
3	原子序	11	由……組成
4	原子質量	12	反應；起作用
5	同位素	13	穩定
6	元素週期表	14	確定；決定
7	電漿	15	指出
8	反應性	16	合成反應

B

Complete the Sentences | 請在空格中填入最適當的答案，並視情況做適當的變化。

reactivity	atomic mass	plasma	chemical property	periodic table
stability	litmus paper	isotope	physical property	atomic number

1　The ＿＿＿＿＿＿ ＿＿＿＿＿＿ of a substance are its physical characteristics, such as its color, shape, or hardness.
物質的物理性質是如顏色、形狀或是硬度的物理特徵。

2　A characteristic of a substance that reacts with other materials and forms new substances is its ＿＿＿＿＿＿ ＿＿＿＿＿＿.
某物質與其他材料反應並生成新物質的特性，稱為化學性質。

3　Fundamental properties of atoms include atomic number and ＿＿＿＿＿＿ ＿＿＿＿＿＿. 原子的基礎性質包含原子序和原子質量。

4　＿＿＿＿＿＿ are atoms that have the same number of protons but different numbers of neutrons. 具有相同的質子數，中子數卻不同的原子稱為同位素。

5　The ＿＿＿＿＿＿ ＿＿＿＿＿＿ is the table that shows the chemical elements arranged by their atomic numbers. 以原子序排列的化學元素表，稱為元素週期表。

6　＿＿＿＿＿＿ is not a solid, liquid, or gas but is the fourth state of matter.
電漿為非固體、液體或氣體的第四類物質。

7　A substance's ＿＿＿＿＿＿ refers to the property that enables it to go through chemical changes more easily than others.
物質的反應性指的是更能幫助化學變化發生的特色。

8　A substance's ＿＿＿＿＿＿ refers to the property that enables it to resist going through chemical changes. 物質的穩定性指的是能幫助避免起化學變化的特色。

C

Read and Choose | 閱讀下列句子，並且選出最適當的答案。

1　What is matter (formed | composed) of?

2　Many elements (react | show) with one another to form compounds.

3　Many compounds (stabilize | determine) after they have been formed.

4　Litmus paper (arranges | indicates) if something is an acid or a base.

D

Look, Read, and Write | 看圖並且依照提示，在空格中填入正確答案。

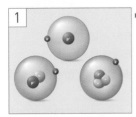 ▸ a form of an atom that has a different numbers of neutrons but the same chemical structure

_____

 ▸ a list that shows the chemical elements arranged according to their properties

_____

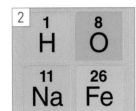 ▸ the number of protons found in the nucleus of an atom

_____

 ▸ a type of paper that is used for testing whether a substance is acid or base

_____

E

Read and Answer | 閱讀並且回答下列問題。 076

Atoms and Their Atomic Numbers

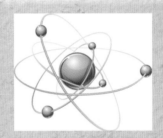

All atoms have different numbers of protons, neutrons, and electrons. The protons are positively charged and are in the nucleus. Neutrons are also in the nucleus. But they have no charge. And electrons orbit the nucleus. They have negative charges. The number of protons and neutrons in an atom is often—but not always—the same.

Every element has a different number of protons. This helps make it different from another element. An element's atomic number is the same as its number of protons. For example, hydrogen has only 1 proton. So this means that it has an atomic number of 1. It is the first element on the periodic table of elements. Helium is the second element. It has an atomic number of 2. This means that it has 2 protons in its nucleus.

There are more than 100 different elements. Scientists often recognize them according to their atomic numbers. Carbon is the basis for all life on Earth. Its atomic number is 6. Oxygen is an important element. Its atomic number is 8. Iron is another important element. 26 is its atomic number. Gold has an atomic number of 79. And uranium's atomic number is 92.

What is true? Write T(true) or F(false).

1 Neutrons have no charge.   _____

2 An element's atomic number is the number of electrons it has.   _____

3 Helium has an atomic number of 1.   _____

4 Oxygen has 8 protons.   _____

Light and Energy

Unit 20 光線與能量

Key Words ⊙ 077

01	**transformation** [͵trænsfɚˈmeʃən]	(n.) 轉換；變化　*transformation into sth. 轉變為某物 *transmutation (n.) 遷變；蛻變；衰變 The **transformation** of the sun's heat into electricity creates solar power. 將太陽的熱度轉換為電力便成了太陽能。
02	**visible light** [ˈvɪzəbḷ laɪt]	(n.) 可見光　*spectrum (n.) 光譜　*RGB color model 三原色光模式 The part of the spectrum you can see is called the **visible light**. 光譜能見的部分稱為可見光。
03	**invisible light** [ɪnˈvɪzəbḷ laɪt]	(n.) 不可見光 Ultraviolet light and infrared light are **invisible light**. 紫外線與紅外線皆是不可見光。
04	**ultraviolet light** [͵ʌltrəˈvaɪəlɪt laɪt]	(n.) 紫外線（**UV**）　*black light 黑光燈；紫外線燈　*UV index 紫外線指數 **Ultraviolet light** is invisible light and causes chemical changes. 紫外線為不可見光，並會引起化學變化。
05	**infrared light** [͵ɪnfrəˈrɛd laɪt]	(n.) 紅外線（**IR**）　*infrared thermography 紅外線成相儀 *IR sensor 紅外線感應器 **Infrared light** is invisible light that is next to visible red waves in the spectrum. 紅外線是在光譜中可見紅波旁的不可見光。
06	**X-ray** [ˈɛksˈre]	(n.) X射線；X光　*to have an X-ray 做X光檢查　*radiograph (n.) X光片 **X-rays** can pass through most objects. X 射線能穿透大部分的物品。
07	**amplitude** [ˈæmpləˌtjud]	(n.) 振幅　*amplitude modulation 振幅調變　*decibel (n.) 分貝（dB） The **amplitude** of a sound wave controls the sound's loudness. 聲音的大小取決於聲音的振幅。
08	**electromagnetic** [ɪˌlɛktromægˈnɛtɪk]	(a.) 電磁的　*electromagnetic induction 電磁感應 *electromagnetic interference 電磁干擾（EMI） When an electric charge moves in a magnetic field, it produces electromagnetic energy. 當電荷於磁場中移動時，便產生了電磁能。
09	**electromagnetic wave** [ɪˌlɛktromægˈnɛtɪk wev]	(n.) 電磁波　*electromagnetic radiation 電磁輻射　*radio wave 無線電波 **Electromagnetic waves** can transfer without matter or through matter. 電磁波可藉由介質傳播，也可在無介質的狀態下傳播。
10	**law of conservation of energy** [ˌkɑnsɚˈveʃən ɔv ˈɛnɚdʒɪ]	(n.) 能量守恆定律　*law of conservation of mass 質量守恆定律 The **law of conservation of energy** states that energy can change forms, but the total amount of energy in a closed system is always the same. 能量守恆定律說明了能量可轉換形式，但封閉系統中的能量總和永遠保持相同。

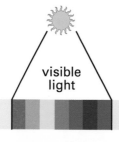

spectrum　invisible light　　**visible light**　　invisible light

infrared light　　　　　　　　　　ultraviolet light

to have an X-ray

transform	轉換；改變
	Energy can be **transformed** into many other forms of energy.
	能量能轉換成多種其他形式的能量。
convert	轉換
	Energy can be **converted** into many other forms of energy.
	能量能轉換成多種其他形式的能量。
diffract [dɪˋfrækt]	繞射
	Waves **diffract** when they collide with an object. 波動撞擊到物體時會發生繞射。
generate	產生
	Dams can **generate** a tremendous amount of energy.
	水壩能產生巨大的能量。
destroy	破壞
	Energy cannot be created or **destroyed** but just changes forms. 能量僅能轉換形式，無法被製造或是破壞。

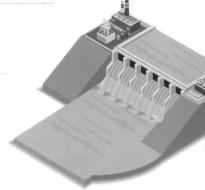

crest	波峰
	The high part of a wave is called the **crest**.
	波動的高點稱為波峰。
trough	波谷
	The low part of a wave is called the **trough**.
	波動的低點處稱為波谷。
wavelength	波長
	The **wavelength** is the distance from crest to crest.
	波峰到波峰的距離稱為波長。

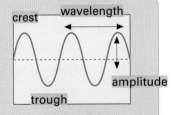

Energy and Environmental Risks 能源與環境風險

greenhouse effect	溫室效應
	The **greenhouse effect** is caused by greenhouse gases, such as carbon dioxide, in the air.
	溫室效應是由空氣中的溫室氣體，如二氧化碳，所造成的。
acid rain	酸雨
	Acid rain can poison animals and vegetation and devastate environments. 酸雨會毒害動植物並破壞環境。
radioactive waste	放射性廢料
	One of the problems associated with nuclear power is **radioactive waste**. 有關核能發電的其中一個問題即是放射性廢料。

Checkup

A

A

Write | 請依提示寫出正確的英文單字和片語。

1 轉換；變化 (n.) _____
2 可見光 _____
3 不可見光 _____
4 紫外線 _____
5 紅外線 _____
6 X射線 _____
7 振幅 _____
8 電磁的 _____

9 電磁波 _____
10 能量守恆定律 _____
11 轉換；改變 (v.) t_____
12 繞射 _____
13 產生 _____
14 波峰 _____
15 波長 _____
16 溫室效應 _____

B

Complete the Sentences | 請在空格中填入最適當的答案，並視情況做適當的變化。

| electromagnetic wave | transformation | visible | ultraviolet light | X-ray |
| law of conservation | electromagnetic | invisible | infrared light | amplitude |

1 The _____ of the sun's heat into electricity creates solar power.
將太陽的熱度轉換為電力便成了太陽能。

2 Ultraviolet light and infrared light are _____ light.
紫外線與紅外線皆是不可見光。

3 _____ _____ is invisible light and causes chemical changes.
紫外線為不可見光，並會引起化學變化。

4 _____ can pass through most objects. X 射線能穿透大部分的物品。

5 The _____ of a sound wave controls the sound's loudness.
聲音的大小取決於聲音的振幅。

6 When an electric charge moves in a magnetic field, it produces
_____ energy. 當電荷於磁場中移動時，便產生了電磁能。

7 _____ _____ can transfer without matter or through matter.
電磁波可藉由介質或無介質來傳播。

8 The _____ _____ _____ of energy states that energy can change
forms, but the total amount of energy in a closed system is always the same.
能量守恆定律說明了能量可轉換形式，但封閉系統中的能量總和永遠保持相同。

C

Read and Choose | 閱讀下列句子，並且選出最適當的答案。

1 Energy can be (destroyed | transformed) into many other forms of energy.
2 Waves (release | diffract) when they collide with an object.
3 Dams can (convert | generate) a tremendous amount of energy.
4 One of the problems associated with nuclear power is (radioactive | acid) waste.

Look, Read, and Write | 看圖並且依照提示，在空格中填入正確答案。

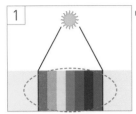

1 ▸ the part of the spectrum the human eyes can see

_____

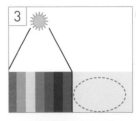

3 ▸ rays of light that cannot be seen and that are shorter than the rays of violet light

_____

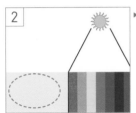

2 ▸ rays of light that cannot be seen and that are longer than the rays of red light

_____

4 ▸ the warming of the Earth's atmosphere that is caused by air pollution

_____

Read and Answer | 閱讀並且回答下列問題。 080

Energy and Environmental Risks

In the modern age, human society runs on energy. Most machines need electricity to operate. Humans have many different ways to create electricity. But some ways are harmful to the environment.

For example, fossil fuels are the most common kind of energy. They include coal, oil, and natural gas. First, people have to mine them from the ground. This can sometimes harm the environment. However, scientists are creating cleaner and more efficient ways to do that these days. So the environment is not damaged as much. But when people burn these fossil fuels, they can release gases that might harm the environment.

Tidal energy is another way to make electricity. This uses the ocean tides to make electricity. But some kinds of tidal energy can kill many fish and other sea creatures. Also, dams can create lots of clean hydroelectric energy. But dams create lakes and change the courses of rivers. So they can change the environment very much.

Nuclear energy is a very powerful form of energy. It is cheap. It is also very clean. But many people are afraid of it because it uses radioactive materials. Also, there have been some accidents at nuclear power plants in the past. But the technology is much better these days. So many countries are starting to build more nuclear power plants now.

Fill in the blanks.

1 Most _____ use electricity.

2 Mining fossil fuels from the ground can sometimes harm the _____.

3 Tidal energy uses the ocean _____ to make electricity.

4 _____ energy is cheap and clean but uses radioactive materials.

Review Test 4

A

Write | 請依提示寫出正確的英文單字和片語。

1	震央	_____	11	漂移 _____
2	震波	_____	12	爆發 _____
3	結晶化	_____	13	使……成化石 _____
4	指標化石	_____	14	大滅絕 _____
5	環礁	_____	15	引起 _____
6	大陸棚	_____	16	摧毀　w_____
7	物理性質	_____	17	穩定 _____
8	原子序	_____	18	由……組成 _____
9	轉換；變化 (n.)	_____	19	轉換　c_____
10	電磁波	_____	20	產生 _____

B

Choose the Correct Word | 請選出與舖底字意思相近的答案。

1 Low tide occurs when the water ebbs.

   a. recedes   b. floods   c. diffracts

2 Energy can be transformed into many other forms of energy.

   a. converted   b. generated   c. crystallized

3 All matter is made of elements.

   a. created   b. composed   c. connected

4 Tsunamis can devastate the coastal areas that they strike.

   a. kill   b. trigger   c. wipe out

C

Complete the Sentences | 請在空格中填入最適當的答案，並視情況做適當的變化。

lithosphere	isotope	metamorphism	ocean floor

1 The _____ is made up of the crust and the upper mantle.
岩石圈是由地殼和上部地函所組成的。

2 _____ refers to the process by which metamorphic rock forms.
變質作用指的是變質岩石的形成。

3 _____ _____ can be divided into three major regions: the continental shelf, the continental slope, and the abyssal plain.
海床分為三種主要區域：大陸棚、大陸斜坡與深海平原。

4 _____ are atoms that have the same number of protons but different numbers of neutrons. 具有相同的質子數，中子數卻不同的原子稱為同位素。

5

Mathematics

Numbers and Computation 數字與計算

| 01 | **factor** [ˈfæktɚ] | (n.) 因數（= divisor） | *multiple (n.) 倍數 *common factor/multiple 公因數／倍數 |
| | | The **factors** of 16 are 1, 2, 4, 8, and 16. 16 的因數是 1、2、4、8 還有 16。 | |

| 02 | **prime number** [praɪm ˈnʌmbɚ] | (n.) 質數 | *coprime (a.) 互質的（= relatively prime） |
| | | A **prime number** is one that can only be divided by itself and 1. 僅能被本身與 1 除盡的叫做質數。 | |

| 03 | **composite number** [kəmˈpɑzɪt ˈnʌmbɚ] | (n.) 合數 | *greatest common factor 最大公因數（GCF） *least common multiple 最小公倍數（LCM） |
| | | **Composite numbers**, like 4 and 6, have more than two factors. 擁有兩個以上的因數即為合數，例如 4 與 6。 | |

| 04 | **base** [bes] | (n.) 底數 | *exponentiation (n.) 指數運算 *logarithm (n.) 對數 |
| | | In 5^2, 5 is called the **base**. 5^2 中，5 稱為底數。 | |

| 05 | **exponent** [ɪkˈsponənt] | (n.) 指數；冪 | |
| | | In 4^3, 4 is the base, and 3 is the **exponent** or power. 4^3 中，4 為底數，3 為指數。 | |

| 06 | **power** [ˈpaʊɚ] | (n.) 次方；冪（= exponent） | |
| | | 5^2 is read "five to the second **power**." 5^2 讀為 5 的二次方。 | |

| 07 | **square** [skwɛr] | (n.) 平方 | |
| | | 5^2 is also read "five **squared**." 5^2 讀為 5 的平方。 | |

| 08 | **cube** [kjub] | (n.) 立方 | |
| | | 4^3 is read "four **cubed**" or "four to the third power." 4^3 讀為 4 的立方或 4 的三次方。 | |

| 09 | **square root** [skwɛr rut] | (n.) 平方根 | *cube root 立方根 *radical symbol 開根號 |
| | | The **square root** of 16 is four. 16 的平方根是 4。 | |

| 10 | **perfect square** [ˈpɝfɪkt skwɛr] | (n.) 完全平方 | *perfect cube 完全立方；完美立方體 |
| | | A **perfect square** is a number that is the square of an integer: 1, 4, 9, 25. 完全平方是一個整數平方的數字，像是 1、4、9、25。 | |

prime number

2, 3, 5, 7, 11, 13, 17 ...

4, 6, 8, 9, 10, 12, 14 ...

composite number

exponent / power

$$5^2 = 25$$

base

perfect square

square	平方 If you **square** 2, the answer is 4. ($2^2 = 4$) 將 2 平方等於 4。
raise to the second power	將……平方 If you **raise** 2 **to the second power**, the answer is 4. ($2^2 = 4$) 將 2 平方等於 4。
cube	立方 If you **cube** 2, the answer is 8. ($2^3 = 8$) 2 的立方等於 8。
raise to the third power	將……立方 If you **raise** 2 **to the third power**, the answer is 8. ($2^3 = 8$) 2 的立方等於 8。
represent	表示 Places to the right of the decimal point **represent** values smaller than 1. 小數點右側處表示數值小於 1。
be simplified	受到簡化 A fraction **is simplified** when its numerator and denominator have no common factor greater than 1. 當分子與分母沒有大於 1 的公因數時，分數即受到簡化。

Word Families 🔊 083

set	集合 The **set** of multiples of 2 is {2, 4, 6, 8...}. 2 的倍數集合為 {2、4、6、8……}。
member	元素 The things in a set are called its **members**. 集合中的數稱為元素。
negative	負的 The numbers to the left of 0 on the number line are **negative**, or **negative** integers. 數線上位於 0 左邊的數字為負值或是負整數。
positive	正的 The numbers to the right of 0 on the number line are **positive**, or **positive** integers. 數線上位於 0 右邊的數字為正值或是正整數。

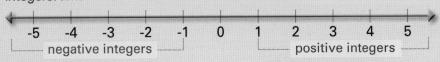

-5 -4 -3 -2 -1 0 1 2 3 4 5
negative integers   positive integers

Abbreviation 縮寫

GCF (greatest common factor) 最大公因數
LCM (least common multiple) 最小公倍數

Numbers 數字

trillion 兆   **billion** 十億
million 百萬   **thousand** 千
hundred 百   **ten** 十
one 一

Checkup

Write | 請依提示寫出正確的英文單字和片語。

1	因數	_____	9	平方根	_____
2	質數	_____	10	完全平方	_____
3	合數	_____	11	將……平方 r	_____
4	底數	_____	12	將……立方 r	_____
5	指數；冪	_____	13	表示	_____
6	次方；冪	_____	14	受到簡化	_____
7	平方	_____	15	集合	_____
8	立方	_____	16	元素	_____

Complete the Sentences | 請在空格中填入最適當的答案，並視情況做適當的變化。

composite number	square	power	perfect square	factor
prime number	exponent	base	square root	cube

1 The _____ of 16 are 1, 2, 4, 8, and 16.
16 的因數是 1、2、4、8 還有 16。

2 A _____ _____ is one that can only be divided by itself and 1.
僅能被本身與 1 除盡的叫做質數。

3 _____ _____, like 4 and 6, have more than two factors.
擁有兩個以上的因數即為合數，例如 4 與 6。

4 In 4^3, 4 is the base, and 3 is the _____ or power.
4^3 中，4 為基數，3 為冪。

5 5^2 is read "five to the second _____."
5^2 讀為 5 的二次方。

6 5^2 is also read "five _____."
5^2 讀為 5 的平方。

7 4^3 is read "four _____" or "four to the third power."
4^3 讀為 4 的立方或 4 的三次方。

8 The _____ _____ of 16 is four.
16 的平方根是 4。

Read and Choose | 閱讀下列句子，並且選出最適當的答案。

1 If you (square | cube) 2, the answer is 4.

2 If you (square | cube) 2, the answer is 8.

3 If you raise 2 to the (second | third) power, the answer is 8.

4 A fraction is (represented | simplified) when its numerator and denominator have no common factor greater than 1.

D

Look, Read, and Write | 看圖並且依照提示，在空格中填入正確答案。

1
2, 3, 5,
7, 11, 13,
17 . . .

▸ a number that can't be divided by any other number except itself and the number 1

_____

3
1, 4, 9,
16, 25, 36,
49, 64 ...

▸ an integer that is the square of an integer

_____

2
4, 6, 8,
9, 10, 12,
14 ...

▸ a number that has more than two factors

_____

4
A={a, b}

▸ one of the distinct objects that make up that set

_____

E

Read and Answer | 閱讀並且回答下列問題。 🔊 084

Square Roots

You have probably multiplied a number by itself before. For example, two times two is four. (2×2=4) Four times four is sixteen. (4×4=16) Five times five is twenty-five. (5×5=25) And ten times ten is one hundred. (10×10=100) When you multiply a number by itself, you are squaring it.

However, what happens when you do an inverse operation? An inverse operation of squaring is finding the square root of a number. When the divisor of a number and the result are the same, then that is the square root of the number.

For instance, the square root of 4 is two. ($\sqrt{4}$=2) Why is that? The reason is that four divided by two is two. (4÷2=2) The divisor and the result are the same. Also, the square root of 49 is seven. Forty-nine divided by seven is seven. And the square root of 100 is ten. One hundred divided by ten is ten.

However, not all square roots are whole numbers. In fact, they are usually irrational numbers. For example, what is the square root of three? It is not a whole number. Instead, it is 1.73205. It actually goes on to infinity because it can never be solved. And how about the square root of six? It is 2.44948. It too goes on to infinity and cannot be solved. Actually, the majority of numbers have square roots that are irrational numbers.

What is true? Write T(true) or F(false).

1   The square root of five is twenty-five.   _____

2   When you multiply a number by itself, you get the square root.   _____

3   Most square roots are whole numbers.   _____

4   The square root of three is an irrational number.   _____

Unit 22 Probability and Statistics 機率與統計

Key Words 🔘 085

01	**probability** [ˌprɑbəˈbɪlətɪ]	*(n.)* 機率　*in all probability 很有可能；十之八九　*likelihood (n.) 可能；可能性
		The odds of something happening are the **probability**. 某事發生的可能性稱為機率。
02	**statistics** [stəˈtɪstɪks]	*(n.)* 統計資料　*data (n.) 數據；訊息　*big data 大數據
		Statistics are facts that are collected from analyzing information expressed in numbers. 從分析的數據資料所蒐集而來的論據,叫做統計資料。
03	**proportion** [prəˈporʃən]	*(n.)* 比例　*to be in/out of proportion to sth. 與某物成／不成比例 *to blow sth. out of proportion 對某事小題大做
		A **proportion** is an equation stating that two ratios are equal to each other. $(\frac{3}{10} = \frac{9}{30})$ 比率相等的等式則為比例。
04	**percent** [pəˈsɛnt]	*(n.)* 百分比　*one hundred percent 完全地；百分之百地
		A **percent** is the ratio of a number to 100. 百分比即為 100 對某數字的比率。
05	**histogram** [ˈhɪstəˌɡræm]	*(n.)* 直方圖　*bar chart 長條圖；柱狀圖　*line chart 折線圖
		A **histogram** is a kind of bar graph that is used to tabulate frequencies. 直方圖為一種用來將頻率表格化的條狀圖。
06	**circle graph** [ˈsɜkl ɡræf]	*(n.)* 圓餅圖（= pie chart）　*infographic (n.) 資訊圖表
		A **circle graph** is used to show how individual data relate to the whole. 用來顯示個別數據與全體的關聯的是圓餅圖。
07	**tree diagram** [tri ˈdaɪəˌɡræm]	*(n.)* 樹狀圖　*Venn diagram 文氏圖　*scatter diagram 散佈圖
		Tree diagrams show all the possible outcomes. 樹狀圖顯示出所有可能的結果。
08	**sampling** [ˈsæmplɪŋ]	*(n.)* 抽樣　*sample (n.) 樣本　*population (n.) 母體 *simple random sampling 簡單隨機抽樣
		A **sampling** is a small part of a group that is selected to be tested or analyzed. 從一群中挑選出來作為試驗或分析的小部分為抽樣。
09	**terminating decimal** [ˈtɜməˌnetɪŋ ˈdɛsɪml]	*(n.)* 有限小數
		A **terminating decimal** is one that stops at a certain place below the decimal point, such as 0.25. 小數點後停於某數,如 0.25,即為有限小數。
10	**repeating decimal** [rɪˈpitɪŋ ˈdɛsɪml]	*(n.)* 循環小數
		A **repeating decimal** is one that continues to infinity, such as 0.33333 . . . 循環小數是無限循環的小數,像是 0.33333……。

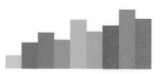

histogram

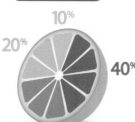

circle graph

10%
20%
40%
30%

tree diagram

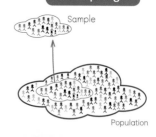

sampling

Sample

Population

cross multiply 交叉相乘
Cross multiply to solve for n in the following problem. ($\frac{n}{10} = \frac{5}{9} \rightarrow n \times 9 = 10 \times 5$)
以交叉相乘來解以下問題的 n 。

eliminate
[ɪˈlɪməˌnet] 消除
To write a percent as a decimal, divide by 100 and **eliminate** the percent sign.
(156.3%=1.563) 欲將百分比寫成小數的形式，要將之除以 100 再消除掉百分比符號。

tabulate
[ˈtæbjuˌlet] 以表格顯示
Tabulate the numbers by using a histogram.
利用直方圖來將數據以表格顯示。

mean 平均值（= average）
The average value of a group is the **mean**. 平均值為一組的平均數值。

median 中位數
The middle number in a sequence of numbers is the **median**.
一連串數字中的中間數字為中位數。

mode 眾數
The number or numbers that occur most often in a group are the **mode**.
一組數字中出現次數最多的則為眾數。

range 區間
The **range** covers the lowest to highest numbers that occur in a set.
區間涵蓋了一組數字中的最高與最低值。

coordinate
[koˈɔrdṇet] 座標
The location of a point on a graph can be determined by its **coordinates**.
圖表上某點的位置能藉由座標來確認。

coordinate axis
[koˈɔrdṇet ˈæksɪs] 座標軸
The **coordinate axis** has an x-axis and a y-axis.
座標軸有 X 軸與 Y 軸。

coordinate plane 座標平面
A **coordinate plane** is the area covered by the x-axis and the y-axis on a graph. 座標平面是由圖表上的 X 軸與 Y 軸所涵蓋之處。

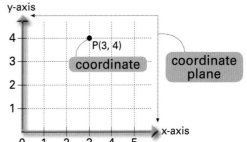

median

1, 2, 3, 4, 5

$\frac{1+2+3+4+5}{5} = 3$

mean

0, 7, 8, 11, 15, 16, 20

1, 1, 2, 2, 2, 2, 4, 5, 5

mode

y-axis

P(3, 4)
coordinate

coordinate plane

x-axis

Checkup

A

Write | 請依提示寫出正確的英文單字和片語。

1	機率	_____	9	有限小數	_____
2	統計資料	_____	10	循環小數	_____
3	比例	_____	11	交叉相乘	_____
4	百分比	_____	12	消除	_____
5	直方圖	_____	13	以表格顯示	_____
6	圓餅圖	_____	14	中位數	_____
7	樹狀圖	_____	15	區間	_____
8	抽樣	_____	16	座標	_____

B

Complete the Sentences | 請在空格中填入最適當的答案，並視情況做適當的變化。

| probability | tree diagram | proportion | repeating decimal | percent |
| statistics | circle graph | histogram | terminating decimal | sampling |

1 The odds of something happening are the _____.
某事發生的可能性稱為機率。

2 _____ are facts that are collected from analyzing information expressed in numbers. 從分析的數據資料所蒐集而來的論據，叫做統計資料。

3 A _____ is an equation stating that two ratios are equal to each other. 比率相等的等式則為比例。

4 A _____ is a kind of bar graph that is used to tabulate frequencies. 直方圖為一種用來條列頻率的條狀圖。

5 _____ _____ show all the possible outcomes. 樹狀圖顯示出所有可能的結果。

6 A _____ is a small part of a group that is selected to be tested or analyzed. 從一群中挑選出來作為試驗或分析的小部分為抽樣。

7 A _____ _____ is one that stops at a certain place below the decimal point, such as 0.25. 小數點後停於某數，如 0.25，即為有限小數。

8 A _____ _____ is one that continues to infinity, such as 0.33333 . . . 循環小數是無限循環的小數，像是 0.33333……。

C

Read and Choose | 閱讀下列句子，並且選出最適當的答案。

1 To write a percent as a decimal, divide by 100 and (cross multiply | eliminate) the percent sign.

2 (Circulate | Tabulate) the numbers by using a histogram.

3 The average value of a group is the (median | mean).

4 The number or numbers that occur most often in a group are the (range | mode).

D

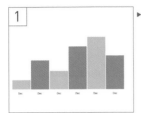

1 ▸ a kind of bar chart that is used to tabulate frequencies

_____

3 ▸ a small group of things taken from a larger group and used to represent the larger group

_____

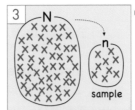

2 ▸ a chart consisting of a circle that is divided into parts to show different amounts of the whole

_____

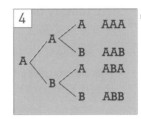

4 ▸ a diagram that shows all of the possible outcomes

_____

E

Read and Answer | 閱讀並且回答下列問題。 ⊙088

Probability and Statistics

The probability of something is the chance that it will happen. This is often expressed as a percentage. For example, if you flip a coin, the probability of it being heads is fifty percent. If you roll a die, the probability of it being the number one is 16.67%, or $\frac{1}{6}$. You can determine the probability by taking the number of ways something can happen and dividing it by the total number of outcomes.

Statistics, on the other hand, is the field of math that collects, organizes, and interprets data. Once data has been collected, one of the easiest ways to analyze it is with graphs. For data that involves probability, circle graphs—or pie charts—are the best to use. These can be divided into 100 percentage points. Perhaps there is a fifty percent chance of something happening, a twenty-five percent chance of something else happening, and a twenty-five percent chance of something different happening. This can easily be shown on a circle graph.

On the other hand, other statistics are best recorded on a bar graph. These are simple charts with an x-axis and a y-axis. For example, perhaps the person is recording some students' best subjects. The classes are English, math, science, and history. These classes go on the x-axis, which is horizontal. The number of students that do well in each class goes on the y-axis, which is vertical. This makes the data easy to see and to interpret.

Fill in the blanks.

1 The chance of something happening is its _____.

2 Statistics is the field of math that collects, organizes, and interprets _____.

3 A _____ _____ is also called a pie chart.

4 A bar graph has an _____ and a y-axis.

Measurement 測量

Key Words 089

01	**metric system** [ˈmɛtrɪk ˈsɪstəm]	(n.) 公制（= metric unit） *decimal system 十進位制 *binary number 二進位制 The **metric system** is a measurement system that is based on multiples of ten. 公制是一種以十為倍數的測量系統。
02	**customary unit** [ˈkʌstəmˌɛrɪ ˈjunɪt]	(n.) 美制單位 *imperial unit 英制單位 **Customary units** of length include inch, foot, yard, and mile. 美制單位的長度單位為英吋、呎、碼與哩。
03	**basic unit** [ˈbesɪk ˈjunɪt]	(n.) 基本單位 *International System of Unit 國際度量衡單位（SI） The **basic unit** of length in the metric system is the meter. 公制中長度的基本單位為公尺。
04	**linear** [ˈlɪnɪə]	(a.) 長度的；線性的 *non-linear (a.) 非線性的 *linear measurement 長度單位 *linear relationship/sequence 直系關係／線性順序 Units that measure length, width, height, and distance are called **linear** units. 測量長、寬、高與距離的單位稱為長度單位。
05	**capacity** [kəˈpæsətɪ]	(n.) 容量 *seating capacity 座位容量 *a capacity crowd/audience 座無虛席 The basic unit of **capacity** in the metric system is the liter. 公制中容量的基本單位為公升。
06	**mass** [mæs]	(n.) 質量 *weight (n.) 重量 The basic unit of **mass** in the metric system is the kilogram. 公制中質量的基本單位為公斤。
07	**conversion** [kənˈvɝʃən]	(n.) 換算 *the conversion of sth. to/into sth. 從某物到某物的換算 In the metric system, the **conversion** of one unit to another simply involves moving the decimal point. (2.195 m = 21.95 dm = 219.5 cm) 欲於公制中將單位換算成另一種，僅需將小數點移位。
08	**unit of time** [ˈjunɪt ɔv taɪm]	(n.) 時間單位 *Olympiad (n.) 奧林匹克周期 *decade (n.) 十年 *century (n.) 世紀 *light year 光年 Hours, minutes, and seconds are **units of time**. 時、分與秒都是時間單位。
09	**elapsed time** [ɪˈlæpst taɪm]	(n.) 實耗時間 *time lag（兩個事件之間的）時間差 The time that has passed by from a given moment is **elapsed time**. 於規定時間中所經過的時間為實耗時間。
10	**prefix** [ˈpriˌfɪks]	(n.) 字首；前綴 *affix (n.) 後綴；詞綴 *metric prefix 公制字首／前綴 "Kilo-" and "centi-" are **prefixes** used in the metric system. 「kilo」、「centi」是公制中所使用的前綴詞。

Metric Unit

centimeter (cm)	meter (m)
kilometer (km)	liter (ℓ)
gram (g)	kilogram (kg)

Customary Unit

mile (mi)	yard (yd)	foot (ft)
inch (in)	pound (lb)	ounce (oz)
pint (pt)	quart (qt)	gallon (gal)

measure
測量
Length can be **measured** in meters and centimeters in the metric system.
長度可藉公制中的公尺與公分來測量。

abbreviate
[əˌbrivɪˈet]
縮寫
Hours, minutes, and seconds are often **abbreviated** to h, min, and sec.
時、分與秒常被縮寫成「h」、「min」與「sec」。

convert
轉換
Convert meters into millimeters. 將公尺轉成公釐。

translate
轉化
You can **translate** 0.5 h to minutes by calculating 0.5 of 60 minutes.
(0.5×60 = 30 min) 你能以計算 60 分鐘的 0.5 倍的方式，來將 0.5 小時轉化成分鐘。

Word Families 🔊 091

Prefixes Used in the Metric System
公制的字首

Kilo- means thousand.
表示「千」

1 kilometer (km) = 1,000 m
1公里＝1000公尺

Hecto- means hundred.
表示「百」

1 hectometer (hm) = 100 m
一百公尺＝100公尺

Deka- means ten.
表示「十」

1 decameter (dam) = 10 m
十公尺＝10公尺

Deci- means tenth.
表示「十分之一」

1 decimeter (dm) = 0.1 m
1分米＝0.1公尺

Centi- means hundredth.
表示「百分之一」

1 centimeter (cm) = 0.01 m
1公分＝0.01公尺

Milli- means thousandth.
表示「千分之一」

1 millimeter (mm) = 0.001 m
1公釐＝0.001公尺

Checkup

A

Write | 請依提示寫出正確的英文單字和片語。

1	公制	9	實耗時間
2	美制單位	10	字首；前綴
3	基本單位	11	測量
4	長度的	12	縮寫
5	容量	13	轉換 c
6	質量	14	轉化 t
7	換算	15	表示「百」
8	時間單位	16	表示「十」

B

Complete the Sentences | 請在空格中填入最適當的答案，並視情況做適當的變化。

mass	linear unit	conversion	metric system	elapsed time
prefix	basic unit	capacity	customary unit	unit of time

1 The _____ _____ is a measurement system that is based on multiples of ten. 公制是一種以十為倍數的測量系統。

2 The _____ _____ of length in the metric system is the meter.
公制中長度的基本單位為公尺。

3 Units that measure length, width, height, and distance are called _____ _____. 測量長、寬、高與距離的單位稱為長度單位。

4 _____ _____ of length include inch, foot, yard, and mile.
美制單位的長度單位為英吋、呎、碼與哩。

5 In the metric system, the _____ of one unit to another simply involves moving the decimal point.
欲於公制中將單位換算成另一種，僅需將小數點移位。

6 The basic unit of _____ in the metric system is the liter.
公制中容量的基本單位為公升。

7 The basic unit of _____ in the metric system is the kilogram.
公制中質量的基本單位為公斤。

8 "Kilo-" and "centi-" are _____ used in the metric system.
「kilo」、「centi」是公制中所使用的前綴詞。

C

Read and Choose | 閱讀下列句子，並且選出最適當的答案。

1 Length can be (abbreviated | measured) in meters and centimeters in the metric system.

2 Hours, minutes, and seconds are often (translated | abbreviated) to h, min, and sec.

3 (Group | Convert) meters into millimeters.

4 Kilo- means (thousand | hundred).

D

Look, Read, and Write | 看圖並且依照提示，在空格中填入正確答案。

 1 ▸ the system of measurement based on the meter and the liter as the basic units of length and volume

_____

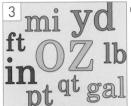 3 ▸ the most commonly used system of measurement in the United States

_____

 2 ▸ relating to length, rather than area or volume

_____

 4 ▸ the time that has passed by from a given moment

_____

E

Read and Answer | 閱讀並且回答下列問題。 092

The Metric System

The metric system is a system of measurement that uses the base-10 system. It measures length, volume, weight, pressure, energy, and temperature. There are several units in the metric system. But, since it uses the base-10 system, converting them is quite easy.

The meter is the unit used to measure length in the metric system. But there are also millimeters, centimeters, decimeters, decameters, hectometers, and kilometers. So, in 1 meter, there are 10 decimeters, 100 centimeters, and 1,000 millimeters. Also, in 1 kilometer, there are 10 hectometers, 100 decameters, and 1,000 meters. The most common units of length are the millimeter, centimeter, meter, and kilometer.

The liter is the unit used to measure volume in the metric system. However, there are also milliliters, centiliters, deciliters, decaliters, hectoliters, and kiloliters. The method to convert them is the same as for meters.

The gram is the unit used to measure mass in the metric system. The most common units of mass are the gram and the kilogram. There are other units, but they are not commonly used.

Finally, the metric system uses Celsius to measure temperature. 0 degrees Celsius is the temperature at which water freezes. 100 degrees Celsius is the temperature at which water boils.

What is NOT true?

1 The meter measures length in the metric system.
2 A decameter is bigger than a centimeter.
3 The liter is used to measure weight in the metric system.
4 Water freezes at 0 degrees Celsius.

Key Words 🔊 093

01	**bisector** [baɪˈsɛktə]	*(n.)* 二等分線　*angle bisector theorem 內分比定理 *perpendicular bisector 垂直平分線 A **bisector** is a line segment that splits an angle into two congruent angles. 二等分線是將一個角度分成兩等分的線段。
02	**congruent figure** [ˈkɑŋgrʊənt ˈfɪgjə]	*(n.)* 全等圖形　*congruent triangles 全等三角形 Figures that have the same shape and size are **congruent figures**. 擁有相同形狀與尺寸的圖形為全等圖形。
03	**similar figure** [ˈsɪmələ ˈfɪgjə]	*(n.)* 相似圖形　*similar triangles 相似三角形 Figures that have the same shape but are different sizes are **similar figures**. 擁有相同形狀，尺寸卻不同的圖形為相似圖形。
04	**corresponding** [ˌkɔrɪˈspɑndɪŋ]	*(a.)* 同位的；對應的　*corresponding angles 同位角 *alternate interior angles 內錯角 The **corresponding** angles of similar triangles are the same as one another. 相似三角形的同位角彼此相同。
05	**proportional** [prəˈpoʃənḷ]	*(a.)* 成比例的　*proportional to sth. 與某物成比例 The lengths of corresponding sides of similar figures are **proportional**. 相似圖形所對應的邊長應為成比例的。
06	**identical** [aɪˈdɛntɪkḷ]	*(a.)* 相同的　*identical to/with sth. 與某物相同　*identical twin 同卵雙胞胎 A polygon can be divided into two **identical** halves by an axis of symmetry. 一個多邊形可藉由對稱軸分為兩個等分。
07	**symmetrical** [sɪˈmɛtrɪkḷ]	*(a.)* 對稱的　*asymmetrical (n.) 不對稱的 A **symmetrical** triangle has an axis of symmetry. 對稱三角形擁有一個對稱軸。
08	**perimeter** [pəˈrɪmətə]	*(n.)* 周長　*area (n.) 面積 The **perimeter** of a figure is the linear distance around that figure. 一個形狀的周長為沿著形狀的線性距離。
09	**circumference** [səˈkʌmfərəns]	*(n.)* 圓周長　*pi (n.) 圓周率　*circular sector 扇形 The **circumference** is the perimeter of a circle. 圓周長為一個圓形的周長。
10	**transformation** [ˌtrænsfəˈmeʃən]	*(n.)* 轉換　*transformation progress 變換過程 **Transformation** is the movement of a figure by translation, rotation, or reflection. 因平移、旋轉或反射所造成的圖形變動稱為轉換。

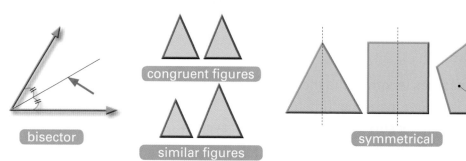

Power Verbs

🔊 094

be congruent to 與……全等

When △ ABC has the same size and shape as △ DEF, we say that
△ ABC is congruent to △ DEF.
當三角形 ABC 與三角形 DEF 的大小形狀皆同時，我們稱三角形 ABC 與三角形 DEF
全等。

bisect 平分

A bisector bisects an angle into two congruent angles.
二等分線能將一個角平分為兩個相等角。

Word Families

🔊 095

two-dimensional figure 平面圖形（= plane figure）

A rectangle is a two-dimensional figure.
長方形為平面圖形。

three-dimensional figure 立體圖形（= solid figure）

A rectangular prism is a three-dimensional figure.
長方柱為立體圖形。

Dimensions 維度	**Circle** 圓

first dimension 第一維度（= line）
second dimension 第二維度（= plane）
third dimension 第三維度（= solid）

chord 弦　　**diameter** 直徑
radius 半徑　　**arc** 弧
circumference 圓周長

first dimension

A　　B

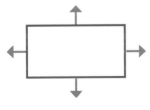

second dimension

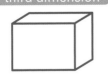

third dimension

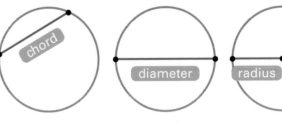

chord　　diameter　　radius

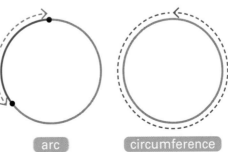

arc　　circumference

Checkup

Write | 請依提示寫出正確的英文單字和片語。

1	二等分線	_____	
2	全等圖形	_____	
3	相似圖形	_____	
4	同位的；對應的	_____	
5	成比例的	_____	
6	相同的	_____	
7	對稱的	_____	
8	周長	_____	
9	圓周長	_____	
10	轉換	_____	
11	與……全等	_____	
12	平分	_____	
13	平面圖形	_____	
14	立體圖形	_____	
15	弦	_____	
16	直徑	_____	

B

Complete the Sentences | 請在空格中填入最適當的答案，並視情況做適當的變化。

identical	bisector	congruent figure	circumference	proportional
similar figure	symmetrical	corresponding	transformation	perimeter

1 A _____ is a line segment that splits an angle into two congruent angles.
二等分線是將一個角度分成兩等分的線段。

2 Figures that have the same shape and size are _____ _____.
擁有相同形狀與尺寸的圖形為全等圖形。

3 Figures that have the same shape but are different sizes are _____
_____. 擁有相同形狀，尺寸卻不同的圖形為相似圖形。

4 The _____ angles of similar triangles are the same as one another.
相似三角形的的同位角彼此相同。

5 The lengths of corresponding sides of similar figures are _____.
相似圖形所對應的邊長應為成比例的。

6 A polygon can be divided into two _____ halves by an axis of symmetry.
一個多邊形可藉由對稱軸分為兩個等分。

7 A _____ triangle has an axis of symmetry.
對稱三角形擁有一個對稱軸。

8 The _____ of a figure is the linear distance around that figure.
一個形狀的周長為沿著形狀的線性距離。

C

Read and Choose | 閱讀下列句子，並且選出最適當的答案。

1 When △ ABC has the same size and shape as △ DEF, we say that △ABC is
(similar | congruent) to △DEF.

2 A bisector (moves | bisects) an angle into two congruent angles.

3 A rectangle is a (two-dimensional | three-dimensional) figure.

4 A rectangular prism is a (two-dimensional | three-dimensional) figure.

D Look, Read, and Write | 看圖並且依照提示，在空格中填入正確答案。

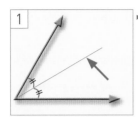
1
▸ a straight line that divides an angle or line into two equal parts

_____

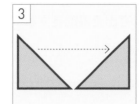
2
▸ figures that have the same shape but are different sizes

_____

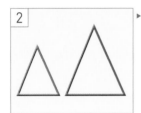
3
▸ the movement of a figure by translation, rotation, or reflection

_____

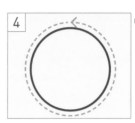
4
▸ the length of a line that makes a circle or other round shape

_____

E Read and Answer | 閱讀並且回答下列問題。 ● 096

Dimensions

The physical world we live in has three dimensions. These three dimensions can all be measured and charted on a graph. They are length, width, and depth.

Length is the first dimension. It is represented by a simple line. On a three-dimensional graph, it is represented by the x-axis, which runs horizontally.

The second dimension is width. When an object exists in two dimensions, it can take the shape of a geometrical figure, such as a square, rectangle, triangle, or circle. In other words, it can be represented in both length and width. On a three-dimensional graph, width is represented by the y-axis, which also runs horizontally.

The third dimension is depth. It is also called height. When an object exists in three dimensions, it can take the shape of a solid figure, such as a cube, pyramid, sphere, or prism. On a three-dimensional graph, depth is represented by the z-axis, which runs vertically.

The fourth dimension is time. Scientists have a name for a cube that exists in four dimensions. They call it a tesseract.

So how many dimensions are there? Scientists are not sure. Some believe that there may be eleven dimensions. Others claim that there are even more. Right now, scientists are searching for extra dimensions. They have not found any yet, but they believe they exist.

Answer the questions.

1   How many dimensions are in the physical world? _____
2   What are these dimensions?   _____
3   What is the fourth dimension?   _____
4   How many dimensions are there?   _____

A

Write | 請依提示寫出正確的英文單字和片語。

1	質數	_____	11	平方	_____
2	合數	_____	12	立方	_____
3	指數；冪	_____	13	消除	_____
4	機率	_____	14	以表格顯示	_____
5	統計資料	_____	15	循環小數	_____
6	公制	_____	16	縮寫	_____
7	美制單位	_____	17	轉換	c_____
8	長度的	_____	18	與……全等	_____
9	成比例的	_____	19	平分	_____
10	相同的	_____	20	半徑	_____

B

Choose the Correct Word | 請選出與鋪底字意思相近的答案。

1 A rectangle is a two-dimensional figure.

   a. plane figure   b. solid figure   c. line

2 A rectangular prism is a three-dimensional figure.

   a. plane figure   b. solid figure   c. line segment

3 Convert meters into millimeters.

   a. Translate   b. Square   c. Abbreviate

4 A bisector bisects an angle into two congruent angles.

   a. represents   b. cubes   c. splits

C

Complete the Sentences | 請在空格中填入最適當的答案，並視情況做適當的變化。

histogram	conversion	similar	base

1 In 4^3, 4 is the _____, and 3 is the exponent or power.
4^3 中，4 為底數，3 為指數。

2 A _____ is a kind of bar graph that is used to tabulate frequencies.
直方圖為一種用來將頻率表格化的條狀圖。

3 In the metric system, the _____ of one unit to another simply involves moving the decimal point.
欲於公制中將單位換算成另一種，僅需將小數點移位。

3 Figures that have the same shape but are different sizes are _____ figures.
擁有相同形狀，尺寸卻不同的圖形為相似圖形。

6

Language •
Visual Arts • Music

Unit 25 Poetry and Stories 詩歌與故事

Key Words 🔊 097

01	**verse** [vɝs]	(n.) 韻文　*blank verse 無韻詩　*to write sth. in verse 用韻文寫某物 Rhymed **verse** is the most commonly used form of **verse**. 最常使用的韻文形式為押韻詩。
02	**prose** [proz]	(n.) 散文　*purple prose 詞句華麗的散文　*prose drama 散文劇 **Prose** is written language in its usual form, in contrast to poetry. 與詩歌比起來，散文是以一般文體著成。
03	**prose poem** [proz `poɪm]	(n.) 散文詩　*narrative/epic/lyric poem 敘事詩／史詩／抒情詩　*elegy (n.) 輓歌 　　　　　　　*classical/modern Chinese poem 舊體詩／新詩 A **prose poem** is poetry written in prose. 以散文形式著作的詩歌稱為散文詩。
04	**rhyme** [raɪm]	(n.) 押韻　*nursery rhyme 兒歌；童謠　*be no/without rhyme 毫無道理 　　　　　*to rhyme with sth. 和某物押韻　*a sense of rhyme 韻律感 Poems often repeat **rhymes** in a regular pattern. 詩歌通常以規律的形式重覆押韻。
05	**stanza** [`stænzə]	(n.) 詩節　*quatrain (n.) 四行詩節　*syllable (n.) 音節 A **stanza** consists of a group of lines that usually has a similar pattern of rhymes. 一個詩節由相似押韻的句子所組成。
06	**couplet** [`kʌplɪt]	(n.) 對句　*Chinese couplet 對子；對聯　*heroic couplet 英雄偶句詩 A **couplet** consists of two lines that rhyme with one another. 一組對句由互相押韻的兩個句子所組成。
07	**rhyme scheme** [raɪm skim]	(n.) 韻式　*alliteration (n.) 頭韻　*assonance (n.) 半押韻 The **rhyme scheme** is the pattern of rhymes that a poem follows. Two common **rhyme schemes** are ABAB and AABB. 韻式是詩歌所遵守的押韻形式。常見的兩種韻式為 ABAB 與 AABB。
08	**meter** [`mitɚ]	(n.) 格律　*iambic pentameter 抑揚格五音步（每行詩有五個韻腳，遵循弱強的格律） Most poems have a regular **meter** or a rhyme scheme. 大多詩歌都有規律的格律或韻式。
09	**free verse** [fri vɝs]	(n.) 無韻詩　*comic/light/satirical verse 打油／諧趣／諷刺詩 **Free verse** is poetry that follows no particular meter or rhyme scheme. 不遵從特定韻律或韻式的詩則為無韻詩。
10	**sonnet** [`sɑnɪt]	(n.) 十四行詩　*epitaph (n.) 悼文；悼亡詩；（尤指）墓誌銘 A **sonnet** is a poem that has 14 lines. 十四行詩為有 14 行的詩。

Verse

... ...

line　And fare the well, my only luve,

And fare thee weel a while!

stanza　And I will come again, my luve,

Though it were ten thousand mile!

rhyme

🔊 098

rhyme

押韻

Many words in poems often **rhyme** with one another.
詩歌中的文字通常互相押韻。

exaggerate
[ɪgˋzædʒəˏret]

誇大

Do not **exaggerate** the pronunciation of the stressed syllables.
請勿刻意誇大重音節的發音。

stress

重讀；強調

Be sure not to **stress** the unstressed syllables when you read a poem.
當你朗讀詩歌時，請勿強調非重音節。

quote

引用

Many famous couplets are still remembered and **quoted** today.
許多著名的對句至今仍存於記憶中並受到引用。

reinforce
[ˏriinˋfɔrs]

強化；加深

In poetry, a rhyme scheme can even **reinforce** the key
idea of a poem. 詩中的韻式有時甚至能強化一首詩的主旨。

Word Families

🔊 099

epic poem	史詩 An **epic poem** is a long poem that tells the tale of a hero and his great deeds. 史詩為述說某位英雄與他偉大事蹟的長篇詩。
allegory [ˋæləˏgorɪ]	寓言（= fable） An **allegory** is a story or poem in which the characters and events are symbols of something else. 故事或詩中的角色與事件作為某物的象徵，則稱為寓言。
stressed syllable	重音節 A **stressed syllable** is spoken in a stronger tone of voice. 重音節要以加重的語調說出來。
unstressed syllable	非重音節 An **unstressed syllable** is spoken in a weaker tone of voice. 非重音節要以弱化的語調說出來。

Rhyme Scheme

Little Lamb, who made thee? – A
Dost thou know who made thee? – A
Gave thee life and bid thee feed – B
By the stream and o'er the mead; – B

AABB

In every cry of every Man, – A
In every Infant's cry of fear, – B
In every voice, in every ban, – A
The mind-forged manacles I hear. – B

ABAB

Sonnet

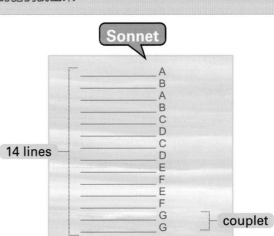

14 lines

A
B
A
B
C
D
C
D
E
F
E
F
G
G

couplet

Checkup

Write | 請依提示寫出正確的英文單字和片語。

1	韻文	_____	9	格律	_____
2	散文	_____	10	十四行詩	_____
3	散文詩	_____	11	史詩	_____
4	押韻 (n.)	_____	12	誇大	_____
5	詩節	_____	13	重讀；強調	_____
6	對句	_____	14	引用	_____
7	韻式	_____	15	強化；加深	_____
8	無韻詩	_____	16	寓言	_____

Complete the Sentences | 請在空格中填入最適當的答案，並視情況做適當的變化。

prose	prose poem	free verse	verse	rhyme
stanza	sonnet	rhyme scheme	meter	couplet

1 Rhymed _____ is the most commonly used form of verse.
最常使用的韻文形式為押韻詩。

2 _____ is written language in its usual form, in contrast to poetry.
與詩歌比起來，散文是以一般文體著成。

3 Poems often repeat _____ in a regular pattern.
詩歌通常以規律的形式重覆押韻。

4 A _____ consists of a group of lines that usually has a similar pattern of rhymes. 一個詩節由相似押韻的句子所組成。

5 A _____ consists of two lines that rhyme with one another.
一組對句由互相押韻的兩個句子所組成。

6 The _____ _____ is the pattern of rhymes that a poem follows.
韻式是詩歌所遵守的押韻形式。

7 Most poems have a regular _____ or a rhyme scheme.
大多詩歌都有規律的格律或韻式。

8 A _____ is a poem that has 14 lines.
十四行詩為有 14 行的詩。

Read and Choose | 閱讀下列句子，並且選出最適當的答案。

1 Many words in poems often (exaggerate | rhyme) with one another.

2 Be sure not to (quote | stress) the unstressed syllables when you read a poem.

3 Many famous couplets are still remembered and (quoted | stressed) today.

4 In poetry, a rhyme scheme can even (consist | reinforce) the key idea of a poem.

D

Look, Read, and Write | 看圖並且依照提示，在空格中填入正確答案。

1

Little Lamb, I'll tell thee,
Little Lamb, I'll tell thee,
He is called by thy name,
For he calls himself a Lamb;
...

▸ writing in which words are arranged in a rhythmic pattern

_____

3

A
B
A
B
C
D
C
D
E
F
E
F
G
G

▸ a poem made up of 14 lines that rhyme in a fixed pattern

_____

2

In every cry of every Man,   – A
In every Infant's cry of fear,   – B
In every voice, in every ban,   – A
The mind-forged manacles I hear.   – B

▸ a regular pattern of rhyme at the end of the lines in a poem

_____

4

Well, son, I'll tell you:
Life for me ain't been no crystal stair.
It's had tacks in it,
And splinters,
And boards torn up,
......

▸ poetry that does not rhyme and does not have a regular rhythm

_____

E

Read and Answer | 閱讀並且回答下列問題。 🔊 100

Types of Poems

Poets have many different types of poems to choose from when they write. They can write very long or very short poems. They can write about many different subjects. And they can write with different rhyme schemes and in different meters.

One of the oldest types of poems is the epic. This is a very long poem. It can often be thousands of lines long. An epic poem is typically about a hero and his adventures. There have been many famous epic poems in history. The *Iliad*, *Odyssey*, *Aeneid*, *Beowulf*, and *Gilgamesh* are just a few of the many epic poems.

On the other hand, many poems are very short. Sonnets are one type of short poem. They are poems with fourteen lines. Usually, the last two lines in a sonnet rhyme. Sonnets can be about many different topics. William Shakespeare wrote many famous sonnets.

Couplets can be long or short poems. Each stanza in a couplet has two lines. The last word in each line rhymes.

Quatrains are very short poems. They only have four lines. And cinquains have five lines. Limericks are also poems with five lines. And haikus are poems with only three lines. The first and third lines have five syllables. And the second line has seven syllables. They are some of the shortest of poems.

What is true? Write T(true) or F(false).

1   Epic poems are short poems.   _____

2   *Beowulf is* a famous sonnet by William Shakespeare.   _____

3   A sonnet has fourteen lines.   _____

4   Quatrains and limericks both have four lines.   _____

Key Words

🔊 101

01	**common noun** [ˈkɑmən naʊn]	(n.) 普通名詞 *abstract noun 抽象名詞 *concrete noun 具體名詞 Common nouns name any person, place, or thing: teacher, school, book. 普通名詞指的是任何的人、地或物，像是老師、學校、書。
02	**proper noun** [ˈprɑpɚ naʊn]	(n.) 專有名詞 *collective noun 集合名詞 *noun phrase 名詞片語 Proper nouns name a specific person, place, or thing: Tom, Seoul, England. 專有名詞指的是特定的人、地或物，像是湯姆、首爾、英國。
03	**active voice** [ˈæktɪv vɔɪs]	(n.) 主動語氣 We use the **active voice** to say what the subject does. 我們用主動語氣來表達主詞做的事。 E.g., He cleaned the room.
04	**passive voice** [ˈpæsɪv vɔɪs]	(n.) 被動語氣 We use the **passive voice** to say what happens to the subject. 我們用被動語氣來表達主詞遭遇的事。 E.g., The room was cleaned.
05	**root** [rut]	(n.) 字根 *prefix (n.) 字首；前綴 *suffix (n.) 字尾；後綴 *stem (n.) 語幹；詞幹 Many words in English have Greek or Latin **roots**. 英文中有許多字擁有希臘或拉丁的字根。
06	**etymology** [ˌɛtəˈmɑlədʒɪ]	(n.) 詞源學 *folk etymology 通俗詞源 （以熟悉的詞取代陌生的詞，而創造新詞的過程） The study of the origins of words is **etymology**. 文字起源的研究為詞源學。
07	**simple sentence** [ˈsɪmpl̩ ˈsɛntəns]	(n.) 簡單句 A sentence with one independent clause is a **simple sentence**. 句子擁有一獨立子句的為簡單句。 E.g., I like her.
08	**compound sentence** [ˈkɑmpaʊnd ˈsɛntəns]	(n.) 合句 A sentence with two or more independent clauses is a **compound sentence**. 句子擁有兩個或以上的獨立子句為合句。 E.g., I like her, but she doesn't like me.
09	**complex sentence** [ˈkɑmplɛks ˈsɛntəns]	(n.) 複句 A sentence with one independent clause and at least one dependent clause is a **complex sentence**. 句子擁有一獨立子句，並至少有一從屬子句的為複句。 E.g., I like her because she is so funny.
10	**compound-complex sentence** [ˈkɑmpaʊnd ˈkɑmplɛks ˈsɛntəns]	(n.) 複合句 A sentence with two or more independent clauses and at least one dependent clause is a **compound-complex sentence**. 句子擁有兩句或以上的獨立子句，且至少有一從屬子句為複合句。 E.g., The girl you like called me, and she asked me for help because she was in trouble.

🔊 102

parse　　　從語法上分析
Parse a sentence by analyzing its grammatical parts.
藉由分析文法的部分來分析句子。

analyze　　分析；解析
Analyze the origins of the words. 分析字詞的起源。

identify　　識別；確認
Identify the dependent and independent clauses in the following sentence.
將下列句子中的從屬與獨立子句區分出來。

clarify　　使清楚；闡明
A complex sentence can clarify the relationship between two separate sentences
by using a conjunction. 複句能藉由連接詞來釐清兩個獨立句子間的關聯。

take　　　採取
English has taken words from many different languages.
英語採取多種不同語言的文字。

borrow　　引入；借用
English has borrowed words from many different languages.
英語從多種不同的語言中借用文字。

Word Families

🔊 103

clause　　　子句
A clause is a sentence with a subject and predicate.
子句為擁有主詞與述語的句子。

dependent clause　　從屬子句
A dependent clause is not a complete sentence and cannot stand
alone as a sentence. 從屬子句不是完整句，且無法獨立成為一個句子。

independent clause　　獨立子句
An independent clause is a clause that can express a complete
thought. 獨立子句為能表達完整思想的子句。

Although he was very sick, he attended the meeting.
└── dependent clause ──┘ └── independent clause ──┘

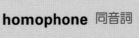

Grammar Terms
文法術語

part of speech 詞類；詞性　**prefix** 字首；前綴　　**suffix** 字尾；後綴

synonym 同義字　　　　　**antonym** 反義字　　　**homophone** 同音詞

simile 明喻　　　　　　　**metaphor** 隱喻

Checkup

Write | 請依提示寫出正確的英文單字和片語。

1	普通名詞	_____	9	複句	_____
2	專有名詞	_____	10	複合句	_____
3	主動語氣	_____	11	從語法上分析	_____
4	被動語氣	_____	12	分析；解析	_____
5	字根	_____	13	識別；確認	_____
6	詞源學	_____	14	使清楚；闡明	_____
7	簡單句	_____	15	子句	_____
8	合句	_____	16	從屬子句	_____

B

Complete the Sentences | 請在空格中填入最適當的答案，並視情況做適當的變化。

root	active voice	compound-complex	complex sentence
etymology	passive voice	compound sentence	simple sentence

1 We use the _____ _____ to say what the subject does.
我們用主動語氣來表達主詞做的事。

2 We use the _____ _____ to say what happens to the subject.
我們用被動語氣來表達主詞遭遇的事。

3 Many words in English have Greek or Latin _____.
英文中有許多字擁有希臘或拉丁的字根。

4 The study of the origins of words is _____. 文字起源的研究為詞源學。

5 A sentence with one independent clause is a _____ _____.
句子擁有一獨立子句的為簡單句。

6 A sentence with two or more independent clauses is a _____
_____. 句子擁有兩個或以上的獨立子句為合句。

7 A sentence with one independent clause and at least one dependent clause is a
_____ _____. 句子擁有一獨立子句，並至少有一從屬子句的為複句。

8 A sentence with two or more independent clauses and at least one dependent
clause is a _____ sentence.
句子擁有兩句或以上的獨立子句，且至少有一從屬子句為複合句。

C

Read and Choose | 閱讀下列句子，並且選出最適當的答案。

1 (Analyze | Compound) the origins of the words.

2 A complex sentence can (clarify | parse) the relationship between two separate
sentences by using a conjunction.

3 English has (followed | taken) words from many different languages.

4 (Borrow | Identify) the dependent and independent clauses in the following
sentence.

D

1 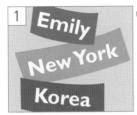 ▸ a word that is the name of a particular person, place, or thing that is spelled with a capital letter

_____

3
He is handsome.

▸ a sentence that has only one verb

_____

2 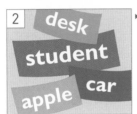 ▸ a word that is the name of a group of similar things, and not of a single person, place, or thing

_____

4
I got up late, so I was late.

▸ a sentence made from two independent sentences joined by "and", "or", or "but"

_____

E

Greek and Latin Roots

English has more words than any other language. Why is this? One reason is that English borrows words from many other languages. Then it turns these words into new English words. Many of these words come from Greek and Latin. These are called roots. By studying roots, a person can learn the meanings of many different words in English.

For instance, the root hydro comes from Greek. It means "water." From that root, we get the words hydrate, dehydrate, hydrant, hydrogen, and many others. The root aster comes from Greek. It means "star." From aster, we get the words asteroid, asterisk, astronomy, astronaut, and many others. Geo also comes from Greek. It means "earth." The words geology, geometry, and geography all come from it.

Of course, there are many roots from Latin, too. For instance, the root vid means to "see." From that root, we get video, visual, visualize, and many others. The root script means to "write." From it, we get transcript, inscription, and others. And port means to "carry." From that root, we get transport, portable, export, and import, among others.

Without borrowing from other languages, English would have very few words. But, thanks to Latin and Greek—and other languages, too—English has many, many words.

Fill in the blanks.

1 English has more _____ than any other language.
2 Geo is a root word that comes from _____.
3 The root vid means to "_____."
4 The root _____ means to "carry."

Common English Sayings and Expressions 常見英文諺語和措辭

Key Words 🔘 105

01	**indeed** [ɪnˈdid]	*(adv.)* 真正地　*indeed（口語）表示驚訝、惱怒、不相信、不感興趣 A friend in need is a friend **indeed**. 患難見真情。
02	**necessity** [nəˈsɛsətɪ]	*(n.)* 需要　*of necessity 勢必　*from/out of necessity 出於需要 **Necessity** is the mother of invention. 需要乃發明之母。
03	**hatch** [hætʃ]	*(v.)* 孵化　*Down the hatch! 乾杯！　*escape/serving hatch 緊急出口／上菜窗口 Don't count your chickens before they **hatch**. 凡事切莫過早下定論。
04	**haste** [hest]	*(n.)* 急忙　*make haste 趕快 　　　　*Marry in haste, repent at leisure. 草率結婚後悔多。 **Haste** makes waste. 欲速則不達。
05	**flock** [flɑk]	*(v.)* 聚集　*to flock to/into/out of . . . 成群結隊去／進／出…… 　　　　*to flock round sb./sth. 把某人／某物團團圍住 Birds of a feather **flock** together. 物以類聚。
06	**worm** [wɝm]	*(n.)* 蟲　*the worm turns 兔子急了也咬人　*worm sth. out of sb. 從某人套出某事 The early bird gets the **worm**. 早起的鳥兒有蟲吃。
07	**deep** [dip]	*(a.)* 深的　*to get into deep water 惹上大麻煩　*deep pockets 財力雄厚 　　　　*still waters run deep 深藏不露　*to go off the deep end 火冒三丈 Beauty is only skin **deep**. 美貌是膚淺的。
08	**put** [pʊt]	*(v.)* 放置　*to put ideas into sb.'s head 使某人產生念頭 　　　　*to put yourself in sb.'s place/position/shoes 處在（某人的）角度考慮 Don't **put** all your eggs in one basket. 別把雞蛋全都放在一個籃子裡。
09	**grass** [græs]	*(n.)* 草　*to put sb. out to grass 迫使某人退休　*grassroots (n.) 平民百姓 The **grass** is always greener on the other side of the hill. 外國的月亮比較圓。
10	**procrastination** [proˌkræstəˈneʃən]	*(n.)* 拖延；耽擱　*positive procrastination 故意耽擱 **Procrastination** is the thief of time. 拖延即浪費時間。

A friend in need is a friend indeed.

Don't count your chickens before they hatch.

Birds of a feather flock together.

The early bird gets the worm.

🔊 106

put off

拖延

Never put off till tomorrow what you can do today. 今日事今日畢。

postpone
[post`pon]

拖延；延期

Never postpone till tomorrow what you can do today. 今日事今日畢。

procrastinate

拖延；耽擱

Never procrastinate till tomorrow what you can do today. 今日事今日畢。

convey

傳達

Most sayings convey a specific meaning.
大多數的諺語多傳達特定的涵義。

moralize
[`mɔrəlaɪz]

教化

Some stories moralize and teach people a lesson.
一些故事可教化並教導人們。

Word Families

🔊 107

proverb

諺語

Proverbs are short sayings that are full of wisdom.
諺語為一些充滿智慧的簡短格言。

oral tradition

口傳歷史

Many sayings are passed down from the oral tradition.
許多諺語是從口傳歷史流傳下來的。

folklore

民間傳說

Some sayings come from folklore.
有些諺語是由民間傳說而來的。

oral tradition

fable

寓言

A fable is a story that often involves animals and
which is told to teach people a lesson.
寓言是一種常以動物為主角，用來教導人們的故事。

parable

寓言

A parable is a short story that teaches a moral or
a religious lesson.
寓言是教導寓意或是宗教教誨的短篇故事。

aphorism
[`æfə,rɪzm]

格言

An aphorism is a wise short expression that says a general truth.
格言為表達真理的智慧短語。

moral

寓意

An important lesson of a story is its moral.
一則故事的重要教訓為寓意。

Checkup

A

Write | 請依提示寫出正確的英文單字和片語。

1	真正地	_____	9	深的	_____
2	需要	_____	10	拖延；耽擱 (n.)	_____
3	孵化	_____	11	拖延；延期 (v.)	_____
4	急忙	_____	12	傳達	_____
5	聚集	_____	13	教化	_____
6	蟲	_____	14	諺語	_____
7	放置	_____	15	民間傳說	_____
8	草	_____	16	格言	_____

B

Complete the Sentences | 請在空格中填入最適當的答案，並視情況做適當的變化。

procrastination	deep	haste	hatch	grass
necessity	worm	flock	put	indeed

1 A friend in need is a friend _____.
   患難見真情。

2 _____ is the mother of invention.
   需要乃發明之母。

3 Don't count your chickens before they _____.
   凡事切莫過早下定論。

4 Don't _____ all your eggs in one basket.
   別把雞蛋全都放在一個籃子裡。

5 The _____ is always greener on the other side of the hill.
   外國的月亮比較圓。

6 Beauty is only skin _____.
   美貌是膚淺的。

7 _____ makes waste.
   欲速則不達。

8 Birds of a feather _____ together.
   物以類聚。

C

Read and Choose | 閱讀下列句子，並且選出最適當的答案。

1 Never (transport｜postpone) till tomorrow what you can do today.

2 Most sayings (conduct｜convey) a specific meaning.

3 Some stories (moralize｜moral) and teach people a lesson.

4 A (proverb｜parable) is a short story that teaches a moral or a religious lesson.

Look, Read, and Write | 看圖並且依照提示，在空格中填入正確答案。

1

Time is money.

▸ a brief popular saying that gives advice about how people should live

_____

3

▸ preserving beliefs, customs, and history, in which parents tell their children about them

_____

2

▸ a short story that usually is about animals and that is intended to teach a lesson

_____

4

▸ to be slow or late about doing something that should be done

_____

Read and Answer | 閱讀並且回答下列問題。 ⊙ 108

Common Proverbs

Proverbs are short expressions that people sometimes use. They typically pass on some type of wisdom. The English language has a very large number of proverbs.

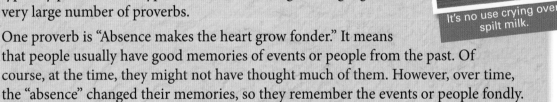

It's no use crying over spilt milk.

One proverb is "Absence makes the heart grow fonder." It means that people usually have good memories of events or people from the past. Of course, at the time, they might not have thought much of them. However, over time, the "absence" changed their memories, so they remember the events or people fondly.

"All that glitters is not gold" is another important proverb. Gold is very valuable, and it glitters brightly. But many other things glitter, too. However, they may not be valuable. In fact, they may even be harmful. So this proverb is a warning. People should be careful because not every shiny, good-looking thing is like gold.

"He who hesitates is lost" is a popular expression. This proverb tells people not to hesitate. They should make a decision and go with it. If they hesitate or wait too long, they might lose an important opportunity.

Finally, "It's no use crying over spilt milk" is another common proverb. Sometimes bad things might happen to a person. But that person should not cry about it. Instead, the person should accept what has happened and move on. That is the meaning of that proverb.

What is NOT true?

1   There are many proverbs in the English language.
2   Proverbs rarely teach some kind of wisdom to people.
3   "All that glitters is not gold" is a proverb that warns people.
4   "It's no use crying over spilt milk" tells people to move on from the past.

Key Words 🔊 109

01 Classical Art
[ˈklæsɪḳl ɑrt]

(n.) 古典藝術　*classicism (n.)（盛行於歐洲18世紀藝術方面的）古典主義

The art of ancient Greece and Rome is often referred to as **Classical Art**. 古希臘與羅馬的藝術通常被稱為古典藝術。

02 order
[ˈɔrdɚ]

(n.) 種類；類型　*column (n.) 圓柱；紀念柱　*pillar (n.) 柱子；支柱

There were three classical **orders** in ancient Greek architecture: the Doric **order**, the Ionic **order**, and the Corinthian **order**. 古希臘建築有三大古典類型，分別是多力克柱式、愛奧尼柱式與科林斯柱式。

03 Doric order
[ˈdɔrɪk ˈɔrdɚ]

(n.) 多力克柱式　*base (n.) 柱礎　*shaft (n.) 柱身　*capital (n.) 柱頭

The **Doric order** column was the oldest and plainest.
多力克柱式為最古老樸素的。

04 Ionic order
[aɪˈɑnɪk ˈɔrdɚ]

(n.) 愛奧尼柱式　*Tuscan order 托斯卡納柱式　*volute (a.) 螺旋形的

The **Ionic order** column was more slender and elegant than Doric order. 愛奧尼柱式比多力克柱式來的纖細，也較為精緻。

05 Corinthian order
[kəˈrɪnθɪən ˈɔrdɚ]

(n.) 科林斯柱式　*composite order 混和柱式
*acanthus (n.)（柱頭上）莨苕葉紋飾

The **Corinthian order** column was the most elaborate.
科林斯柱式是最複雜精巧的。

06 proportion
[prəˈporʃən]

(n.) 比例　*in/out of proportion 比例協調／失調地

In Greek architecture, balance and **proportion** were the most important qualities of art. 希臘建築中，均衡與比例為藝術中最重要的特點。

07 symmetrical
[sɪˈmɛtrɪḳl]

(a.) 對稱的　*asymmetric (a.) 不對稱的

Greek buildings are often well balanced and **symmetrical**.
希臘建築通常為均衡且對稱。

08 column
[ˈkɑləm]

(n.) 圓柱　*a column of smoke 煙柱　*spinal column 脊柱；脊椎

The **columns** had to be in proportion to all of the other parts of the building in ancient Greek architecture.
古希臘建築中，圓柱要與建物的其他部份成比例。

09 Gothic Art
[ˈgɑθɪk ɑrt]

(n.) 哥德式藝術　*Gothic fiction 哥德小說（始於歐洲18世紀的文學派別）

Gothic Art was an expression of the ideas of the medieval church.
哥德式藝術為中世紀教堂概念的一種呈現。

10 linear perspective
[ˈlɪnɪɚ pɚˈspɛktɪv]

(n.) 線性透視法　*foreshortening (n.) 前縮透視法　*vanishing point 消失點
*in/out of perspective 透視比例正確的／失真的

Linear perspective allowed painters to make their paintings look more realistic. 線性透視法能讓畫家的畫作更加寫實。

Classical Orders

Doric order

Ionic order

Corinthian order

work out	發展 The Greeks **worked out** the rules for the proportion of the human body in sculpture. 希臘人在雕刻上成功發展出人體比例的規則。
be influenced by	受⋯⋯的影響 Roman architecture **was influenced by** the Greeks. 羅馬建築受到希臘人的影響。
be inspired by	受⋯⋯的啟發 The Gothic cathedral **was inspired by** Christianity. 哥德式教堂是受基督教所啟發。
dedicate	奉獻 The Parthenon temple was **dedicated** to the goddess Athena Parthenos. 帕德嫩神廟是獻給雅典娜女神的。
honor	榮耀 The Pantheon was built to **honor** the Roman gods. 萬神殿是建造來榮耀羅馬眾神的。
strive	努力；奮鬥 Many classical artists **strived** to create ideal works of art. 多位古典藝術家為了要創作出理想的藝術品而努力不懈。

decorative	裝飾性的 **Decorative** vases were common during the Classical Period. 裝飾性花瓶在古典時期中很常見。
ornate	華麗的 Some Greek columns can be very **ornate**. 一些希臘圓柱相當的華麗。

dome	圓頂 The Pantheon in Rome has a concrete **dome** with an oculus that is open to the sky. 羅馬的萬神殿有一個水泥圓頂，上頭有向天的眼狀天窗。
oculus [ˈɑkjuləs]	眼狀天窗 An **oculus** is a circular opening in the center of a dome. 眼狀天窗是位於圓頂中心的圓形開口。
arch	拱門 The Pantheon in Rome has a number of **arches**. 羅馬的萬神殿有許多拱門。

Pantheon in Rome

oculus

Checkup

A

Write | 請依提示寫出正確的英文單字和片語。

1	古典藝術	_____
2	等級；類型	_____
3	多力克柱式	_____
4	愛奧尼柱式	_____
5	科林斯柱式	_____
6	比例	_____
7	對稱的	_____
8	圓柱	_____
9	哥德式藝術	_____
10	線性透視法	_____
11	發展	_____
12	受……的啟發	_____
13	以……為奉獻	_____
14	努力；奮鬥	_____
15	華麗的	_____
16	眼狀天窗	_____

B

Complete the Sentences | 請在空格中填入最適當的答案，並視情況做適當的變化。

Ionic order	linear perspective	order	Classical Art	proportion
Doric order	Corinthian order	column	Gothic Art	symmetrical

1 There were three classical _____ in ancient Greek architecture.
古希臘建築有三大古典類型。

2 The _____ _____ column was the oldest and plainest.
多力克柱式為最古老樸素的。

3 The _____ _____ column was the most elaborate.
科林斯柱式是最複雜精巧的。

4 The _____ _____ column was more slender and elegant than Doric order. 愛奧尼柱式比多力克柱式來的纖細，也較為精緻。

5 In Greek architecture, balance and _____ were the most important qualities of art. 希臘建築中，均衡與比例為藝術中最重要的特點。

6 Greek buildings are often well balanced and _____.
希臘建築通常為均衡且對稱。

7 The _____ had to be in proportion to all of the other parts of the building in ancient Greek architecture. 古希臘建築中，圓柱要與建物的其他部份成比例。

8 _____ _____ allowed painters to make their paintings look more realistic. 線性透視法能讓畫家的畫作更加寫實。

C

Read and Choose | 閱讀下列句子，並且選出最適當的答案。

1 The Greeks (worked | strived) out the rules for the proportion of the human body in sculpture.

2 Roman architecture was (influenced | honored) by the Greeks.

3 The Gothic cathedral was (depicted | inspired) by Christianity.

4 The Parthenon temple was (dedicated | represented) to the goddess Athena Parthenos.

D

 ► the quality of having two parts that match exactly

_____

 ► a long post made of steel, stone, etc., that is used as a support in a building

_____

 ► a style of art that was common in medieval Europe

_____

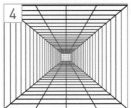 ► a way of showing depth or distance in a painting or drawing

_____

E

Read and Answer | 閱讀並且回答下列問題。 ● 112

Classical Art

The ancient Greeks loved art. They made all kinds of works of art. This included pottery, paintings, sculptures, and murals. The Greeks even considered their buildings to be works of art. So they made beautifully designed buildings as well.

Many examples of pottery have survived from ancient Greece. Pottery in ancient Greece had two functions. People used it to eat or drink from. And they used it for decorations. Many Greek ceramics have beautiful pictures painted on them. These pictures often show stories from Greek mythology.

Sculpture was highly prized in ancient Greece. The Greeks made sculptures from either stone or bronze. Many stone sculptures have survived to today. But few bronze sculptures have. The Greeks depicted the people in sculptures exactly as they looked in real life.

As for architecture, many Greek buildings still exist today. One important feature of these buildings is their columns. The Greeks made three types of columns: Doric, Ionic, and Corinthian. Doric columns were the simplest. They had very plain designs. Ionic columns had flutes, or lines, carved into them from the top to the bottom. They were also more decorative than Doric columns. Corinthian columns were the most decorative ones of all. Their tops—called capitals—often had flowers or other designs on them. And they also had flutes.

Answer the questions.

1 What kinds of works of art did the ancient Greeks make?

_____

2 What pictures did the Greeks often paint on their pottery?

_____

3 What did the Greeks make sculptures from? _____

4 What were the three types of columns the Greeks made?

_____

Unit 29

From Baroque Art to Realism 巴洛克藝術到寫實主義

Key Words 🔘 113

01	**Baroque Art** [bəˋrok ɑrt]	(n.) 巴洛克藝術　*Baroque painting/music/architecture 巴洛克繪畫／音樂／建築

Baroque Art is known for its dramatic contrast of light and shade.
巴洛克藝術以誇張的光影對比而聞名。

02	**chiaroscuro** [kɪ͵ɑrəˋskjuro]	(n.) 明暗對照法　*shading (n.)（繪畫）陰影處理　*cross-hatching (n.) 交叉線法

Chiaroscuro refers to the contrast between light and dark in a painting.
明暗對照法指的是圖畫上明暗的對比。

03	**grotesque** [groˋtɛsk]	(a.) 風格怪異的　*absurd (a.) 荒謬的；荒唐的　*monstrous (a.) 駭人聽聞的

Baroque Art may seem very dramatic and **grotesque** at first.
巴洛克藝術起初看似誇張而怪異。

04	**contortion** [kənˋtɔrʃən]	(n.) 扭曲　*contortionist (n.) 軟骨功表演者　*distortion (n.) 失真；扭曲；曲解

The **contortion** of bodies created many of the grotesque statues.
身體的扭曲創造出許多怪異的雕像。

05	**Rococo Art** [rəˋkoko ɑrt]	(n.) 洛可可藝術（= Late Baroque Art）　*chinoiserie (a.) 中國風的

Rococo Art is characterized by its decorative and lighthearted look that uses pastel colors.
洛可可藝術以它的裝飾性及淡彩繪成的輕鬆愉快畫面為特色。

06	**pastel** [pæsˋtɛl]	(n.) 淡而柔和的色彩　*a pastel tone 淡雅的色調　*pastel (n.) 彩色粉筆

Pastels are colors that appear both soft and pale.
淡彩為柔和而淡的顏色。

07	**Neoclassical Art** [͵nioˋklæsɪkḷ ɑrt]	(n.) 新古典藝術　*revival (n.) 復甦；復興

Jacques-Louis David was a highly influential French painter of Neoclassical Art.
雅克-路易・大衛為新古典藝術中，具有高度影響力的法國畫家。

08	**Romantic Art** [rəˋmæntɪk ɑrt]	(n.) 浪漫派藝術　*romantic (n.) 浪漫主義者　*Symbolism (n.) 象徵主義

One of the most important subjects in **Romantic Art** was nature.
浪漫派藝術中最重要的主題之一為自然。

09	**etching** [ˋɛtʃɪŋ]	(n.) 蝕刻版畫　*woodcut (n.) 木刻；木版畫　*tempera (n.) 蛋彩畫

Etchings are pictures printed from a metal plate that are created through the use of acid. 蝕刻畫是以強酸腐蝕過的金屬板所印製的圖畫。

10	**exaggeration** [ɪg͵zædʒəˋreʃən]	(n.) 誇張　*without exaggeration 毫不誇張　*hyperbole (n.) 誇飾法

Exaggeration of physical characteristics was one element of Romantic Art. 浪漫派藝術的其中一個要素為身體特徵的誇大。

chiaroscuro

contortion

Baroque Art

Rococo Art

evoke
[ˈɪvok]

喚起；引起
Baroque Art often **evokes** an emotional and dramatic feeling in the viewer.
巴洛克藝術常會引起觀眾情感與激情上的感受。

revive
[rɪˈvaɪv]

復興；甦醒
Neoclassical Art **revived** classical forms and subjects.
新古典藝術復興了古典的形式與主題。

contort

扭曲
The artist **contorted** the statue into a grotesque shape.
藝術家將雕像扭曲成一種怪異的形狀。

depict

描繪
People are **depicted** in ways that are not real in Romantic Art.
浪漫派藝術中，人類以失真的方式受到描繪。

etch

蝕刻
Artists **etch** works by using acid. 藝術家利用酸來蝕刻作品。

contrast

對比
Many artists **contrast** light with dark shades in their work.
許多藝術家在作品中以陰影來對比出光線。

Art Movements
藝術運動

Classical Art 古典藝術	**Realism** 寫實主義
Gothic Art 哥德式藝術	**Impressionism** 印象主義
Renaissance Art 文藝復興藝術	**Expressionism** 表現主義
Baroque Art 巴洛克藝術	**Abstract Art** 抽象主義
Rococo Art 洛可可藝術	**Cubism** 立體主義
Neoclassical Art 新古典藝術	**Dadaism** 達達主義
Romantic Art 浪漫派藝術	**Pop Art** 普普藝術

Neoclassical Art

Romantic Art

Impressionism

Abstract Art

Checkup

A

Write | 請依提示寫出正確的英文單字和片語。

1	巴洛克藝術 _____	9	蝕刻畫 _____
2	明暗對照法 _____	10	誇張 _____
3	風格怪異的 _____	11	喚起；引起 _____
4	扭曲 (n.) _____	12	復興；甦醒 _____
5	洛可可藝術 _____	13	扭曲 (v.) _____
6	淡彩 _____	14	描繪 _____
7	新古典藝術 _____	15	蝕刻 _____
8	浪漫派藝術 _____	16	使……對比 _____

B

Complete the Sentences | 請在空格中填入最適當的答案，並視情況做適當的變化。

Rococo Art	etching	exaggeration	contortion	pastel
Romantic Art	grotesque	Neoclassical Art	Baroque Art	chiaroscuro

1 _____ _____ is known for its dramatic contrast of light and shade.
巴洛克藝術以誇張的光影對比而聞名。

2 Baroque Art may seem very dramatic and _____ at first.
巴洛克藝術起初看似誇張而怪異。

3 The _____ of bodies created many of the grotesque statues.
身體的扭曲創造出許多怪異的雕像。

4 _____ _____ is characterized by its decorative and lighthearted look that uses pastel colors. 洛可可藝術以它的裝飾性及淡彩繪成的輕鬆愉快畫面為特色。

5 _____ are colors that appear both soft and pale.
淡彩為柔和而淡的顏色。

6 One of the most important subjects in _____ _____ was nature.
浪漫派藝術中最重要的主題之一為自然。

7 _____ are pictures printed from a metal plate that are created through the use of acid. 蝕刻畫是以強酸腐蝕過的金屬板所印製的圖畫。

8 _____ of physical characteristics was one element of Romantic Art.
浪漫派藝術的其中一個要素為身體特徵的誇大。

C

Read and Choose | 閱讀下列句子，並且選出最適當的答案。

1 Baroque Art often (etches | evokes) an emotional and dramatic feeling in the viewer.

2 Artists (etch | evoke) works by using acid.

3 Neoclassical Art (revived | reviewed) classical forms and subjects.

4 The artist (contrasted | contorted) the statue into a grotesque shape.

Look, Read, and Write | 看圖並且依照提示，在空格中填入正確答案。

 1 ▸ the use of areas of light and darkness in a painting

_____

 3 ▸ a pale or light color

_____

 2 ▸ the act of twisting something into an unusual shape

_____

 4 ▸ a picture made by putting ink on an etched piece of metal and then pressing paper against the metal

_____

Read and Answer | 閱讀並且回答下列問題。 116

From Baroque to Realism

From around the late sixteenth century to the early eighteenth century, there was a new type of art in Europe. It was called Baroque. There were Baroque artists in every European country. So they all had slightly different styles. But there were many similarities that Baroque artists shared.

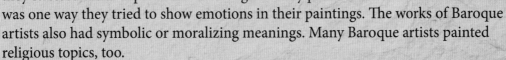

For one, there were often contrasts between light and dark in Baroque paintings. The artists also focused on movement. And they stressed facial expressions in the figures they painted. This was one way they tried to show emotions in their paintings. The works of Baroque artists also had symbolic or moralizing meanings. Many Baroque artists painted religious topics, too.

One very important characteristic was that Baroque artists were realists. So they painted their subjects as realistically as possible. They knew about perspective. So they could show things such as size and distance. They were also able to use the space in their paintings very well. This ability made many Baroque artists quite famous. Today, people still admire the works of artists such as El Greco, Rembrandt, and Caravaggio.

What is NOT true?

1 The Baroque Period ended during the seventeenth century.
2 Baroque paintings have contrasts between light and dark.
3 Many Baroque paintings showed people's emotions.
4 El Greco and Rembrandt were two Baroque artists.

A World of Music 音樂的世界

Key Words 🔊 117

01	**bass clef** [ˋbes klɛf]	*(n.)* 低音譜號 The **bass clef** is also known as the F clef. 低音譜號又以 F 譜號為人所知。
02	**treble clef** [ˋtrɛbḷ klɛf]	*(n.)* 高音譜號 The **treble clef** is also called the G clef. 高音譜號又稱為 G 譜號。
03	**staff** [stæf]	*(n.)* 五線譜（ **= stave** ）　*numbered musical notation 簡譜 Musical notes are placed on lines or between the lines of a **staff**. 音符位於五線譜的線上或線間。
04	**grand staff** [grænd stæf]	*(n.)* 大譜表　*Gongche notation 工尺譜（中國民間傳統記譜法之一） A **grand staff** has two staves, a treble clef staff and a bass clef staff. 大譜表上有兩個五線譜，分別是高音譜與低音譜。
05	**time signature** [taɪm ˋsɪgnətʃɚ]	*(n.)* 拍號（ **= measure/meter signature** ）　*time (n.) 節拍（ = beat ） 　*rhythm (n.) 節奏 The **time signature** shows how many beats are in each measure. 拍號顯示每個小節有幾拍。
06	**scale** [skel]	*(n.)* 音階　*sharp (n.) 升記號　*flat (n.) 降記號 A **scale** is a fixed sequence of musical notes moving from low to high or high to low. 音階為從低到高或從高到低的固定音符順序。
07	**chord** [kɔrd]	*(n.)* 和弦　*to strike a chord 引起共鳴；扣動心弦　*harmony (n.) 和聲 When you play a **chord**, you play several notes at a time. 當你彈奏和弦就是一次彈奏多個音。
08	**triad** [ˋtraɪəd]	*(n.)* 三和弦　*root note 根音　*major/minor triads 大／小三和弦 Three-note chords, also called **triads**, are common in popular music. 三和弦又稱為 triads，在流行音樂中很常見。
09	**counterpoint** [ˋkaʊntɚˌpɔɪnt]	*(n.)* 對位法　*fugue (n.) 賦格曲　*canon (n.) 卡農曲 A characteristic of Baroque music is **counterpoint**. 巴洛克音樂的一個特色為對位法。
10	**string quartet** [strɪŋ kwɔrˋtɛt]	*(n.)* 弦樂四重奏　*string/wind instrument 弦／管樂器 　*percussion (n.) 打擊樂器 A **string quartet** usually consists of a viola, a cello, and two violins. 弦樂四重奏通常包含了一把中提琴、一把大提琴還有兩把小提琴。

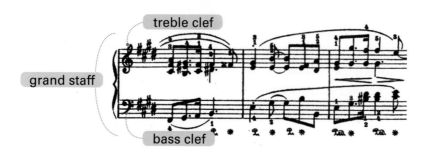

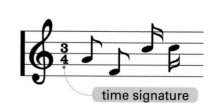

time signature

🔊 118

distinguish 區別
[dɪˈstɪŋgwɪʃ]
Bach was **distinguished** for the passionate spirit of his church music.
巴哈以其教堂音樂中的慷慨激昂精神為人所熟知。

involve 包括；包含
Church music typically **involves** vocal soloists, a choir, and an organ or other instruments. 教堂音樂通常包括獨唱者、唱詩班與一把風琴或是其他樂器。

follow 跟隨
Follow the meter signature to play at the right speed.
跟著拍號便能以正確的速度演奏。

pay attention to 留意
Pay attention to the meter signature to play at the right speed.
留意拍號便能以正確的速度演奏。

Word Families 🔊 119

oratorio 清唱劇（以宗教為主題）
[ˌɔrəˈtorɪo]
An oratorio is a long piece of music with a religious theme and includes an orchestra, a choir, and soloists.
清唱劇為以宗教為題的長篇樂曲，其中有管弦樂團、唱詩班與獨唱者。

cantata 康塔塔（短篇清唱劇）
A cantata is a short musical work for singers and instruments.
康塔塔是為歌唱家與樂器所作的短篇音樂劇。

sonata 奏鳴曲
Sonatas generally have three sections: the exposition, the development, and the recapitulation. 奏鳴曲通常分為三部分，分別為呈示部、發展部與再現部。

Musical Instructions 音樂指導

Largo（= very slow）最緩板
Adagio（= slow）慢板／柔版
Andante（= moderate）行板
Moderato（= medium）中板
Allegro（= fast）快板
Presto（= very fast）急板
Prestissimo（= as fast as you can go）最急板

Notes and Rests 音符與休止符

whole note 全音符
whole rest 全休止符
half note 二分音符
half rest 二分休止符
quarter note 四分音符
quarter rest 四分休止符
eighth note 八分音符
eighth rest 八分休止符

Checkup

Write | 請依提示寫出正確的英文單字和片語。

1	低音譜號	_____	9	對位法	_____
2	高音譜號	_____	10	弦樂四重奏	_____
3	五線譜	_____	11	區別	_____
4	大譜表	_____	12	包括；包含	_____
5	拍號	_____	13	跟隨	_____
6	音階	_____	14	留意	_____
7	和弦	_____	15	清唱劇	_____
8	三和弦	_____	16	奏鳴曲	_____

B

Complete the Sentences | 請在空格中填入最適當的答案，並視情況做適當的變化。

triad	time signature	staff	grand staff	bass clef
chord	counterpoint	scale	string quartet	treble clef

1 Musical notes are placed on lines or between the lines of a _____.
   音符位於五線譜的線上或線間。

2 A _____ _____ has two staves, a treble clef staff and a bass clef staff.
   大譜表上有兩個五線譜，分別是高音譜與低音譜。

3 The _____ _____ shows how many beats are in each measure.
   拍號顯示每個小節有幾拍。

4 A _____ is a fixed sequence of musical notes moving from low to high or high to low. 音階為從低到高或從高到低的固定音符順序。

5 When you play a _____, you play several notes at a time.
   當你彈奏和弦就是一次彈奏多個音。

6 Three-note chords, also called _____, are common in popular music.
   三和弦在流行音樂中很常見。

7 A characteristic of Baroque music is _____.
   巴洛克音樂的一個特色為對位法。

8 A _____ _____ usually consists of a viola, a cello, and two violins.
   弦樂四重奏通常包含了一把中提琴、一把大提琴還有兩把小提琴。

C

Read and Choose | 閱讀下列句子，並且選出最適當的答案。

1 Bach was (distinguished | composed) for the passionate spirit of his church music.

2 Church music typically (involves | places) vocal soloists, a choir, and an organ or other instruments.

3 (Take | Pay) attention to the meter signature to play at the right speed.

4 (Sonatas | Cantatas) generally have three sections: the exposition, the development, and the recapitulation.

D

Look, Read, and Write | 看圖並且依照提示，在空格中填入正確答案。

1  ▸ a sign on a stave which shows that the notes are above middle C

_____

3  ▸ a set of notes played or sung in order, going up or down

_____

2  ▸ a sign on a stave which shows that the notes are below middle C

_____

4  ▸ a group of four instruments with strings that play together

_____

E

Read and Answer | 閱讀並且回答下列問題。 🔊 120

The Classical Period of Music

The years between 1750 and 1820 saw some of the greatest music ever created. This time is now called the Classical Period of music. Among the composers who wrote during this period were Mozart, Beethoven, Haydn, and Schubert.

Mozart

Beethoven

By 1750, people were getting tired of the Baroque Period. So they worked on new forms of music. Thus arose the Classical Period. It has several important characteristics. For one, the mood of the music often changed. In a single piece of music, there was not just one mood anymore. Instead, the mood could suddenly change anytime during a piece. The same was true of the rhythm of the music. Music from this period followed several different rhythmic patterns. There were often sudden pauses. Or the music would suddenly go from being very slow to very fast or from very soft to very loud.

Also, music from the Classical Period has beautiful melodies. The works the composers created are typically easy to remember. Of course, they are still sophisticated works. But the ease with which people can remember them has helped increase their popularity. Even today, the works of composers from this period are among the most popular of all classical music.

Fill in the blanks.

1   The Classical Period of music lasted from _____ to 1820.
2   The _____ Period came right before the Classical Period.
3   The mood of the music during the Classical Period could often _____ suddenly.
4   Many compositions from the Classical Period are _____ to remember.

Review Test 6

A

Write | 請依提示寫出正確的英文單字和片語。

1 韻文 _____		11 十四行詩 _____
2 散文 _____		12 強化；加深 _____
3 主動語氣 _____		13 複句 _____
4 被動語氣 _____		14 拖延；延期 p_____
5 急忙 _____		15 傳達 _____
6 聚集 _____		16 受……的啟發 _____
7 風格怪異的 _____		17 奉獻 _____
8 扭曲 (n.) _____		18 喚起；引起 _____
9 音階 _____		19 復興；甦醒 _____
10 和弦 _____		20 對位法 _____

B

Choose the Correct Word | 請選出與鋪底字意思相近的答案。

1 Many classical artists strived to create ideal works of art.
   a. tried   b. represented   c. honored

2 Never put off till tomorrow what you can do today.
   a. analyze   b. postpone   c. evoke

3 English has borrowed words from many different languages.
   a. revived   b. conveyed   c. taken

4 People are depicted in ways that are not real in Romantic Art.
   a. influenced   b. described   c. composed

C

Complete the Sentences | 請在空格中填入最適當的答案，並視情況做適當的變化。

indeed	couplet	root	order

1 A _____ consists of two lines that rhyme with one another.
   一組對句由互相押韻的兩個句子所組成。

2 Many words in English have Greek or Latin _____.
   英文中有許多字擁有希臘或拉丁的字根。

3 A friend in need is a friend _____. 患難見真情。

4 There were three classical _____ in ancient Greek architecture.
   古希臘建築有三大古典類型。

140

Index

ANSWERS
AND
TRANSLATIONS

A

1 producer   2 consumer   3 investor
4 entrepreneur   5 marketplace   6 distribution
7 consumption   8 opportunity cost   9 demand
10 supply   11 produce   12 reap   13 inflation
14 deflation   15 scarcity   16 Gross Domestic Product

B

1 Entrepreneurs   2 investor   3 marketplace
4 Distribution   5 consumption   6 opportunity cost
7 supply   8 demand

C

1 manufacture   2 consume   3 distributed
4 Inflation

D

1 producer   2 consumer   3 entrepreneur
4 opportunity cost

E 基礎經濟

　　在自由市場經濟中，由公司來決定生產的產品與數量，然而，他們在乎的是獲利，便不願生產過多或過少，只想生產剛好的數量。因此，他們會特別留意供需法則。

　　該法則說明了當產品供不應求時，價格則會上漲。若是供過於求的話，價格則會下跌。公司多想取中間值，他們要供跟求都剛剛好。

　　不過公司需要考慮進去的還有其他因素。一旦產品生產，他們就要送到市場上，民眾才能購買產品，這就稱為物流，多以貨車、火車、船隻與飛機來運輸。若無有效的物流系統，即使是受歡迎的產品都會銷售不佳。

　　產品一旦上市，就必須受到使用，也就是讓民眾買走它們。購買的數量取決於許多事，如供給與需求，價格也是另一個重要的因素。

以下何者為「是」？請在空格中填入「T」或「F」。
1 公司關心是否獲取利潤。 (T)
2 供需法則在經濟面上很重要。 (T)
3 供過於求通常會造成價格上漲。 (F)
4 物流就是將產品賣給客戶。 (F)

A

1 topographic map   2 contour   3 Arctic Circle
4 Antarctic Circle   5 Tropic of Cancer
6 Tropic of Capricorn   7 absolute location
8 relative location   9 elevation   10 desertification
11 denote   12 identify   13 utilize   14 line of latitude
15 line of longitude   16 equator

B

1 topographic map   2 Tropic of Cancer
3 Tropic of Capricorn   4 Antarctic Circle
5 Arctic Circle   6 Relative location
7 absolute location   8 elevation

C

1 mark   2 utilize   3 identified   4 Cancer

D

1 contour   2 Arctic Circle   3 absolute location
4 desertification

E 地球的氣候區

　　地球上總共有三大氣候區，分別是熱帶、溫帶與寒帶氣候區。

　　熱帶氣候區位於赤道附近，基本上，就在北回歸線與南回歸線之間。熱帶氣候區大致上全年氣候炎熱，熱帶氣候區中的許多地方氣候潮濕，但又不全然是如此。

　　溫帶氣候區則是三大氣候區中最大的區域。其中一個溫帶氣候區位於北回歸線與北極圈之間，另一個則在南回歸線與南極圈之間。全球多數人口居住於溫帶氣候區。溫帶氣候區既不過於炎熱也不過於寒冷，終年都能感受四季的變化。這些區域的天氣通常不會太過極端。

　　寒帶氣候區則位於北極圈與南極圈。這些地區的天氣終年酷寒，鮮少有人與動物居住在此地。

填空
1 地球上總共有三大氣候區，分別是熱帶、溫帶與寒帶氣候區。 (temperate)
2 熱帶區的氣候多為炎熱而潮濕。 (wet)
3 其中一個溫帶地區位於南回歸線與南極圈之間。 (Antarctic Circle)
4 鮮少有人與動物居住在極地區。 (Few)

A

1 Ice Age   2 Stone Age   3 Bronze Age   4 Iron Age
5 covenant   6 polytheism   7 monotheism
8 Hebrew   9 Code of Hammurabi   10 Fertile Crescent
11 domesticate   12 tame   13 worship   14 practice
15 wander   16 establish

B

1 New Stone Age   2 Bronze Age   3 Fertile Crescent
4 monotheism   5 polytheism
6 Code of Hammurabi   7 Hebrew   8 covenant

C

1 domesticate   2 tamed   3 wandered   4 Old

D

1 Ice Age   2 Iron Age   3 polytheism   4 monotheism

E 以色列的故事

　　中東以前有許多不同的宗教，人們常向許多神祇祈求，有山神、河神、湖神與海神，各種神都有。然而，有一個宗教開始只崇拜單一神祇。

　　有一位叫做亞伯蘭的男子，據說他是諾亞與亞當的後裔。他住在一處稱做迦南的地方，神明耶和華在那裡和亞伯蘭立下約定。耶和華承諾給他很多後代子孫，並表示要將他現居之處永遠贈與他們，代價就是亞伯蘭只能崇拜耶和華。亞伯蘭答應了，並將名字改成了亞伯拉罕，意思就是「諸國之父」。

　　亞伯拉罕的後裔與他的兒子以撒都成了以色列人。以撒與他的妻子利百加不久後生下一對雙胞胎，取名為雅各與以掃。雅各的子孫創立了以色列的 12 支派，將城市耶路撒冷變成政治權力的樞紐。他們強盛了一段時期，後來為埃及降服且奴役。摩西後來就是在埃及解放以色列人，讓他們在多年後又重回應許之地。

以下何者為非？（1）
1 多數中東人僅崇拜唯一神祇。
2 亞伯蘭只信仰耶和華。
3 以撒是亞伯拉罕的兒子。
4 以色列人將耶路撒冷作為首都。

Unit
04 ● Asian Civilizations (p. 24)

A
1 Indus Valley civilization 2 reincarnation 3 Veda
4 raja 5 dynasty 6 Middle Kingdom 7 pictograph
8 tsar 9 warlord 10 Shinto 11 reincarnate
12 be restricted to 13 centralize 14 unify / unite
15 shogun 16 samurai

B
1 Indus Valley 2 reincarnation 3 raja 4 dynasty
5 Middle Kingdom 6 Warlords 7 pictographs
8 czar

C
1 reincarnated 2 restricted 3 centralized
4 unified

D
1 Indus Valley civilization 2 reincarnation 3 Veda
4 Shinto

E 早期的印度河文明
　　古老的文明在印度河流域一處建立，即今日的印度與巴基斯坦，此文明又稱作哈拉帕文明，大約從西元前 2500 年持續到西元前 1500 年。
　　印度河流域文明的人們大多耕種土地，所以他們曉得農業的訣竅，這使他們免於流浪。不過他們不只是農夫，他們還建造了多個城市。考古學家發現多處曾是城市的遺跡，他們造了宮殿、廟宇、浴場與其他建物。他們還將城市規劃成棋盤狀，以方格的形狀呈現。
　　印度河流域的人民在其他方面也相當進步，他們製陶、以銅與青銅製作物品，甚至還有他們自己的一套書寫系統。此系統是依據象形文字而來，但目前尚未得以翻譯。
　　印度河流域是世界上最早出現文明的地方之一，有關此地的資訊甚少，但研究學者在此地的知識上每年都有所斬獲。

閱讀並回答下列問題。
1 印度河流域的文明叫做什麼？
　(The Indus Valley civilization. The Harappan civilization.)
2 印度河流域中的城市裡有什麼？
　(Palaces, temples, baths, and other buildings.)
3 印度河流域中的人民以什麼製作器具？
　(Copper and bronze.)
4 印度河流域中的人民使用何種類型的書寫系統？
　(One based on pictographs.)

Unit
05 ● Ancient Greek and Roman Civilizations (p .28)

A
1 Minoan 2 Mycenaean 3 Phoenician 4 city-state
5 acropolis 6 Hellenistic 7 monarchy 8 oligarchy
9 Pax Romana 10 Edict of Milan 11 reign / rule
12 oppress 13 confer 14 consul 15 tyrant
16 dictator

B
1 Mycenaeans 2 Minoans 3 city-states
4 acropolis 5 Hellenistic 6 monarchy 7 oligarchy
8 Pax Romana

C
1 reigned 2 oppressed 3 granted 4 spread

D
1 Phoenician 2 monarchy 3 acropolis
4 Edict of Milan

E 羅馬：從共和國到帝國
　　根據傳說，羅繆勒斯與雷摩斯兄弟倆於西元前 753 年建立了羅馬。羅馬逐漸強盛壯大，直到西元前 620 年伊特魯里亞人攻取此國。伊特魯里亞人統治羅馬有 111 年之久。在西元前 509 年時，羅馬人推翻國王驕傲者塔克文，重獲自由。
　　羅馬人建立一種稱為共和國的新政府。在此種體制之下，他們選出一小群人作為領袖，稱為羅馬貴族，多達 300 人可受選進入元老院。羅馬共和國體制持續有 500 年之久。
　　羅馬開始越來越強盛，很快就控制了整個義大利半島。它與迦太基的布匿戰爭從西元前 264 年打到了西元前 146 年，羅馬贏得了勝利，成為整個地中海的霸主。羅馬共和國很快地龐大起來，但也變得腐敗。一名叫做尤利烏斯・凱薩的將軍挑戰元老院的權威，並成為了一位獨裁者，然而他卻在西元前 44 年遭到謀殺，而共和國則是由三位領袖統治。他們互相鬥爭，最後由屋大維贏得勝利，成為首位羅馬的皇帝。共和國已不復存在，成為了羅馬帝國。

* Etruscan 伊特魯里亞人   overthrow 推翻

以下何者為「是」？請在空格中填入「T」或「F」。
1 羅馬於西元前 753 年被伊特魯里亞人征服。（F）
2 羅馬元老院有 300 位成員。（T）
3 羅馬與迦太基打布匿戰爭。（T）
4 尤利烏斯・凱薩成為首位羅馬皇帝。（F）

Review Test 1

A
1 distribution 2 consumption 3 topographic map
4 Antarctic Circle 5 Ice Age 6 Bronze Age
7 Indus Valley civilization 8 dynasty 9 Hellenistic
10 oligarchy 11 manufacture 12 scarcity
13 denote 14 utilize 15 domesticate
16 Code of Hammurabi 17 reincarnate
18 be restricted to 19 reign / rule 20 oppress

B
1 (b) 2 (a) 3 (b) 4 (c)

C
1 demand 2 absolute location 3 monotheism
4 pictographs

A

1 caravan 2 Bedouin 3 Muhammad 4 prophet
5 Ramadan 6 Mecca 7 caliph 8 bazaar
9 Ottoman Empire 10 sultan 11 flourish
12 prohibit 13 dedicate / devote 14 reveal
15 decline 16 Muslim

B

1 caravan 2 Bedouins 3 Mecca 4 prophet
5 caliph 6 bazaar 7 Ottoman Empire 8 sultan

C

1 devoted 2 forbidden 3 dedicated 4 revealed

D

1 caravan 2 Ramadan 3 prophet 4 Hajj

E 伊斯蘭教的傳播

　　伊斯蘭教的創立者穆罕默德於 632 年辭世。他去世時,穆斯林還很少,也沒有什麼土地。穆罕默德去世後,伊斯蘭教開始快速傳播。

　　穆罕默德辭世不久後,穆斯林領袖們選出哈里發來治理伊斯蘭教社會。在最初的四位哈里發的統治下(從 632 年到 661 年),伊斯蘭教的傳播普及整個阿拉伯半島。伊斯蘭教在 661 年攻下中東的波斯與非洲近東的埃及。伍邁葉王朝從 661 年 750 年統治整個伊斯蘭世界,將伊斯蘭教傳播至整個北非。一個伊斯蘭教的軍隊在 711 年時越過地中海,進入了西班牙,並在短短幾年內就佔領了西班牙。穆斯林向北走進入了法國,不過鐵鎚查理在 732 年時,於圖爾附近擊潰了伊斯蘭教的軍隊,停止了穆斯林的北征。

　　此時,穆斯林無法攻下東邊的拜占庭帝國,多次前往君士坦丁堡也總是敗下陣來。然而後來鄂圖曼帝國從東方崛起,威脅到了拜占庭帝國。到了 15 世紀,拜占庭帝國衰弱不堪,鄂圖曼人於 1453 年征服了他們。他們將君士坦丁堡定為首都,他們在那裡統治著一個龐大的伊斯蘭教帝國到 20 世紀。

* the reigns of first four caliphs
　　最初的四大哈里發(阿布・伯克爾、歐麥爾、奧斯曼、阿里)

填空

1 伊斯蘭教的創立者是穆罕默德。(Muhammad)
2 最初的四位哈里發從 632 年統治到 661 年。(632)
3 鐵鎚查理於杜爾附近擊潰了穆斯林。
　(Charles Martel)
4 鄂圖曼帝國擊敗了拜占庭帝國。(Ottoman)

A

1 feudalism 2 Catholic Church 3 Magna Carta
4 Black Death 5 guild 6 Reformation
7 Counter-Reformation 8 Protestant 9 Inquisition
10 execution 11 infect 12 clash 13 reform
14 spilt 15 declare 16 bishop

B

1 Feudalism 2 Catholic Church 3 Guilds
4 Inquisition 5 Reformation 6 Counter-Reformation
7 Protestants 8 executions

C

1 infected 2 clashed 3 reform 4 declared

D

1 Magna Carta 2 Black Death 3 Reformation
4 monastery

E 宗教改革

　　數個世紀以來,天主教會掌管了歐洲的生活。但教會裡許多的神父腐敗不堪,對利益與優沃生活的關注,遠勝過宗教。有些人對此感到不滿,其中一位就是馬丁・路德。 1517 年時,他在德國威登堡的教堂門上發表了 95 條有關他對教會不滿的論綱,這就是新教徒宗教改革的開始。

　　路德起初僅想整頓羅馬教會,並無意自立門戶。但教會視他為異教徒並開除了他。此舉造成了德國的宗教分裂,許多德國人對教會心生不滿,卻依舊當基督教徒。很快地,宗教改革如火如荼地展開,在德國,天主教徒與基督教徒相互攻擊。直到 1555 年,該年,奧格斯堡宗教合約讓每位德國貴族可以選擇成為天主教徒或新教徒。

　　就當德國遭遇問題的同一時間,宗教改革也很快地橫掃整個歐洲。像是約翰・喀爾文和烏利希・慈運理也各自主導反抗教會。新教徒教派很快便成立了。有路德教派、長老教派、浸信會,還有喀爾文教派。而在英國,當國王亨利八世脫離羅馬天主教會時,英國還創立了英國國教派。

*heretic 異教徒　excommunicate 開除　sect 宗派

以下何者為非? (2)

1 馬丁・路德開始新教徒的宗教改革。
2 馬丁・路德終身為天主教徒。
3 約翰・喀爾文是宗教改革的另一位領袖。
4 英國國教會是在英國創立的。

Unit 08 • The Enlightenment and the French Revolution (p.42)

A

1 Enlightenment 2 rationalism 3 geocentric
4 heliocentric 5 divine right
6 French Revolution 7 Estates-General 8 Bastille
9 Napoleon 10 Waterloo 11 execute 12 behead
13 overcome 14 seize 15 exile 16 guillotine

B

1 Enlightenment 2 rationalism 3 heliocentric
4 divine right 5 French Revolution
6 Estates-General 7 Napoleon 8 Waterloo

C

1 beheaded 2 executed 3 seized 4 exiled

D

1 geocentric 2 heliocentric 3 divine right
4 Bastille

E 法國大革命

　　法國 18 世紀時，生活對大部分人民來說是困苦的。法國的統治者是國王，他藉由神授君權來掌權，也就是神選擇了國王來治理國家。這表示國王可以為所欲為。法國還有主掌龐大權力的貴族，大多神職人員也都生活富裕，而其他人則是生活困苦。他們貧苦，沒有土地也沒有自由。

　　在 1780 年間，世界正在改變。美國人贏得革命英國的勝利，獲得自由。法國人也想要如此。路易十六與妻子瑪麗·安東尼是暴虐的統治者，他們對人民課以重稅，人民則對貧苦的生活感到厭倦。因此，他們在 1789 年的 7 月 14 日起義，猛烈攻擊位於巴黎的巴士底監獄。他們解放犯人，奪取該地的武器，法國大革命已揭開序幕。

　　法國大革命非常激進暴力，路易十六在革命期間遭到斬首，還有更多的貴族與教士遭到殺害，數千人死於革命期間。最後，君主政體崩解，但法國卻無如人民所盼那樣成為民主國家。反而是由一名將軍—— 拿破崙·波拿巴成為法國君王。他帶領法國與許多歐洲國家作戰，一直到他在 1815 年遭到擊敗為止。

閱讀並回答下列問題。
1 法國哪兩種人的生活富足？
　(Nobles and the clergy.)
2 法國大革命開始時，由誰統治法國？
　(King Louis XVI and Marie Antoinette.)
3 法國大革命何時開始？ (July 14, 1789.)
4 法國大革命結束後由誰統治法國？
　(Napoleon Bonaparte.)

Unit 09 • The Age of Imperialism (p.46)

A

1 imperialism 2 nationalism 3 Great Power
4 rivalry 5 alliance 6 armistice
7 Russian Revolution 8 communism 9 civil war
10 totalitarianism 11 take control of 12 adopt
13 modernize 14 tyrannize 15 oppress
16 confederation

B

1 Imperialism 2 Nationalism 3 Great Powers
4 rivalries 5 alliances 6 armistice
7 Russian Revolution 8 civil war

C

1 took 2 taken 3 adopt 4 tyrannized

D

1 armistice 2 civil war 3 communism
4 totalitarianism

E 世界大戰

　　幾個世紀以來，歐洲國家互相征戰。但從 1914 年到 1918 年出現了一種截然不同戰爭型態，也就是世界大戰。當時的人民將之稱為世界大戰，也就是後來的第一次世界大戰。人民剛開始以為這僅是另一場戰爭，當戰爭結束時，數百萬人死亡，許多人被戰爭的屠殺給嚇壞了。

　　第一次世界大戰開始前，許多歐洲國家相互結盟，若其他國家遭遇到麻煩，承諾要彼此保護。在 1914 年的 6 月 28 日，奧匈帝國的費迪南大公於薩拉耶佛遭到暗殺，奧地利人很快就向塞爾維亞宣戰。但由於不同的聯盟關係，原本小型的戰爭轉變成大規模的戰爭。由德國、奧匈帝國、鄂圖曼帝國主導的同盟國，還有由英國、法國、俄國領導的協約國各據一方。

　　德國人迅速地偷襲了法國，卻無法再前進，雙方都僵持不下，於是開始了塹壕戰。雙方在這四年來都成功殺害許多士兵，坦克車與飛機也首次被用在作戰上，當然也有化學武器。這場戰爭最後終於是結束了，卻沒有真正結束掉戰爭。大概 20 年後又發生了第二次世界大戰，這一次的戰爭比第一次世界戰爭來的更加慘烈。

* horrify 驚嚇 carnage 大屠殺 trench warfare 塹壕戰

以下何者為「是」？請在空格中填入「T」或「F」。
1 第一次世界大戰死了很少人。 (F)
2 費迪南大公是德國人。 (F)
3 英國是協約國的成員。 (T)
4 首台坦克車用於第一次世界大戰。 (T)

A

1 independence   2 NATO   3 Warsaw Pact
4 arms race   5 civil disobedience   6 anti-Semitism
7 apartheid   8 refugee   9 globalization
10 terrorism   11 suppress   12 convince
13 have a rival with   14 terrorize   15 genocide
16 martial law

B

1 independence   2 Warsaw Pact   3 arms race
4 civil disobedience   5 Anti-Semitism
6 Refugees   7 Globalization   8 Terrorism

C

1 suppressed   2 convince   3 raced   4 terrorize

D

1 NATO   2 civil disobedience   3 apartheid
4 Holocaust

E 全球化

　　第二次世界大戰後，世界大幅地轉變，而此多歸因於新的科技。像是噴射機的研發，增進人民旅行的速度。電信通訊也有所進步，電腦與網路的發明，使人與人的聯繫變得更加簡單。

　　全球化擴展開來，世界成了一個更小的地方。在過去，一個國家所發生的事很少會影響到其他國家，或是需要很久的時間之後影響才會發酵。不過現在的世界已經不一樣了，拜全球化之賜，一個地方所發生之事能影響周遭。

　　多虧有全球化，人們現在能更便利地與其他國家的人做生意。當你來到超市，能見到不同國家的各種產品。

　　這些都是因為全球化，近來人們也聽聞越來越多有關其他國家的資訊，這讓人們對其他國家有更深入的了解。在全球化的時代，還沒有發生任何的世界大戰，世界變得更加豐富。全球化對世界當然是有益的。

填空

1 第二次世界大戰後有更多新科技的研發。
(World War II)
2 世界因全球化而變的更加小。 (world)
3 近來與其他國家的人做生意變的更加簡單。 (easier)
4 自全球化以來，世界變的更加豐富。 (richer)

Review Test 2

A

1 caravan   2 prophet   3 Reformation   4 Protestant
5 Enlightenment   6 Bastille   7 imperialism
8 civil war   9 refugee   10 globalization
11 prohibit   12 dedicate / devote   13 execution
14 Inquisition   15 behead   16 banish   17 oppress
18 take over   19 have a rival with   20 persuade

B

1 (a)   2 (b)   3 (a)   4 (c)

C

1 prophet   2 Catholic Church   3 French Revolution
4 Great Powers

A

1 taxonomy   2 Monera kingdom
3 Protista kingdom   4 Fungi kingdom
5 Plantae kingdom   6 Animalia kingdom
7 Arthropoda   8 Mollusca   9 classification
10 Chordata   11 be based on   12 come from
13 classify / categorize   14 Annelid
15 Echinodermata   16 Platyhelminthes

B

1 Taxonomy   2 classification   3 Protista   4 Monera
5 Animalia   6 Plantae   7 Arthropoda   8 Chordata

C

1 based   2 classified   3 categorized   4 Protista

D

1 Monera kingdom   2 Fungi kingdom   3 Arthropoda
4 Mollusca

E 生命五界

　　地球上有眾多生物，科學家將所有型態的生物分成五界，每一界都有各自的特色。

　　第一界是原核生物界，當中約有一萬種物種。此界的生物是單細胞的原核生物，包含了各類的細菌與某些藻類。

　　第二界是原生生物界，當中約有 25 萬種物種。此界的生物包含了原生動物與某些種類的海藻。

　　第三界則是真菌界，當中約有十萬種物種。此界中的生物類似植物，但它們不藉光合作用來製造養分。蘑菇為此界的物種。

　　第四界是植物界，當中約有 25 萬種物種。植物、樹木、花朵與灌木叢都為此界中的物種。

　　第五界是動物界，擁有逾一百萬種物種，是最大的界。它是由多細胞的動物所組成的。

以下何者為「是」？請在空格中填入「T」或「F」。
1 生物分成五大界。 (T)
2 原核生物界有 25 萬種物種。 (F)
3 蘑菇屬於真菌界。 (T)
4 植物界物種數量是最多的。 (F)

A

1 genetics   2 chromosome   3 cell division
4 mitosis   5 meiosis   6 dominant   7 recessive
8 mutation   9 natural selection   10 regulate
11 duplicate   12 take place   13 mutate   14 comprise
15 inheritance   16 epithelial tissue

B

1 chromosomes   2 DNA   3 Cell division
4 mitosis   5 meiosis   6 recessive   7 mutation
8 Natural selection

C

1 regulate   2 duplicates   3 mutate   4 comprised

D

1 chromosome   2 DNA   3 dominant gene
4 genetics

E 格萊高爾‧孟德爾

近期的科學家能活用遺傳學，他們能改變植物的基因結構，讓它們生產更多的水果或稻穀，有些甚至還可以抵抗疾病。但遺傳學領域僅有逾一百年的歷史，非常年輕。而它是由一位名叫格萊高爾‧孟德爾的修道士所開始的。

格萊高爾‧孟德爾對園藝很有興趣，尤其喜歡在花園中種植豌豆。在此過程中，他注意到有些豌豆叢有不同的特徵。有些高有些矮，花朵的顏色也不同。還有其他不同之處，想知道原因的他便開始用豌豆做起了實驗。

孟德爾開始為植物進行雜交，由此了解了顯性基因與隱性基因。他創造出擁有不同植物基因的混種。他種植許多代的豌豆並從中學到很多。孟德爾所習得的便是現代遺傳學的基礎。

孟德爾大部分的研究在 1850 年到 1860 年間進行。人們起初忽略他的成果，一直到 20 世紀初人們才開始深入探討他的研究。那時他們才明白他的成果有多麼偉大。

填空

1 格萊高爾‧孟德爾是遺傳學之父。 (genetics)
2 格萊高爾‧孟德爾在豌豆植物上作實驗。 (pea)
3 格萊高爾‧孟德爾學到顯性與隱性基因。 (dominant)
4 格萊高爾‧孟德爾的研究一直到 20 世紀才受到關注。
　(twentieth)

Unit 13 ● Plant Growth (p.64)

A
1 long-day plant　2 short-day plant　3 angiosperm
4 gymnosperm　5 seed leaf　6 self-pollination
7 cross-pollination　8 wind-pollinated
9 animal-pollinated　10 germination
11 self-pollinate　12 cross-pollinate　13 fertilize
14 thrive　15 tropism　16 perennial

B
1 Short-day　2 Angiosperms　3 Gymnosperms
4 seed leaf　5 cross-pollination　6 Wind-pollinated
7 Animal-pollinated　8 germination

C
1 cross-pollinate　2 fertilized　3 thrive
4 phototropism

D
1 long-day plant　2 self-pollination　3 germination
4 annual (plant)

E 授粉與發芽

所有植物必然會繁殖，這讓它們能繁衍後代以長成成熟的植物。植物的繁殖有兩項重要步驟，首先是授粉，第二個則是發芽。

大多植物兼具雄性與雌性生殖器官，然而它們需要彼此接觸，也就是藉由授粉來繁殖。植物的雄蕊必須與雌蕊接觸，而這可藉由多種方式來完成。有時風會將花粉吹至另一處，不過成效不彰，多為像蜜蜂、蝴蝶與其他昆蟲類的動物來替植物授粉。當牠們穿梭於植物間，花粉會沾到身上，所以當牠們停駐在新植物上時，會有些花粉掉落，植物大多是如此授粉。當花粉從雄蕊到雌蕊處，植物便已授粉並能夠開始繁殖。

另一個重要的步驟為發芽。植物種子成型後便會發芽。植物種子剛開始是休眠狀態的，當它們發芽時便回復生氣並開始生長。若情況良好，種子會長成幼苗，成熟，最後成為一株植物。
* dormant 休眠的

以下何者為非？ (4)
1 授粉步驟在發芽之前。
2 大多植物兼具雄性與雌性器官。
3 昆蟲常替植物授粉。
4 形成植物種子就是發芽。

Unit 14 ● Ecosystems (p.68)

A
1 diversity　2 interaction　3 keystone species
4 carbon cycle　5 nitrogen cycle　6 symbiotic
7 parasitic　8 mutual　9 commensalism
10 succession　11 interact　12 circulate　13 undergo
14 take root in　15 parasite　16 mutualism

B
1 Diversity　2 interaction　3 carbon cycle
4 nitrogen cycle　5 Symbiotic　6 Parasitic
7 Mutual　8 succession

C
1 interact　2 circulates　3 undergo　4 root

D
1 keystone species　2 carbon cycle
3 nitrogen cycle　4 commensalism

E 碳循環與氮循環

碳是最重要的元素之一，所有生物都是由碳所構成的。但它不停地改變型態，這稱為碳循環。碳在大氣中最常以二氧化碳的型態出現，這是由一個碳原子加上兩個氧原子而成的化合物。植物吸入二氧化碳並利用它來製造養分，碳也因此成了植物的部分。植物枯萎死亡掩埋後，經過時間也許轉變成了像煤炭或石油的化石燃料。後來人們燃燒這些化石燃料，釋放二氧化碳回到空氣中。

另一個重要的元素是氮，也有氮循環的存在。我們呼吸的空氣大約有百分之八十是氮，它是空氣中最常見的元素。我們對氮的需求不如對氧氣，但它依然相當重要。

土壤中常有氮，而植物從土壤中獲得氮。當人類與動物食用植物時，植物便釋放氮到體內。人類與動物體內的細菌會將氮轉化成身體可用的。等人類與動物死亡並分解後，氮又回到了土壤或是空氣中，便能再次受到利用。

閱讀並回答下列問題。
1 所有生物是由什麼構成的？ (Carbon.)
2 有些植物會轉變為何？ (Fossil fuels.)
3 大氣中的氮佔了多少？ (80%.)
4 能把體內氮轉化成身體可用的為何？ (Bacteria.)

15 • The Human Body and the Immune System (p. 72)

A
1 immune system 2 lymphatic system 3 antibiotic
4 infection 5 contagious 6 epidemic
7 communicable disease 8 vaccination
9 bacterial 10 viral 11 clog 12 communicate
13 immunize 14 paralyze 15 disable 16 antibody

B
1 immune system 2 lymphatic 3 Antibiotics
4 infection 5 contagious 6 bacterial 7 Viral
8 vaccination

C
1 clogged 2 immunize 3 paralyze 4 antibodies

D
1 immune system 2 viral disease 3 epidemic
4 communicable disease

E 免疫系統

　　人體每日都受到細菌、病毒與其他入侵者的侵襲。身體的免疫系統負責對抗這些不速之客，以維持人體的健康。免疫系統是由不同的細胞、組織和器官所組成的。

　　白血球細胞非常重要，它也稱做白血球，活動於淋巴管中。白血球有兩種類型，第一種是噬菌細胞，用來消滅侵略生物。第二種是淋巴細胞，能幫助人體記憶各種侵略生物。如此便能在以後消滅它們。

　　抗原時常侵襲人體，人體因而產生抗體。抗體對抗抗原，若抗體獲勝，它們便會永遠存於體內。這使得未來人體能再次對抗疾病，對於對抗病毒相當有用。

　　人體生來就對某些疾病免疫，這稱為先天性免疫。但也有後天性免疫，發生於當人體辨認出威脅時，自行學會如何對抗病毒。還有多虧了疫苗，民眾能對許多疾病免疫。接種疫苗有助於提升免疫系統的效力。

* phagocyte 噬菌細胞　　lymphocyte 淋巴細胞

以下何者為「是」？請在空格中填入「T」或「F」。
1 免疫系統能讓人生病。 (F)
2 白血球就是紅血球細胞。 (F)
3 人體偶爾會產生抗體。 (T)
4 人通常生來就有先天性免疫。 (T)

Review Test 3

A
1 Arthropoda 2 Mollusca 3 genetics
4 chromosome 5 cross-pollination
6 wind-pollinated 7 carbon cycle 8 nitrogen cycle
9 immune system 10 contagious 11 be based on
12 sort 13 natural selection 14 regulate
15 self-pollinate 16 fertilize 17 commensalism
18 succession 19 infect 20 paralyze

B
1 (c) 2 (b) 3 (a) 4 (a)

C
1 Protista 2 Cell division 3 germination
4 Symbiotic

16 • Earth's Surface (p. 78)

A
1 mantle 2 lithosphere 3 asthenosphere
4 Pangaea 5 plate tectonics 6 Moho
7 seismograph 8 seismic wave 9 focus
10 epicenter 11 drift 12 shift 13 separation
14 collide 15 erupt 16 continental drift

B
1 mantle 2 lithosphere 3 asthenosphere
4 Pangaea 5 seismograph 6 Seismic waves
7 Moho 8 focus

C
1 drifting 2 erupt 3 collide 4 shifting

D
1 lithosphere 2 plate tectonics 3 seismic waves
4 epicenter

E 火山爆發

　　有時火山會突然爆發，噴射出許多灰燼、氣體與熔岩，可能會造成許多人死亡。是什麼造成火山爆發的呢？

　　在地球深處有很大的壓力，地底的溫度也相當高；事實上，溫度高到能將石頭熔化。地底下所熔化的石頭稱為岩漿，岩漿不斷地想往地表上移動。地底下有叫做岩漿庫，是岩漿聚集之處。這些岩漿庫通常在火山下方，最後地下的壓力實在太大，岩漿爆出到地表，造成了火山爆發。當火山爆發，常噴出灰燼與氣體。也可能會噴出岩漿，地表上的岩漿稱為熔岩，它通常由沿著火山邊緣慢慢流下，最後冷卻硬化。

　　爆發的規模取決於壓力釋放的多寡。有些火山壓力較小，釋放少量的熔岩。有些則驟然爆發，它能噴射數哩，將灰燼噴入空氣中。將熔岩與氣體噴得很遠，為最危險的火山爆發類型。維蘇威火山、喀拉喀托火山與聖海倫火山都曾經驟然噴發，造成許多人死亡。

填空
1 地底下熔化的石頭稱為岩漿。 (magma)
2 岩漿聚集之處稱為岩漿庫。
　(magma chambers)
3 火山爆發時會噴發出許多灰燼、氣體與熔岩。 (ash)
4 維蘇威火山、喀拉喀托火山與聖海倫火山是三座驟然噴發，充滿爆發力的火山。 (volcanoes)

17 • Earth's Rocks and Fossils (p.82)

A
1 rock cycle 2 plate boundary 3 composition
4 crystallization 5 metamorphism 6 igneous rock
7 sedimentary rock 8 index fossil 9 fossil record
10 mass extinction 11 crystallize 12 fossilize
13 petrify 14 date 15 go extinct 16 extrusive rock

B
1 plate boundary 2 composition 3 mass extinction
4 Metamorphism 5 Igneous rocks
6 Sedimentary rocks 7 fossil record 8 Index fossils

C
1 crystallizes 2 fossilize 3 date 4 Extrusive

D

1 rock cycle 2 crystallization 3 index fossil
4 mass extinction

E 大滅絕

每隔一段時間，地球上便會發生一次大滅絕。大滅絕發生時，極多物種即刻絕種。科學家發現在地球的歷史上，起碼發生過五次大滅絕。有高達 95% 的地球生物於大滅絕中死亡。最後一次的大滅絕約於六千五百萬年前發生，科學家將之稱為「白堊紀—第三紀滅絕事件」。

六千五百萬年前的地球面貌相當不同，沒有人類，反而是由恐龍主宰陸地與海洋，此時期稱為白堊紀時期。接著突然發生大滅絕，連科學家們也無法確切了解發生何事。但大多數人相信，是行星或是彗星撞上地球造成地球的驟變。大量的塵土飄入空氣中，遮住了太陽。陽光完全透不進地球，造成許多植物枯萎，以植物為食的動物跟著死亡，食用動物為生的動物也死亡。

「白堊紀— 第三紀滅絕事件」造成了全數恐龍絕種。半數的其他物種也跟著死亡。當然也不是所有生物都滅亡了，事實上有些生物還蓬勃地生長。「白堊紀— 第三紀滅絕事件」後，哺乳動物數量大增，最終進化出人類。若無「白堊紀—第三紀滅絕事件」，也許不會有人類的出現。

* Cretaceous Period 白堊紀

以下何者為非？(4)
1 地球上起碼發生了五次大滅絕。
2 「白堊紀—第三紀滅絕事件」約發生於六千五百萬年前。
3 全數恐龍於「白堊紀—第三紀滅絕事件」滅亡。
4 大多數哺乳動物於「白堊紀—第三紀滅絕事件」中死亡。

Unit 18 ● Oceans and Ocean Life (p. 86)

A
1 current 2 ocean floor
3 continental shelf 4 continental slope
5 abyssal plain 6 trench 7 tsunami 8 tide
9 coral reef 10 atoll 11 ebb 12 recede 13 flood
14 trigger 15 devastate 16 plankton

B
1 Currents 2 Ocean floors 3 continental slope
4 abyssal plain 5 trench 6 tide 7 atoll
8 Coral reefs

C
1 ebbs 2 floods 3 trigger 4 devastate

D
1 continental shelf 2 tsunami 3 plankton 4 atoll

E 海洋資源與保護

海洋覆蓋了約 71% 的地表，裡頭有許多資源能使人類獲益。

首先，海洋是魚產和海鮮的重要來源，各國漁夫前往海上捕魚供人食用。然而人們過度捕撈，使得魚貨量減少。因此，人們要多加注意，勿在區域內過度補魚。反而應少量補魚，讓更多魚生長並重新居於海洋中。

海底還有許多珍貴的資源，像是從海底多處地方抽出石油與天然氣。但再次呼籲，人類要注意。湧出的石油有時會大量漏入水中，造成魚類、鳥類與其他海洋生物的死亡。

海底甚至有大量的特定礦產，金、銀與其他貴金屬未來皆可能受到開採。人們還可以利用海洋獲得能量，潮汐發電在未來能提供便宜且充裕的能量。不過我們要好好照茯海洋，它們雖擁有多樣的資源，但也需要我們的保護。

閱讀並回答下列問題。
1 海洋覆蓋了多少的地表？(71%.)
2 近來魚群面臨了何事？(They are becoming smaller.)
3 石油漏入海洋中會發生何事？
(Fish, birds, and other sea creatures can die.)
4 潮汐發電能有何用處？(It could provide cheap and abundant energy in the future.)

Unit 19 ● Matter (p. 90)

A
1 physical property 2 chemical property
3 atomic number 4 atomic mass 5 isotope
6 periodic table 7 plasma 8 reactivity
9 stability 10 litmus paper 11 be composed of
12 react 13 stabilize 14 determine 15 indicate
16 synthesis reaction

B
1 physical properties 2 chemical property
3 atomic mass 4 Isotopes 5 periodic table
6 Plasma 7 reactivity 8 stability

C
1 composed 2 react 3 stabilize 4 indicates

D
1 isotope 2 atomic number 3 periodic table
4 litmus paper

E 原子與原子序

所有原子皆有不同數目的質子、中子與電子。帶正電的質子與不帶電的中子皆位於原子核中，而帶負電的電子則環繞著原子核。質子與中子的數目通常是一樣的，但不是絕對。

每一個元素皆有不同數目的質子，使元素能互異於彼此。一個元素的原子序與質子數目會是相同的。舉例來說，氫僅有一個質子，也就表示原子序為 1，是元素週期表的首個元素。氦為第二個元素，原子序為 2，代表原子核中有兩個質子。

元素有超過一百種，科學家多以原子序來辨識它們。碳為地球上所有生物的根本，它的原子序為 6。氧是個重要的元素，原子序為 8。鐵是另一個重要元素，原子序是 26。金的原子序是 79，鈾則是 92。

以下何者為「是」？請在空格中填入「T」或「F」。
1 中子不帶電。(T)
2 元素的原子序則是電子的數目。(F)
3 氦的原子序為 1。(F)
4 氧有 8 個質子。(T)

A

1 transformation　2 visible light　3 invisible light
4 ultraviolet light　5 infrared light　6 X-ray
7 amplitude　8 electromagnetic
9 electromagnetic wave
10 law of conservation of energy　11 transform
12 diffract　13 generate　14 crest　15 wavelength
16 greenhouse effect

B

1 transformation　2 invisible　3 Ultraviolet light
4 X-rays　5 amplitude　6 electromagnetic
7 Electromagnetic waves　8 law of conservation

C

1 transformed　2 diffract　3 generate　4 radioactive

D

1 visible light　2 infrared light　3 ultraviolet light
4 greenhouse effect

E 能源與環境風險

　　現代生活中，人類仰賴能源生活，多數機器均需要電力才能運作。人類有許多不同製造電力的方法，然而有些方法卻對環境有害。

　　舉例來說，化石燃料為最普遍的能源，包含了煤礦、石油與天然氣。首先，人們需要從地底開挖它們，此舉有時會破壞到環境。不過近來科學家們為此想出更乾淨、更有效的方法，環境便不會受到如此大的傷害。但當人們燃燒化石燃料時，會釋出可能危害到環境的氣體。

　　另一個發電方式是潮汐發電，利用海洋潮汐來產生電力。不過有一些潮汐能源會使許多魚類和海洋生物死亡。水壩也能產生許多乾淨的水力發電的能源，但它需要造湖，改變河道，大幅地改變了環境。

　　核能發電是個強力的能源形式，價格低廉又非常乾淨。不過由於它使用放射性原料而使許多人感到憂心，而且幾間核能發電廠在過去也曾發生過意外。不過近來科技進步，所以許多國家正開始建造更多的核能發電廠。

填空

1 多數機器均需要電力。 (machines)
2 從地底開挖化石燃料有時會傷害到環境。 (environment)
3 潮汐發電是利用海洋潮汐來產生電力。 (tides)
4 核能發電價格低廉又乾淨，不過使用的是放射性材料。
　 (Nuclear)

Review Test 4

A

1 epicenter　2 seismic wave　3 crystallization
4 index fossil　5 atoll　6 continental shelf
7 physical property　8 atomic number
9 transformation　10 electromagnetic wave
11 drift　12 erupt　13 fossilize　14 mass extinction
15 trigger　16 wipe out　17 stabilize
18 be composed of　19 convert　20 generate

B

1 (a)　2 (a)　3 (b)　4 (c)

C

1 lithosphere　2 Metamorphism　3 Ocean floors
4 Isotopes

A

1 factor　2 prime number　3 composite number
4 base　5 exponent　6 power　7 square　8 cube
9 square root　10 perfect square
11 raise to the second power
12 raise to the third power　13 represent
14 be simplified　15 set　16 member

B

1 factors　2 prime number　3 Composite numbers
4 exponent　5 power　6 squared　7 cubed
8 square root

C

1 square　2 cube　3 third　4 simplified

D

1 prime number　2 composite number
3 perfect square　4 member

E 平方根

　　你或許曾將一個數目乘以它自己，像是 2 乘 2 等於 4、4 乘 4 等於 16、5 乘 5 等於 25，還有 10 乘 10 等於 100。當你將一個數字自乘，也就是在將它平方。

　　然而，當你反過來做時會如何呢？平方的逆向運算便是找出該數的平方根。當一個數字的除數與答案是相同的，即為平方根。

　　舉例來說，4 的平方根為 2。理由為何呢？理由即在於 4 除以 2 等於 2，除數與答案是相同的。還有 49 除以 7 等於 7，所以 49 的平方根是 7。 100 除以 10 等於 10，故平方根為 10。

　　但也不是所有平方根都為整數，事實上通常為無理數。例如 3 的平方根是多少呢？它不是整數，而是 1.73205，實際上為無限小數，為無理數。那 6 的平方根呢？答案是 2.44948，實際上為無限小數，答案依然為無理數。大多數字的平方根實際上皆為無理數。

* irrational number 無理數　infinity 無限

以下何者為「是」？請在空格中填入「T」或「F」。

1 5 的平方根是 25。 (F)
2 當你自乘一個數字即得到平方根。 (F)
3 大多平方根為整數。 (F)
4 3 的平方根為無理數。 (T)

A

1 probability　2 statistics　3 proportion　4 percent
5 histogram　6 circle graph　7 tree diagram
8 sampling　9 terminating decimal
10 repeating decimal　11 cross multiply
12 eliminate　13 tabulate　14 median　15 range
16 coordinate

B

1 probability　2 Statistics　3 proportion
4 histogram　5 Tree diagrams　6 sampling
7 terminating decimal　8 repeating decimal

C

1 eliminate　2 Tabulate　3 mean　4 mode

D
1 histogram　2 circle graph　3 sampling
4 tree diagram

E　機率與統計
某事的機率即是發生的可能性，常以百分比表示。舉例來說，若你擲銅板，正面的機率為 50%。若你擲骰子，擲出點數 1 的機率為 16.67% 或是六分之一。你能藉由記下事物發生數，並將結果除以其總數來測定機率。

統計在另一方面說來，是蒐集、統整與分析數據的數學領域。一旦蒐集了資訊，其中一個最簡易的分析方式便是利用圖表。與機率有關，並最適合的圖表有一圓形圖或稱圓餅圖，皆能分成 100 個百分點。可能某事發生機率有 50%，另一件事發生機率有 25%，再另外一件事的發生機率也是 25%，都可簡易地顯示在圓餅圖上。

另一方面，條狀圖最適用於其他統計資料，而它們為有 X 軸與 Y 軸的簡易圖表。舉例來說，有人正在紀錄幾位學生表現最好的科目，科目有英文、數學、自然科學與歷史。這些科目位於水平狀的 X 軸上，而學生表現良好科目的數據則在垂直的 Y 軸上。而這能使數據清楚又易於分析。

填空
1 某事發生的可能性是機率。(probability)
2 統計是蒐集、統整與分析數據的數學領域。(data)
3 圓形圖又稱作圓餅圖。(circle graph)
4 條狀圖有 X 軸與 Y 軸。(x-axis)

Unit 23 ● Measurement (p .108)

A
1 metric system　2 customary unit　3 basic unit
4 linear　5 capacity　6 mass　7 conversion
8 unit of time　9 elapsed time　10 prefix
11 measure　12 abbreviate　13 convert　14 translate
15 Hecto-　16 Deka-

B
1 metric system　2 basic unit　3 linear units
4 Customary units　5 conversion　6 capacity
7 mass　8 prefixes

C
1 measured　2 abbreviated　3 Convert　4 thousand

D
1 metric system　2 linear　3 customary unit
4 elapsed time

E　公制
公制是以十進位的測量系統，能測量長度、容積、重量、壓力、能量與溫度。公制中有許多單位，不過由於它使用十進位制，便易於轉換。

公制中的公尺是用來測量長度的單位，長度單位的還有公釐、公分、分米、十公尺（公丈）、一百公尺（公引）和公里。所以 1 公尺等於 10 分米，等於 100 公分，等於 1000 公釐。 1 公里等於 10 公引，等於 100 公丈也等於 1000 公尺。最常見的長度單位為公釐、公分、公尺與公里。

公制中的公升是用來測量容積的單位。單位內還有毫升、釐升、分升、十升（公斗）、一百升（公石）與千升（公秉）。轉換單位的方式與公尺的方式相同。

公制中的公克是用來測量質量的單位。最常見的質量單位為公克與公斤，還有一些其他不常用到的單位。

最後公制中用攝氏是來作為測量溫度的單位。水於攝氏零度時結冰，而於攝氏 100 度沸騰。

以下何者為非？(3)
1 公制中的公尺是用於測量長度的。
2 十公尺大於一公分。
3 公制中的公升是用來測量重量的。
4 水於攝氏零度時結冰。

Unit 24 ● Geometry (p. 112)

A
1 bisector　2 congruent figure　3 similar figure
4 corresponding　5 proportional　6 identical
7 symmetrical　8 perimeter　9 circumference
10 transformation　11 be congruent to　12 bisect
13 two-dimensional figure　14 three-dimensional
figure　15 chord　16 diameter

B
1 bisector　2 congruent figures　3 similar figures
4 corresponding　5 proportional　6 identical
7 symmetrical　8 perimeter

C
1 congruent　2 bisects　3 two-dimensional
4 three-dimensional

D
1 bisector　2 similar figures　3 transformation
4 circumference

E　維度
我們所居住的物質世界有三維空間，此三維可在圖表上測量與繪製。它們也就是長度、寬度與深度。

長度為第一維度，可以以一條簡單的直線表示。但在立體圖中則以水平的 X 軸呈現。

第二維度則是寬度。當一物體存於二維空間中，便擁有幾何圖形的型體，如正方形、長方形、三角形與圓形。也就是說它能以長寬來表現。寬度在立體圖中則以同樣水平的 Y 軸來呈現。

第三維度則為深度，又稱為高。當某物體存於三維空間時，會有像是立方體、三角錐、球體與角柱體般的立體形狀。在立體圖中，深度則以垂直的 Z 軸呈現。

第四維度則是時間。科學家替存於第四維度中的立方體命名為「超立方體」。

那到底有多少維度呢？科學家們尚未確定。有些人認為可能有 11 維，有些則聲稱要來的更多。科學家目前正在尋找更多維度，雖然目前尚未發現，但他們深信這是存在的。

閱讀並回答下列問題。
1 物質世界有幾維空間？(Three.)
2 此三維為哪三維？
　(Length, width, and depth or height.)
3 第四維為何？(Time.)
4 總共有幾維？
　(No one is sure. / Scientists do not know for sure.)

A
1 prime number 2 composite number 3 exponent
4 probability 5 statistics 6 metric system
7 customary unit 8 linear 9 proportional
10 identical 11 square 12 cube 13 eliminate
14 tabulate 15 repeating decimal 16 abbreviate
17 convert 18 be congruent to 19 bisect
20 radius

B
1 (a) 2 (b) 3 (a) 4 (c)

C
1 base 2 histogram 3 conversion 4 similar

25 ● Poetry and Stories (p. 118)

A
1 verse 2 prose 3 prose poem 4 rhyme
5 stanza 6 couplet 7 rhyme scheme 8 free verse
9 meter 10 sonnet 11 epic poem 12 exaggerate
13 stress 14 quote 15 reinforce 16 allegory

B
1 verse 2 Prose 3 rhymes 4 stanza 5 couplet
6 rhyme scheme 7 meter 8 sonnet

C
1 rhyme 2 stress 3 quoted 4 reinforce

D
1 verse 2 rhyme scheme 3 sonnet
4 free verse

E 詩歌的種類

　　詩人在作詩時，有許多文體可選擇。他們能寫下極長或極短的詩，或是許多不同的主題，還能以各種韻式與格律來著作。

　　其中一種最古老形式的詩為史詩，是一種極長篇的文體，長度可達數千句之長。史詩通常是有關於一位英雄與他的冒險，歷史上就有許多著名的史詩——《伊利亞德》、《奧德賽》、《伊尼亞斯》、《貝武夫》與《鳩格米西史詩》，這些僅為史詩中的一些例子而已。

　　另一方面，也有許多短詩。十四行詩即是短詩的其中一種。此種有十四個句子的文體，通常最後兩句會押韻。十四行詩能有各種主題，威廉·莎士比亞便寫了許多著名的十四行詩。

　　對句則可長可短。對句中的每個詩節有兩句，每個句子最後的字必定互相押韻。

　　四行詩為極短詩，僅有四個句子。五行詩則有五個句子，五行打油詩也是五個句子的詩。僅有三個句子的為俳句詩，它的首句與第三句有五個音節，第二句則有七個音節；以上為最短詩的其中幾種。

以下何者為「是」？請在空格中填入「T」或「F」。
1 史詩為短詩。 (F)
2 《貝武夫》為著名的十四行詩，由威廉·莎士比亞所著。 (F)
3 十四行詩有十四個句子。 (T)
4 四行詩與五行打油詩同樣擁有四個句子。 (F)

26 ● Grammar and Usage (p. 122)

A
1 common noun 2 proper noun 3 active voice
4 passive voice 5 root 6 etymology
7 simple sentence 8 compound sentence
9 complex sentence
10 compound-complex sentence 11 parse
12 analyze 13 identify 14 clarify 15 clause
16 dependent clause

B
1 active voice 2 passive voice 3 roots
4 etymology 5 simple sentence
6 compound sentence 7 complex sentence
8 compound-complex

C
1 Analyze 2 clarify 3 taken 4 Identify

D
1 proper noun 2 common noun
3 simple sentence 4 compound sentence

E 希臘與拉丁字根

　　英語的文字比其他語言要來的多，理由為何呢？其中一個理由為英文從其他語言中借用文字，再將之轉成新的英文字。這些字有很多都是從希臘文與拉丁文而來，稱為字根。人可藉由研讀字根來學習英文中多種字詞的意義。

　　舉例來說，字根「hydro」起源於希臘文，代表「水」的意思。由此我們可得「hydrate（水化合物）」、「dehydrate（脫水）」、「hydrant（消防栓）」、「hydrogen（氫氣）」與其他字。字根「aster」起源於希臘文，表示「星星」之意。由此我們可得「asteroid（小行星）」、「asterisk（星號）」、「astronomy（天文學）」、「astronaut（太空人）」與其他字。字根「Geo」也是起源於希臘文，代表「陸地」的意思。「geology（地質學）」、「geometry（幾何學）」、「geography（地理學）」皆起源於此。

　　也有許多字根是起源於拉丁文。舉例來說，字根「vid」代表「看」的意思。由此我們可得「video（影片）」、「visual（視覺的）」、「visualize（使形象化）」與其他字。字根「script」代表「寫」的意思。由此我們可得「transcript（文字記錄）」、「inscription（題辭）」與其他字。還有「port」代表「運輸」的意思。由此我們可得「transport（交通）」、「portable（便攜的）」、「export（出口）」、「import（進口）」與其他字。

　　英語若無借用其他語言，將會相當貧乏。多虧有拉丁語和希臘語以及其他語言，英語才有如此多的字詞。

填空
1 英語的文字比其他語言要來的多。 (words)
2 字根「geo」是起源於希臘文。 (Greek)
3 字根「vid」代表「看」的意思。 (see)
4 字根「port」代表「運輸」的意思。 (port)

A

1 indeed 2 necessity 3 hatch 4 haste 5 flock
6 worm 7 put 8 grass 9 deep 10 procrastination
11 put off / postpone / procrastinate 12 convey
13 moralize 14 proverb 15 folklore 16 aphorism

B

1 indeed 2 Necessity 3 hatch 4 put 5 grass
6 deep 7 Haste 8 flock

C

1 postpone 2 convey 3 moralize 4 parable

D

1 proverb 2 fable 3 oral tradition
4 procrastination

E 常見諺語

　　諺語為人們有時會使用的短語，通常傳遞某類智慧。英語中有大量的諺語。

　　有一句話說：「距離產生美」，指的是人們通常對於過去的人、事、物懷抱美好記憶。當時他們當然並不會那麼想，然而要經過時間，「距離」改變了他們的記憶，他們便會深情地回想人事物。

　　「閃閃發亮的並非都是黃金」是另一句重要的諺語。黃金非常珍貴並閃閃發亮，但也有許多不一定珍貴卻會發亮的東西，事實上還可能有害。所以這句諺語是在警告人們，不是所有好看、閃亮之物都如黃金般珍貴。

　　「猶豫者多失」為一常見用語。這句話告訴人們切勿遲疑，應做出決定並順應它。若遲疑等待過久，可能會失去重要的機會。

　　最後，「覆水難收，悔恨無益」是另一句很重要的諺語。有時人會遭遇不好的事，不過無需悔恨。相反地，要接受事實並生活下去便是這句諺語的意義。

以下何者為非？(2)
1 英語中有許多諺語。
2 諺語僅教導某類的智慧。
3「閃光的並非都是黃金」是一句警語。
4「覆水難收」是要告訴人們忘記過去並活在當下。

A

1 Classical Art 2 order 3 Doric order
4 Ionic order 5 Corinthian order 6 proportion
7 symmetrical 8 column 9 Gothic Art
10 linear perspective 11 work out
12 be inspired by 13 dedicate 14 strive 15 ornate
16 oculus

B

1 orders 2 Doric order 3 Corinthian order
4 Ionic order 5 proportion 6 symmetrical
7 columns 8 Linear perspective

C

1 worked 2 influenced 3 inspired 4 dedicated

D

1 symmetrical 2 column 3 Gothic Art
4 linear perspective

E 古典藝術

　　古希臘人熱愛藝術，他們製作各種的藝術品，包含了陶器、繪畫、雕刻與壁畫。希臘人甚至視他們的建築物為藝術品，所以也建造了很多美輪美奐的建築。

　　古希臘留存下許多陶器樣本。古希臘的陶器有兩個用處，用於飲食還有裝飾。許多希臘的陶器上有美麗的圖畫，圖畫多為訴說希臘神話。

　　雕刻在古希臘更是受到讚賞。希臘人以石頭或青銅來雕刻，許多石雕存留至今，銅雕則不然。希臘人所雕出來的人就像是現實生活中的人一樣栩栩如生。

　　至於建築，許多希臘建築留存至今。這些建築的其中一個特點就是它們的圓柱，希臘人有三種類型的圓柱——多力克柱式、愛奧尼柱式與科林斯柱式。多力克柱式為最簡單的單純設計。愛奧尼柱式上從上到下有雕刻的凹槽或是線條，比多力克柱式要來的多裝飾。科林斯柱式為這三種中最多裝飾的柱式。又稱為柱頭的頂部常有雕花或是其他設計，也有凹槽的設計。

* **flute** 柱子上的凹槽

閱讀並回答下列問題。
1 古希臘人製作何種類型的藝術品？
　(Pottery, paintings, sculptures, murals, and buildings.)
2 希臘人通常在陶器上畫什麼？
　(Stories from Greek mythology.)
3 希臘人用什麼雕刻？(Stone and bronze.)
4 希臘人所製作的柱式為哪三種？
　(Doric, Ionic, and Corinthian.)

A
1 Baroque Art   2 chiaroscuro   3 grotesque
4 contortion   5 Rococo Art   6 pastel
7 Neoclassical Art   8 Romantic Art   9 etching
10 exaggeration   11 evoke   12 revive   13 contort
14 depict   15 etch   16 contrast

B
1 Baroque Art   2 grotesque   3 contortion
4 Rococo Art   5 Pastels   6 Romantic Art
7 Etchings   8 Exaggeration

C
1 evokes   2 etch   3 revived   4 contorted

D
1 chiaroscuro   2 contortion   3 pastel
4 etching

E 由巴洛克到寫實主義

　　大約從 16 世紀後期到 18 世紀初期，歐洲出現了一種稱作巴洛克的新型態藝術。每個歐洲國家都有巴洛克的藝術家。他們的風格皆有小小的差異，但巴洛克藝術家間依然擁有許多共同點。

　　舉例來說，巴洛克繪畫中總會有明暗的對比。藝術家們還著重於動作，他們強調畫中人物的臉部表情，此為表現畫中情感的一個方法。巴洛克藝術家的作品通常有象徵或道德上的意義，許多巴洛克藝術家也繪製以宗教為題的畫作。

　　非常重要的一點是巴洛克藝術家們是寫實主義者，因此他們都會盡可能寫實地描繪主題。他們懂透視畫法，所以能展現出畫中物的大小與距離等等。他們還能在作品中善用空間，此能力讓許多巴洛克藝術家相當出名。直到今天，如葛雷柯、林布蘭和卡拉瓦喬之流的藝術家作品依然受到讚賞。

以下何者為非？(1)
1 巴洛克時期於 17 世紀中結束。
2 巴洛克畫作擁有明暗的對比。
3 巴洛克畫作表現人類的情感。
4 葛雷柯與林布蘭為兩位巴洛克藝術家。

A
1 bass clef   2 treble clef   3 staff   4 grand staff
5 time signature   6 scale   7 chord   8 triad
9 counterpoint   10 string quartet   11 distinguish
12 involve   13 follow   14 pay attention to
15 oratorio   16 sonata

B
1 staff   2 grand staff   3 time signature   4 scale
5 chord   6 triads   7 counterpoint   8 string quartet

C
1 distinguished   2 involves   3 Pay   4 Sonatas

D
1 treble clef   2 bass clef   3 scale   4 string quartet

E 音樂的古典時期

　　在西元 1750 年到 1821 年間，出現了一些最偉大的音樂創作。這段時期稱為音樂的古典時期，此時期中的作曲家有莫札特、貝多芬、海頓與舒伯特。

　　1750 年時，人們對巴洛克時期感到厭倦，便開始創作新樂風，造就古典時期的崛起。此時期有許多特點，其中一點便是音樂的調子時常轉變。一首樂曲中不再只有單一曲調，調子反而能任意轉換。樂曲的節奏也是如此，此時期的音樂節拍有多種型式，常有驟然中止或是音樂從極慢到極快，或是從柔和轉變成非常大聲。

　　古典時期的音樂擁有美妙的旋律，作曲家所創作的作品特別容易記得。當然這些作品為精心之作，不過民眾能輕易記住這些曲子也使得這些曲子普及化。甚至到了今日，此時期作曲家的作品也是古典音樂中最為人所熟知的。

填空
1 音樂的古典時期從 1750 年到 1820 年。 (1750)
2 巴洛克時期在古典時期之前。 (Baroque)
3 古典時期的音樂曲調常突然轉變。 (change)
4 許多古典時期的曲子容易記得。 (easy)

Review Test 6

A
1 verse   2 prose   3 active voice   4 passive voice
5 haste   6 flock   7 grotesque   8 contortion
9 scale   10 chord   11 sonnet   12 reinforce
13 complex sentence
14 put off / postpone / procrastinate   15 convey
16 be inspired by   17 dedicate   18 evoke
19 revive   20 counterpoint

B
1 (a)   2 (b)   3 (c)   4 (b)

C
1 couplet   2 roots   3 indeed   4 orders